Gin Soaked Boy

A tale of love, laughter and depression hidden behind a bottle of alcohol

Sandeep Mathew

Leadstart
INKSTATE

ISBN 978-93-5667-561-2

First published in India 2023 by Leadstart Inkstate
A brand of One Point Six Technologies Pvt. Ltd.

Unit no. 26, Ground Floor, A1, Shram Safalya,
Wadala Truck Terminal Road, Near Post Office,
Antop Hill, Mumbai - 400037.
Phone: +91 96999 33000
Email: info@leadstartcorp.com
www.leadstartcorp.com

Editor: Roona Ballachanda
Cover: Ilaya Raja
Layouts: Sathish Kumar

To all those who are committed to improving mental health awareness,

This book is dedicated to you.

May the pages within help you identify some of the signs of mental illness and empower you to take action and help those in need.

We all deserve to move forward.

Contents

Acknowledgement

This book is an attempt to decode depression. According to the World Health Organization, nearly 10% of the world's population is affected by mental health issues. And nearly two-thirds of people who need treatment never seek help from a health professional due to stigma and discrimination. This book aims to leave the reader with an insight to this elusive illness and intervene either for themselves, or for anyone around that may be displaying any one of the 12 symptoms mentioned across the 12 chapters in this book.

Each chapter is made up of 2 acts. The First Act covers the protagonist in his childhood when he is nothing short of a prodigy, and the Second Act draws a sharp polarization to this as he begins to display signs of depression.

Heartfelt gratitude to Gayathri Devadasan, Yukti Goel and Mahima Gupta Didwania, all psychologists by profession, who have proofread these Second Acts of the book.

Once the reader has decided to take that first step of making an intervention, the safety plan at the end of this book provides more guidance. Thanks to Gayathri Devadasan for creating this and Unilever's head of transformation for health and well-being, Sunita Wazir, for providing the initial idea.

Thanks to all those who contributed towards this book. Sonia Mackwani, Founder Director – Touching Lives, Alternative Healing Therapist and Author, for her partnership and the incredible work she does every day with *Touching Lives*. Supriya Jain for giving this book the structure it has. Asha Esther, one of my favorite artists, who designed the cover. Lastly, Atanu Ghosh, the ideal sparring partner and one who never fails to stretch creative boundaries.

Credit to my coterie of childhood and lifelong friends who have been a source of inspiration for this book. Sushma, Aashica, Noel, Anand, Arun, Niroop, Hari, Karthik, Jeetu, Giridhar, Aparna, Pratyoosh, Prakash. And so many more. You know who you are.

Can't say enough for my family who put up with so much, most of all my doggedness to get this book out and the entire team at LeadStart who made it possible.

Lastly, thanks to my best friend, Bala. They say a good friend is someone who gets you out of jail while your best friend is someone sitting next to you in jail, saying, "dude, we are screwed." Bala always made sure to sit next to me, no matter the circumstance.

Foreword

I was only seven or eight, when I first heard of the word depression. I was in my grandmother's house helping her clean vegetables. I was mesmerized with the water turning green and muddy and small worms swirling in it, when the doorbell rang. It was her fourth-floor neighbor. His eyes were red, and his tears ran down his cheeks despite all his attempts to stay collected. *My mother!* He whispered out of his mouth, and it was enough for my grandmother to understand. My grandmother immediately wore a scarf and asked me to stay put until she came back. I was left with the green water and the floating worms; now dead.

I do not know how much time passed but as a child I could sense something terrible must have happened to the man's mother. She was no less than a saint, said my grandmother sobbing herself continuing to teach me to cut the vegetables deftly. The woman was a single mother and had spent her life raising her son and all this was only possible because of only one thing – her unshakeable faith in God. I had certainly heard many times about this woman as someone who meditates and stays in her practice 24/7. She was a beautiful image in my mind. A holy soul, the other neighbors always confirmed. But I had never seen or met this lady ever until her body was taken down in an ambulance. From the balcony of third floor, I saw her for the first time. A small skeletal figure shrunken into herself, her lipless open mouth and her pale skin. Through the white blanket, her fingers were visible, and they held chanting beads. She had died but had not let go of her beads. To my child's mind, it was an impression that one must surely die in the same way and for that one must live life in the same way. Years later, the story had changed. People remembered the lady saying she chronic depression. She died in depression. Wait! Didn't she die in meditation?

We all have grown understanding depression in one form or another. Just as my life went on by cleaning the vegetables while someone died due to depression or not, the imprints of such events in our own lives remain very much in our subconscious mind impacting our lives implicitly. Take a moment and sit and think when was the first time you heard of it?

The good news is, we are now open to understanding any form of illness – mental or physical holistically. We are ready to use both the mainstream and alternative methods of healing and recovery. Today, we can engage in our own inner work, we are in the position to live an inquiry and informed based life and we are only getting closer to understanding our own patterns, behaviors, wounds and traumas and the very advance methods and support systems to heal them. Humans have personal wounds and collective wounds and many a times they are so shared that we miss on identifying behaviors catalyst to chronic conditions. Today a trauma can be healed through psychotherapy, through alternative methods, through eastern-western traditional practices, through shamanic work, through energy work understanding that traumas could be ancestral and an eclectic approach to both medicines and meditations can not only heal our wounds but also lead to a healthy quality of life.

In my practice – I always encourage people to do their Self-Work. This book is a step toward that. The author's intention is to support reader to understand our own lives and our loved ones who matter to us. Written in a form of 12 chapters signifying the 12 signs of depression in a story format, the book is an attempt to demystify this elusive illness. It is a poignant story that will resonate with anyone who is curious about depression and provide insight to how we could save each other, support each other, and lead mindful relationships.

The book will make you vulnerable in a good way for it brings you closer to your own potential of holding another human being as you are being held by this book.

You journey into your mental health can begin with this book.

– Sonia Mackwani

Prologue

I had just landed in Bangalore when I received the call from Aishvarya to go up to your house to check up on you. The moment she uttered your name, I couldn't help but fear the worst. I redirected the Uber to your house instead of mine, which was not unusual for there have been quite a few times when I have come straight to see you after landing in Bangalore. But this time, I was gritting my teeth and clenching my fingers in the hopes that I would indeed see you, and that the quiver I heard in Aishvarya's voice was just a misunderstanding.

No, no, no, no. You better not have Raj. You just... better not have.

I reached the street, but my mind was so foggy that I just couldn't locate your house. I walked up and down that street, recalling all those places where we used to go for a smoke, but your house was nowhere to be found. I called up Aishvarya and she told me to look for a house where a crowd may have gathered. I called up Vinay, who I knew stays very close to Raj's house, and asked him if he could help me find your house.

With Vinay's help, we finally spotted your house, and I heaved a sigh of relief for when I saw that there was no crowd surrounding it. Your parents looked and talked the way they always did, asking me and Vinay about our lives and whereabouts since they hadn't seen us for a few years.

Ten minutes into the conversation, I couldn't take the suspense anymore and asked them, "Where is Raj?" And just as casually as they had spoken till then, your mom said, "He passed away yesterday."

I was gutted. I could feel the wind getting knocked out of me. But I asked again, disbelieving, "He passed away? Yesterday?" And once again, in the very same tone, they said, "Yes, he did. You didn't know? We thought that is the reason you came here." My shock turned to rage.

This was something I was supposed to know? Why are they talking as if this is something normal? How the hell was I supposed to know? I couldn't even find his damned house! And why is no one else here? Why is Raj himself not here? He is gone forever, and I don't even get to see him one last time?

"Where is the body?" I somehow managed to gather myself and asked.

"It is in the hospital. We will bring it here tomorrow."

"What happens after that?"

"We will do a puja in the morning and then take him to crematorium by eleven."

"That soon?"

"Yes, given what has happened to him, it is best to take care of the body quickly."

What happened to him? What the hell did he do? All those conversations about hanging on to a gun, threatening to overdose on drugs, the depression he couldn't deal with any longer… did he actually go through with it? And why didn't he say something to me? I've been speaking with him almost every week. He only had a leg injury. Why am I here? I don't live in Bangalore anymore. What am I even doing in his house?

My mind was flooded with these thoughts. I could see your parents talking, but I had stopped hearing a single word coming out of their mouths.

Thankfully, Vinay was there with me. Not only did he have the presence of mind to find your house, but he also knew when it was time to leave. We drove to a bar nearby. I made a few calls en-route to explain what had happened. Every time I spoke to someone, I almost choked up, but somehow, I held it together, explaining the news I had just received from your parents.

Sushmita started crying. Thomas and Gajan made plans to travel to Bangalore. A lot was happening. Yet, nothing was happening.

At the bar, I had the first quiet moment since receiving the news. It was there that I cried for the first time.

I don't remember when I last cried. So many deaths, so many breakups, so many disappointments in life, but I don't think I cried through any of those. But you made me cry, Raj. For the first time, at that bar, and countless times after that.

Vinay and I raised a toast to you. We toasted to your smile, your wisdom, and those never-ending conversations with you. But we couldn't wrap our head around what happened.

Did you really die? Could that have even happened? Or was there something else to this? Your mom was the only one doing the talking, was there something wrong with her?

So many unanswered questions, but for a moment, the song in the background silenced us. It was the Green Day song that you would sing every time you called us on our birthdays.

It's something unpredictable, but in the end it's right.
I hope you had the time of your life.

– Sachin, January 10, 2020 –

Chapter 1

Reckless Behavior

First Act.
1993

Enter Raj

"Rajaaaa…" boomed a voice from the kitchen, through the living room, up the stairs, through a second living room, all the way to Raj's bedroom.

Raj woke up with a start. It was not the voice that woke him, but the mechanical twang, that of a screeching instrument aspiring to throw melancholy into complete disarray. It was that specific tone that he could recognize anywhere, anytime. The tone his mom used as the last straw, one that could not be defied by any means.

Raj must have slept through the first few times she called out his name. With this tone now, he had no choice but to run downstairs.

"What an excellent idea!"

"Imagine all the money we will save by sending the children on bicycles instead of the school bus."

Raj heard his mom and his neighbor aunty talking to each other as he approached the kitchen. It was almost the end of summer holidays, and he longingly looked at the 'Phantom' and 'Mandrake' comics tossed on the living room sofa as he made his way to the kitchen.

Raj was a voracious reader, a sharp mind with keen acumen but a day dreamer. He pored through comic books in such a way that his mind would take him into the story, as if he were a character enacting the script within those colorful 2-inch boxes. His eyebrows would twitch, lips move subtly, hushing under each breadth of the character's signature lines. Like all kids his age engaging in pretend play, Raj would pretend-play with his favorite characters in the comic books.

He couldn't wait to return to his beloved St Anthony's school, which was located in a quaint part of eastern Bangalore, after the holidays. All his friends were there, all the stories they had to exchange about their individual experiences from the two-month-long summer break, and, of course, make the long-awaited revisit to the library to get more comics. Raj had recently been introduced to all the western publications of comics from the school's library, which were way better than the 'Chanda Mama' and 'Tinkle' his mom got for him.

Those books seemed like utter nonsense now, and he couldn't wait to get back to school just to get hold of more comics. He wanted to know so much more about Mandrake's house, Xanadu. How lovely it would be to have a house like that one day! He wanted to read more about Phantom and his pets, Devil the wolf and Hero the horse. Imagine having a wolf for a pet!

"Raj!" his mom squealed when she saw him entering the kitchen, evaporating his daydreams of Xanadu and Devil into mist.

"Yes, Amma, what is it?"

"Ok listen, you have to get ready immediately. We are taking you to school."

"School? Today is Sunday. School reopens tomorrow."

"No, not St. Anthony's. You are going to MK Jnanadhara School."

"I'm going to what?"

"MK Jnana…."

"That sounds like one of those school Chanda Mama would go to. I'm not going to any school like that. And that too on a Sunday. Come on, Amma!"

"Raj, this is for an entrance exam at this new school that has opened up here. Your atthe from the US also called to tell me that this is a very reputed school and much better than St. Anthony's. And more importantly, your Appa will buy you that BMX bicycle that your cousins in the US ride, because this school is so close by that you can just bike there."

Raj's atthe was his aunt who lived in Los Angeles in the US. She was his dad's older sister and someone who seemed to remote control guide Raj's family all the way from the US. She worked as a rocket scientist, just like Raj's dad, and as a single mother to two children, seemed to be a powerful and intelligent woman whose advice, Raj noticed, his parents usually followed.

"But Amma, I don't want to leave St. Anthony's. All of my best friends are there," Raj tried a futile attempt at changing his mom's mind.

"Raj, you are just twelve years old, about to start 6th grade. You haven't even met your best friends yet!"

Enter Sachin

"Ma'am finished!" said Raj as he handed over his paper to the elderly, bushy-haired class teacher.

"Let me have a look. Oh no. You haven't answered enough questions in the math section. You poor kid. You're probably weak in math. Hmm, let's see what we can do here."

The bushy-haired teacher tapped the shoulder of the student sitting in front of Raj.

"Son, what's your name?"

"Sachin, ma'am."

Sachin had a friendly demeanor and a welcoming embrace. He would sometimes appear shallow and even a touch arrogant, but those who became friends with him, somehow felt comfortable sharing, staying and basking in his reassuring comfort knowing he would be that one person they could always count on. As years would go by, Sachin would become a keeper of good friends, a maker of shared memories, and through his days with Raj, come closest to understanding the complexities that lay beneath him.

"Sachin, can you help this boy in the math section?"

Raj and Sachin exchanged a glance, their eyes widening with the same thought, "She wants us to cheat?"

"Um… sure, ma'am. Here you go. This is how you solve question five."

"Um... ok, thanks," mumbled Raj and got back to his paper.

Raj knew the answer to question five just as he did for all the remaining questions. He was the best performing math student at St. Anthony's. He was intentionally underperforming in the entrance test because he didn't want to leave his school and his friends there.

But because of the bushy-haired teacher, he started answering all the questions, lest she once again embarrasses him or Sachin or any other kid in the class.

By the time the bell rang, Raj had answered a lot more questions than he had originally planned to. In his mind, the results still didn't matter. He was never going to leave St. Anthony's.

"How did it go?" asked his mom, waiting eagerly for him outside.

"Ok, I suppose," shrugged Raj.

"Ok, great. Let's hope you get in. Then we can get you the BMX cycle as well."

Raj was fuming out of both ears – he didn't like this bribe business and wished his mom would understand that St. Anthony's was a much cooler school compared to this one, where he still couldn't pronounce the name correctly.

Moreover, he knew all this bribing was just his mom's doing as his Appa would never resort to something like that. Raj's Appa was a bit of an enigma to Raj. He was always around at home. He seemed to go to the office after Raj left to school and would return before Raj came back from school. So, Raj would always see him at home, but rarely heard him speak. He had very few conversations with him. His dad only seemed to talk to his mom, and a lot of times, Raj would feel that the things his mom is telling him are actually coming from his dad rather than his mom. And when it came to buying things, Raj would always simply ask his dad directly, and his dad almost always simply got what he asked for. So, he knew, if he wanted a bike, his dad would get it for him. This whole bribe to change a school was completely unnecessary and one of those things he just humored his mom with. Raj always felt it was better to allow his mom to feel she was in control, when most often, it was the other way around as Raj knew exactly what she was up to.

Just as Raj and his mom were about to leave, Raj saw her. Shoulder length, poky straight hair that seemed forced into pigtails held together by at least a dozen pink rubber bands. Sharp facial contours with a prominent nose, was her most distinct feature. The prettiest girl Raj had ever seen, walked out of a neighboring classroom.

Her skin was radiant white. Raj thought that girls with that skin color existed only in his Mandrake and Phantom comic books. He was so caught up in a trance that he didn't even realize that she had been crying. The girl caught him staring at her and stopped crying. Their eyes met as she walked past him.

"Don't you agree, Raj?" said Raj's mom, snapping him out of his daydream.

"Yes… um… let's hope I get into this school," replied Raj, dazed.

Enter Aishvarya

"Raj, this new school uniform is much better than the St. Anthony's one," said Raj's mom as she fastened his tie.

"Thanks, Amma," smiled Raj.

"And it is so good to see you so happy about your new school. Just a week back, I was worried you would be making a fuss about leaving St. Anthony's. I wonder what changed your mind?"

"Like you said Amma, seems like I'm going to be meeting my best friends in this new school," sniggered Raj as he mounted his brand-new BMX, complete with 'shock absorbers'. He had exploited his mom's 'bribe' to full effect.

At the new school, Raj ran into Sachin, the same kid who had helped him during the entrance test. He noticed they were of the same average height and sported very similar hairstyles, a partition on one side separating a tuft of wavy hair on the other side.

Both Raj and Sachin were glad they knew at least one person in this new school. They started talking and Raj learnt Sachin was from Kerala, while he himself was a native of Tamil Nadu. Though that technically meant they were outsiders, they always identified as hard core Bangalorean.

Their conversation trickled over to hobbies, and watching TV usually topped the short list that anyone possessed at their age. And when it came to watching TV, there was just one channel, Doordarshan, that was the sole source of entertainment for everyone in the house. The previous night, one of the most provocative shows till date was aired on the channel: the rerun of the recently concluded Miss World contest.

It was only aired because Aishwarya Rai, a participant from India, had won the Miss World title. Just a few months back, Sushmita Sen had won the Miss Universe title. It was the first time that women from India had won both the titles. 'Ash' and 'Sush' were all they both could talk about till they found their classroom.

Once they entered their classroom, Raj started looking around for the short-haired girl. He hoped—and prayed—that she too had managed to clear the entrance test and joined his new school. Fortunately, he spotted her sitting right on the first bench, next to another pretty girl. Raj couldn't help but wonder that his shift to this new school was turning out to be a much better decision than continuing at St. Anthony's.

The bell rang, and as the class began to settle down, the class teacher walked in. It was the bushy-haired teacher. She introduced herself as Emma ma'am, the geography teacher, and asked the rest of the class to introduce themselves one by one.

Front bench girl went first, "Aishvarya, ma'am." The name got etched onto Raj's brain; he thanked the stars that she cleared her entrance exams. Little did he know then that Aishvarya had not just cleared those exams but would go on to hold the first rank in every school year till they graduated from MK Jnanadhara.

Her bench-mate went next, "Sushmita, ma'am." Sachin, who was sitting next to Raj, sniggered, "Looks like we have an Ash and a Sush in our class as well."

Aishvarya and Sushmita stood out from the rest of the girls in class and knew about it as well. They were good looking and smart. They were each alpha girls in their own right, though in very different ways. Aishvarya carried a smidge of maturity that made her a favorite among the teachers and eventually a favorite among the parents of the other students in class as well. If there was one student that every parent in class would want her kid to be like, it was Aishvarya.

Sushmita on the other hand was an understated leader. While Aishvarya was more in-your-face kind of smart, Sushmita's intellect ran many levels deep. Every time someone would have a conversation with Sushmita, it would feel like she knows so much more about the topic, and even about the person she is speaking with. While Aishvarya intimidated some even before they could start a conversation with her, Sushmita intimidated within the first sentence of the conversation, and at far superior levels to Aishvarya.

All the students in the school were divided into four houses: green, blue, red and yellow. Each house had its own house captain, and luckily for Raj, he was made the captain of the Green house while Aishvarya was captain of the Blue house.

The captains were given various responsibilities, which they were expected to perform together. One of them was to inspect all the classrooms at the end of each day to ensure they were neat and tidy. On his very first classroom inspection round, Raj found himself next to Aishvarya.

Raj's heart rate shot to a level it had never been to before the moment they were alone in the classroom. He went about inspecting the class, moving as far away from Aishvarya as possible, worried she may hear his labored breathing.

Aishvarya broke the awkward silence.

“It was interesting to learn geography today,” she said, referring to Emma ma’am and her geography lesson earlier in the day.

Which part of India are you from?” Raj replied almost instinctively.

“I’m from Coorg.”

“That explains why your skin tone is so fair,” Raj said and immediately added, “must have to do with all the pork you guys eat,” in an attempt at a joke, hoping it would slow down his heart rate.

“There is no connection between my skin tone and pork,” Aishvarya replied, completely missing the point.

“I was just joking… sorry…. Anyway, if you would like to travel to any of the other metros in India, which one would it be?” Raj continued along the line of questioning to keep the conversation going.

“Maybe… Kolkata.”

“Why?”

“Seems like a nice and calm place… unlike Bangalore!”

Second Act.
2009

Reckless behavior on the bridges of Kolkata

"Kolkata is mayhem! I'm on the Howrah bridge and there isn't a nosier place on earth I've been to. And there's garbage thrown everywhere.... So much for being the most famous bridge in India! I keep walking up and down, trying to figure out what the big deal about this bridge is all about. Why do people keep staring at me? Are they staring at my jacket? I wonder if it's because of the gun I'm hiding in there"

Raj blurted out to confused Sushmita on the other end of the phone before abruptly hanging up. It wasn't the first time he had had a conversation like this.

He had repeatedly called Sushmita ever since he moved to Kolkata a few months back, shocking her and even making her tear up on some occasions.

He had just completed his MBA from one of India's leading business schools and was soon after offered a plush job at an MNC. His first posting was in Kolkata where he received a grandiose welcome. His accommodation was a vintage, British-era guesthouse, and he had a chauffeur-driven white Ambassador car to take him any place he'd like.

He loved the special treatment he received in Kolkata, but he hated the city.

The thing nobody told me about Kolkata is how freaking hot it is. Horses sweat, men perspire, women glow, and I drench. Every day has turned into a never-ending battle to stay dry. The perpetual sticky feeling is alleviated by the odd cold scotch or the discreetly timed crotch wipe. In the past month, I have learnt a lot of things about my bladder. The neurons which control my piss pot are very sensitive to heat, VERY! The gleeful lightness after peeing! It virtually occupies my day. The unwashed masses are starting to bug me a bit. A few minutes outside my car, and I smell like I have crawled out of Shrek's anus. He is green, so I'm guessing his poo smells a bit! Bengali bacteria derive their bliss from baptizing my balls. I spot a bimbo at the bar. Alas, all bacchanalian thoughts of backending her over the balcony have been blown to bits due to the burden of my bladder, full of beer. I'm headed for the bathroom now. My Mumbai heart bellows thoughts of my Bangalorean being... of a bright, blue and brilliant sun... of breezy, bitter and beautiful rain.

Oh, how I miss good weather!

Raj's job in Kolkata entailed hobnobbing with some of the biggest businessmen there, and many of them offered Raj surreptitious gifts to curry favors from his company. One of them was a goon who offered Raj his gun.

The new job, the money, the attention, it was all a heady cocktail for Raj. He was having the time of his life.

What made it even more entertaining were the calls he made to Sushmita, reveling in his newfound glory and tormenting her relentlessly.

It was all fun and games for him, but Sushmita was scared out of her wits. She would sometimes stay on the phone with Raj until he reached his hotel, worried that he would do something silly, something irreversible, if she didn't.

She tried everything to get him out of Kolkata. She didn't like the person he was being in the city. She even tried reaching out to his parents and convincing him through them. But none of it worked.

Raj stayed in Kolkata for a year, and called Sushmita almost every day, concocting conversations that were entertaining only for him. Sushmita could never figure out whether what he was saying was the truth or just fantasies. It was an act he kept up for the next decade.

One fine night, Sushmita received a message from Raj. It read: I'm done! I can't take this anymore.

Sushmita stayed up the entire night, trying to get through to Raj. Finally, she got through to him in the morning.

"Raj, are you ok? Where are you?"

"I'm in Chennai. I've been posted here now."

"Thank God! What happened to the gun?"

"What gun?"

Sushmita never learnt the true story behind the gun. Raj denied or digressed from the topic every time she brought it up. She thought it didn't matter though. At least he was out of Kolkata.

Little did she know, the reckless behavior with the gun was just the beginning.

Chapter 2

Substance Abuse

First Act.
1994

Enter the supporting cast.

As MK Jnanadhara entered its second year, many new faces joined the school. Raj and Sachin checked out the noticeboard for the list of students—both old and new—who would be their classmates in the 7th grade. As they went through the list, Sachin noticed something.

"Raj, your name is not on the list!"

"No, it's right there. Raghavendra."

"What? Your name is… Raghavendra! Why does everyone call you Raj then!"

"Well, my parents call me Raj at home, but its popularity in school is all thanks to Vinay. He spotted me once at a CD lending library which also happens to be called Raj, and the owner there is called Raj, and he knows me as Raj since my parents started my membership there with him. So, when Vinay heard Raj call me Raj at Raj, it was too amusing for him to let it go and he made sure everyone in school started calling me that. Besides, it's so much simpler than Raghavendra! I don't blame anyone for just using Raj."

Vinay was one of the students, who along with Sachin and Raj, was continuing from the previous year. Vinay was a walking encyclopedia of sorts and knew specific details about certain topics, which was resourceful in an age when Google wasn't around. His knowledge about things and ability to link people to events led him to christen everyone in class with a nickname. Some were surreptitious in meaning, that it sometimes took years for people to figure out what the names really meant. For instance, he bestowed upon Aishvarya the moniker 'Battery' and everyone in class assumed it was because her full name was Aishvarya Aiyappanna, or AA, which was like the AA batteries used in remotes and such. However, Vinay had a hidden meaning to it. AA was a reference to Aishvarya's bra size. Not too many boys knew about bra sizes then, and the best they could come up with was something crass like 'Manchester' for Aishvarya. Vinay was ahead of his time. Luckily for Aishvarya, neither name stuck, and she was simply known as Ash.

As Raj and Sachin headed towards their class, Raj froze when he saw the first new face. Most boys their age hadn't sprouted any facial hair yet, but this new kid had a thick chin trap.

"Who is that uncle!" Raj exclaimed.

"Hi, my name is Naveen," the uncle-like student greeted them when he saw them.

"Or you can call him China," chipped in Vinay.

"China? Why?" Raj asked, confused.

"Because Chilly Hanging In Naveen's Ass," said Vinay and promptly burst into laughter.

Naveen simply smiled sheepishly, and the nickname stuck.

Naveen stood out amongst his classmates. He was tall, broad shouldered, and physically far ahead for his age. He required a shave every morning while the rest of the boys in class barely sprouted a fuzz. However, he was mentally dull. Not in the biologically challenging sort of way, but just a bit slow to react at times. Just as Vinay had proven while christening him China.

"Hi, my name is Gajan Mahalingam," another new student cut in.

Before Raj and Sachin could react, he had moved on to another student, "Hi, my name is Gajan Mahalingam."

Vinay whispered to Raj and Sachin, "Ok, that guy does not need a nickname!"

Gajan was as tall as China but had a lanky frame. He sported short, spiky hair and seemed to be bursting with energy. He went around introducing himself to everyone in class without waiting for anyone to introduce themselves back or have any conversation with them. That gave a first impression of being shallow and even a tad bit annoying. However, Gajan was anything but that. He was incredibly warm and genuinely cared for the people around him. It came from a fundamental sense of being deeply god-fearing and behaved as if every action of his was judged by a higher power. He worked hard at studies, at sport, and always gave maximum effort to anything that came his way. This eventually turned him into one of the most when rounded students at the school.

Raj noticed Gajan had taken a seat next to Aishvarya, and as if on cue, Vinay quipped, "Our new class teacher, Padmini ma'am, has assigned seats to everyone. No more sitting where you feel like, and she has intentionally paired the new kids with class toppers, and hence Gajan with Aishvarya."

Raj grunted and looked around to see if he had been assigned a new bench partner as well, and to his dismay, he had to sit with a new student, Thomas.

Thomas was of average height, similar to Raj, and uncannily sported a similar hairstyle as well. And in the years that followed, many would confuse Thomas, Raj and Sachin given how similar they looked. Thomas had moved from Dubai and was exposed to a different culture from what he found himself at in MK Jnanadhara. For instance, the music he listened to was classic rock bands like The Rolling Stones, Pink Floyd and Led Zeppelin. He eventually turned out to be the best bench partner for Raj, since he introduced him to all these bands and Raj fell in love with them instantly. They would spend all day talking about discographies, song lyrics and new album releases. The rest of the class could hardly follow their conversation, making the pair form a tight bond with the exclusivity. It was all the music Raj and Thomas would listen to for the rest of their lives, and the school bench marked the beginning of their friendship.

Of all the new students who had joined the 7th grade, none made as much of an impact as Dev. Dev was tall, good looking and exuded confidence and clarity in thought that betrayed his age. While introducing himself in class, he said that his purpose in life was, "to make people laugh." It sounded trivial to some of the other students, but in the days that followed, nobody else brought their purpose alive as much as Dev.

He would frequently crack smart and witty jokes that made everyone laugh. When it came to Dev, the students laughed with him, unlike China who the students laughed at.

However, Dev's comedy was not limited to the classroom, and he was phenomenal on stage, successfully making wider audiences crack up.

A new auditorium had been set up in school and Sachin, inspired by the Malayalam slapstick comedy shows his parents watched on TV, decided to host a skit at the new auditorium.

He assembled a cast that consisted of Aishvarya, Sushmita, Thomas and Dev. Among them, Dev had the smallest role in terms of dialogue, but he needed to be on stage for the entire duration. He was put in-charge of the microphone on stage, so that he could move it around for the rest of the cast as required.

With just this small part, Dev single-handedly made the skit a resounding success.

"The things you were doing with the microphone, at one point acting like it was an ice cream cone, was hilarious! The crowd just loved it!" Raj praised at the end of the skit.

Later in the year, an inter-house competition among the students of all the houses of the 7th grade was announced. Each house was tasked with organizing a skit about a famous scientist.

Raj, the green house's captain, picked Nicolas Copernicus and set about researching for the skit. However, as the preparations progressed, something dawned on Raj. He realized he was not comfortable on stage. Unlike the rest of his friends who seemed to love the limelight, he didn't want to play even a supporting character in the skit, let alone Nicolas Copernicus.

He was competitive nevertheless and wanted to ensure he got the best scores. So, he approached Dev to play the protagonist. Dev was in the blue house, and though this was an inter-house competition, Raj knew that Dev, more than any other student in class, loved to put on a show on stage. He knew Dev would accept and also ensure his skit was a success. It was unconventional, but Raj had his way. Remained inconspicuous in the background, and yet ensured great results.

Padmini ma'am decided to enroll the school into a prestigious inter-school theatre competition known as NIE. The skits hosted by Sachin and the acting talent of newcomers like Dev didn't go unnoticed. Padmini ma'am organized a skit called 'Bus Stop' and cast Aishvarya, Sushmita, Thomas, China, Vinay, Gajan, Sachin and Dev, who were thereafter referred to as the Bus Stop crew.

Dev was offered the lead role. His character had to speak in Kannada, a language he wasn't familiar with, since he had moved to Bangalore from Kolkata only that year. Despite the time crunch, he learnt the language and played the role so well that he was nominated for the Best Actor award at the end of the show.

He did not go on to win the Best Actor award, but 'Bus Stop' did win Best Play, catapulting the nascent two-year-old school to being recognized as one of the best performing arts schools of Bangalore.

Sachin and Dev had been bitten by the theatre bug, and they would go on to host many shows in the years to come, partly given their interest in theatre, and partly as an excuse to keep the Bus Stop crew together.

Scene change: PT Class

PT or Physical Training was everyone's favorite class because they got to play outside on a fifty-square-meter dusty patch. As if the outdoors were not exciting enough, they had an old, bald man with a waist so large he struggled to tie his own shoelaces to teach them 'Physical Training'. He did anything but that and would constantly be the butt of jokes amongst the students.

"You three, walk in pairs" and "stop making noise like pigeon pollution" were some of his classics. In the years to come with social media and memes, it felt as though the 'Indian Teacher' jokes were modeled on this very PT teacher.

A PT curriculum was practically non-existent, and after shouting at a few kids, the PT teacher would leave them to their own devices.

One day, during one such PT class, the students decided to have a race. They organized themselves at the starting point and braced themselves for the run. The finish line was drawn just a few meters before the school compound.

When the mark was given and the students began to run, Raj gave it all he had. He was so competitive that he didn't slow down near the finish line, and promptly went smashing against the compound wall.

All the kids started laughing at him. Embarrassed, Raj looked at them and was about to pick a fight when he realized that something was wrong with his arm. It started hurting a lot, and he cringed as the pain got worse by the moment.

"Sir! Sir! Something happened to Raj's arm," shouted a few students as they ran towards the PT teacher.

"You silly fellow, why didn't you slow down near the finish line?" he exclaimed angrily.

Raj, still in agony, looked up at him and replied calmly, "Because I came first."

Scene change: Science class

The next day, Raj walked into class with a cast on his arm. The first period was the science class and the students had to present a science project. Everyone carried a fair bit of equipment with them, but Raj just carried a small bag and a can of Coke.

Gajan, who would grow up to be a design engineer, was most curious about everybody's projects. When he noticed Raj, he asked with concern, "You couldn't carry anything else because your arm is broken?"

"Not at all, this can is my science experiment!"

The students started setting up and demonstrating their respective projects. When Raj's turn came, Gajan and Sachin exchanged a nervous glance, unsure of what Raj was about to do.

Raj took out a detergent bottle and a beaker from his bag and poured the liquid from the detergent bottle into the beaker. Then he opened the can of Coke and put it inside the beaker such that the detergent liquid came up to the brim of the Coke can. He left it that way for a while and soon, everyone could see the transparent detergent liquid turning black.

Raj removed the Coke can from the beaker and hoisted it up to show that the metal layer of the can had dissolved and what was left behind was the layer of plastic out of which all of the Coke had drained out into the detergent in the beaker. Raj went on to explain that plastic used formed a semi-permeable membrane through which the Coke flows out.

All the students stared blankly at each other. They had never heard of a semi-permeable membrane before.

Sure enough, with one functioning hand, a beaker, some detergent liquid and a can of coke, Raj aced the Science project.

Scene change: Library class

Raj looked forward to library class the most. For a whole hour, he could sit and read any book of his choice undisturbed. The library at MK Jnanadhara had so many more books than the one at St. Anthony.

Raj soon discovered that comics could be a lot more interesting than Phantom or Mandrake. There was Archie's and Jughead! Raj loved these comics, especially the ones with Betty. He would catch himself daydreaming about her and shake his head in disbelief that he had a crush on a fictitious animated character. There was something about the 'girl-next-door' in shorts he admired, especially the strips on a sunny day when Betty would step outside her house barefoot.

But the library housed more than just comic books.

Raj was introduced to Hardy Boys and Nancy Drew and the Famous Five. He loved all of them. Their exciting adventures made up for what Raj thought his real world enormously lacked in. He would envision himself playing one of the characters in the books he read, hoping one day some of them may indeed come true.

It was during the library period when Raj discovered that he was a faster reader than everyone else in his class. He had the fastest frequency of picking books off the shelf, making some of the other students wonder if he really was reading everything. He became a voracious reader and was soon running out of books to read in the school library.

Scene change: Mobile library

Just as Raj was exhausting the collection at the school library, the Mobile library came as a godsend. It was a van that would drive up to this street a few blocks from school every day in the evening, and the students would walk up to it and pick out the books of their choice.

The Mobile library van had a more varied collection than the school library.

But what Raj liked more than that was that he could walk all the way to the street where the van was parked, with Aishvarya. This fifteen-minute walk turned out to be the favorite part of his day. Due to the assigned seating and reduced house captain duties, Raj did not get too many opportunities to talk with Aishvarya in school.

While the walks to the Mobile Library were great, there were always one too many students walking along with them, and Raj wished he had more alone time with Aishvarya.

The Archie comics move.

On one such visit to the Mobile Library, Raj handed an Archie comic to Aishvarya, saying it was a book he bought because he really liked the stories in it and that he wanted Aishvarya to read it.

Aishvarya took the comic book home and noticed that written on the first page was Raj's name and phone number. She was confused as to what this meant. Did Raj want her to call her, or did he write his name and phone number in all the books he owned?

Not knowing what to do, she went to Sushmita's house and asked for advice.

"Call him, of course," said Sushmita.

"But what if he thinks I'm weird to call him? Or, what if he thinks I like him? I'm too scared," replied Aishvarya.

"Fine, then I'll do it."

"Noooooo!"

"It's fine, I'll fake the conversation," Sushmita said as she dialed Raj's number.

"Hello, can I speak with Santosh please?" she asked when he picked up the call.

"Santosh? There is no one here by that name," replied Raj.

Sushmita apologized for having dialed a wrong number but kept the conversation going without revealing her true identity.

The entire time they talked, Aishvarya was squealing with excitement in the background, oblivious to the fact that Raj was engaged in a riveting conversation with Sushmita, without even knowing who she really was.

This marked the beginning of a long and complicated relationship between Raj and Sushmita.

The prank call made Aishvarya realize that she was fond of Raj. However, she couldn't convince herself to call him. Instead, she returned his Archie comic book with her number written next to his on the front page.

Scene change: English class

Raj was good at most subjects, but English was his best subject. The top honors in their English class were usually shared among Raj, Aishvarya and Sushmita. Aishvarya, however, aced every other subject, making her the overall first rank holder in the 7th grade.

Raj's proficiency in English had everything to do with his habit of reading, for which the English teacher loved him. She would constantly single him out in class and praise him endlessly. She would also single out the ones who did not perform well, namely China, who was always at the receiving end of her ire.

Once, during an English test, they were tasked with writing an advertisement for a watch. China borrowed Gajan's watch and spent the duration of the test drawing an exact replica of that watch. That was it. That was his advertisement. It was a great drawing, but not what the English teacher wanted, and she promptly reprimanded him in class.

On another occasion, she asked a student to read an essay written by China. It was so poorly written that all the students had a good laugh at China's expense.

Poor China, bookish learning was never his thing. He turned into the class jester, a role he always held within the Bus Stop crew.

Raj was the opposite of China. He was bright, and he devoured books. And with very little effort, grades came by for him, making all the teachers, especially the English teacher, adore him.

Learning to drink and smoke – Part 1

Datta, one of the new students in class, was known for drinking and smoking. Some of the other students in class got curious about this and Datta offered them beer in Pepsi bottles and a few drags of the cigarettes he used to carry on him.

Thomas and Sachin, among the group of curious students, tried them out and absolutely hated it.

Datta, being more experienced, explained to them that it never felt good the first few times, but eventually you figured out what the fuss was all about.

Soon enough, Thomas and Sachin began to spend every evening with Datta, trying to appreciate smoking, while the rest of the students walked up to the Mobile library.

One day, Raj got to know about the things Thomas and Sachin were up to. He was furious. He called them aside and yelled at them.

Thomas and Sachin tried telling him all the things that Datta had told them and asked Raj to join them as well.

"Never!" shouted Raj, "I will never drink and smoke like you guys."

Second Act.
2010

Substance abuse

"Dude, you've got to come home right now," Raj screamed into the phone the moment Sachin picked it up. "The house is on fire."

"Dude, I told you, I can't come home and drink with you today. I'm out with my office colleagues. Please stop it with this nonsense."

"Listen, Sachin, I'm not kidding. The house is on fire, and you need to get here right away."

Sachin hung up on Raj and got back to watching the movie with his new team. He had just been posted to Chennai for work as the Area Sales Manager. Raj had been notorious for his outlandish stories lately, like the time he scared the shit out of everyone when he casually brandished a gun in Kolkata barely a year ago. Sachin found it hard to take his current outburst too seriously.

The phone rang again, "Dude, you've got to come home right now, the house is on fire!"

"Hey man, calling me and saying the same thing over and over again is not going to help."

"Dude, I'm telling you, the house is on fire. You have to come home right now."

Knowing fully well that the calls would not stop till he went home, and faintly worried that the story might just be true, Sachin profusely apologized to his new team and left the theatre to get home.

He hailed an auto and started towards the apartment he had recently moved into with Raj, who had been posted in Chennai after spending the last year in Kolkata.

When he reached the building, he saw a fire truck parked outside, spraying water into the top floor, the same floor where his shared apartment was.

The moment he saw the truck, Sachin jumped out of the auto and ran up the stairs. As he climbed up the four flights of stairs, he could see the other residents of the building outside their doors, talking frantically amongst each other.

"It seems he set the house on fire willingly," said one.

"They are saying there were sparks from the AC," whispered another.

Upon reaching the entrance of the house, Sachin saw Raj sitting comfortably on the sofa in the hall, smoking a cigarette, with a bottle of Jack Daniels placed on the table in front of him.

"What the hell is going on!" burst Sachin.

"Hey dude, thanks for coming. The house was on fire. There are firemen in your room right now."

Sachin ran into his room to see all of his clothes and books scattered all over the place. And soaking wet.

One of the firemen made his way towards him and asked, "Do you live here?"

"Yes," said Sachin, visibly shivering with fear and rage.

"We managed to douse out the fire and salvage as many of the things as possible inside the house. Your friend outside said there were sparks from the AC that caused this, but we've seen enough of such house fires, and we can tell you that this was no accident."

"What do you mean?"

"Your friend went to bed with a cigarette in his hand, which is what started the fire. His room is the most damaged and that is where the fire started. You can see his bed is burnt to a crisp."

"Ok, sir, I understand. Thanks for your trouble. Do I need to pay you anything for this?"

"You don't have to pay anything, but we have to report it like it is. This was a callous drinking negligence by your friend outside."

"Sir, please don't report it that way. Can you just say that this was an accident?"

"Who will believe it! Look outside your door. All of your neighbors have been coming one by one to see the tamasha here, and the first thing they see is that fellow drinking and smoking in the hall."

"I understand. Let me deal with him."

Sachin rushed to the hall and grabbed the bottle from the table, but Raj stopped him, "No, don't remove this. They must know that I was drinking and therefore didn't notice the sparks from the AC."

"What rubbish, Raj! You know how terrible this looks!" Sachin forcefully removed the bottle from the table and took it into his room, all the while eyeing the neighbors outside who were witnessing the scuffle between the two friends.

"Sir, our landlord will only believe the official report. It would really matter a lot if you called this an accident. Please let me know what can be done."

"Ok, you pay Rs. 1000 to each of us here for the effort we have put in, and I'll will see what can be done."

"There are 4 of you here. That's a lot of money."

"Well, you think all this water and the truck outside comes free of charge?"

"Ok, ok, just give me some time to get the money. I'll give it to you outside."

Sachin ran as fast as he could to the nearest ATM to get the money and came back to give it to the firemen who had packed up and were sitting in their trucks by then.

He went up to find Raj in the hall; the Jack Daniels was back on the table and the glass next to it refilled.

"What is wrong with you, Raj! I just took that bottle away and you've brought it back here again. And you're drinking with the door wide open? Can't you see that all the neighbors can see this?"

"That is the whole point dude. If they see this, they will believe that I was drinking and didn't realize the AC was sparking."

"Man, nobody believes that. It's a stupid story," said Sachin, shutting the door, "now let's get out of here because the place stinks."

"I am not going anywhere. I've been waiting to have a drink from this bottle."

"You mean this has just been lying here and you aren't drunk?"

"Of course, I'm drunk! I was out drinking with colleagues and pretty smashed before I came home itself. You know I don't drink alone right! I was just ensuring the bottle is visible to be consistent with my story. But after staring at it for so long, I really need have a drink."

"Are you seriously going to sit in this smoke and soot and drink?"

"Of course, are you going to join in?"

Chapter 3

Unstable career

First Act.
1995

Learning to drink and smoke – Part 2

Over the summer holidays, Raj began drinking and smoking as well. His new best friend, Thomas, loved playing snooker, and would hang out all the time at a snooker parlor called Prime Time, chain-smoking the entire time he was there.

Raj figured he was good at snooker and found himself at Prime Time as often as Thomas, and there was only so much he could resist before giving the cigarette a try himself. Soon, after an entire day of snooker, they began going out for beers in the evening. This became a routine for both for many years to come.

When school resumed after the summer holidays, they would try to cut classes to go out for a smoke.

On one occasion, Dev joined them outside for a smoke. When they got back, Padmini ma'am was waiting for the trio at the entrance. She asked them where they were, and Raj and Thomas said they were playing pen fight on the table and the pen went flying out the window and so they went out to fetch it.

Padmini ma'am looked at Dev and asked what he was doing there. Dev calmly replied, "Ma'am, it was my pen."

The three of them came very close to being rusticated from the school. When Aishvarya got to know about this, she waited for the moment she was with Raj on one of their walks to the Mobile Library and reprimanded him for his newfound habit. Some of the students who noticed Aishvarya's concern dismissed it as just another goody two shoes act by the class topper. Only Sushmita, Aishvarya's closest friend, knew that it was more than that. Aishvarya liked Raj a lot and was worried he was about to embark on a path there may be no turning back from.

There was a lot that Raj wanted to tell Aishvarya about his newfound passion for smoking. But during Aishvarya's sudden outburst, the words escaped him. At times like this, he chose to write. It was as if the thoughts in his head and the feelings in his heart manifested into the words that ebbed out of his fingers, through the pen, and onto the paper in front of him. And as the ink dried on the paper, he felt calmer, like he had transferred his discomfort out of his body and onto the paper to achieve Zen status. He picked up the diary his mom had given him in which he would write every time he had a moment and began to write as he was having one right then.

It so happens that today is International Anti-Smoking Day, the day where it is officially allowed for a bunch of holier-than-thou people to freely parade on the streets, dispensing information about the oh-so-gory effects of tobacco. They say that peer pressure is the single biggest reason that people start smoking, so we have days like this where we try to curb peer influence by influencing people with placards instead. C'mon nothing is absolutely black or white, there are shades of grey in almost everything. You want proof?

Smoking is the single biggest preventable cause of death. What about car accidents? They cause more deaths, don't they? Should we walk everywhere? What, that is not preventable. Who decides that? YOU?

There are an estimated 1.3 billion smokers and half of them (some 650 million people) are expected to die prematurely of a tobacco-related disease. The tobacco industry also employs more than 100 million people worldwide. Would you rather they beg on the streets? Don't blame those poor employees if they light up then!

The Department of Health, which leads in the observance of smoking related health issues, has issued a warning against the long-term effects of cigarette smoking. Hitler once said the Aryans are the only pure race, America in the early 19th century thought slaves were the next best thing after Swiss cheese. Yeah, but surely the DoH's word must be absolute. Far be it for me to make up my own mind.

"Long-term smoking has been linked to various health problems and has been found to aggravate existing health conditions," the DoH said. Various health problems… MY problems! What's yours?

Don't brush this off as the biased opinion of a smoker, I do agree with plenty of rules. Like different smoking sections, I have no problem with that. Why should I harm others? Underage smoking should be curbed, packs should come with warnings... yada yada yada... but pray tell me when I sit alone on a cold, rainy afternoon minding my own business, smoking my own cigarette... why must you ruin my view with your stupid placard?

Official quote: "People always come up to me and say that my smoking is bothering them... Well, it's killing me!" - Wendy Liebman

Video games

Video game consoles were one of the by-products of India's 1991 liberalization and they started making their way into India from China. Super Mario, Contra, Tank, and the likes were doing their rounds through gaming devices like Dendy and Sega. Raj was the first in class to buy a Dendy game console. Sachin soon followed with a Sega, and the practice of exchanging video game cartridges between the two began.

The rest of the class split themselves into playing these video games at either one of their houses.

Raj was the undisputed champion of video games. Nobody from class could match him on any of them. He seemed to be naturally gifted at maneuvering the digital world. This finesse at video games trickled over to his programming skills in the computer lab, where Raj wrote some of the best C++ codes in class.

Now, in addition to the English teacher, the computer teacher adored him. He seemed to wield unimaginable powers over her.

Once, the students had an exam at the computer lab and while waiting outside the lab for the previous batch to finish, some of the students egged Raj to turn off the main switch outside.

He actually did it and when the computer teacher rushed out to see what had happened, he innocently replied, saying, "Sorry, ma'am, I was trying to turn on the lights in the corridor and it seems I switched off the mains."

"Oh, that's ok, Raj," the teacher said and simply turned the mains back on and instructed the students inside to redo their programs in case they hadn't saved their work.

Raj could literally get away with anything with these teachers.

Sometimes reality seems like life in slow motion. Playing Tomb Raider for three days non-stop will do that to you. Does that invisible line that divides the realms of imagination and real life reside only in frail minds? Are we flirting with madness?

There seems to be a definable point of no return, on the other side of which everything seems perfect. Isolated beyond compassion, Insulated beyond boredom. Within my own private castle there is no place for either. Should we join the living? Should we just sit hand in hand soaking in this perfect world we have created? Just some more random thoughts that are better off in my diary. Not a kindred soul to be bothered by these wasteful imaginations.

Windows 95

In 1995, Microsoft launched their seminal operating system, Windows 95, that revolutionized personal computing. Raj needed to be first in line in this department as well and convinced his dad to buy him a personal computer.

Having a home PC made Raj a whiz at coding. For the Computer class year-end assignment, he created the front end for what is now Skyscanner.net. Sachin created something similar, along the same lines as what is now Booking.com. They both had one of the best projects in class. However, when they compared their codes, Sachin noticed one specific function that Raj had that totally beat Sachin's code. This function was 'undelete.'

Sachin's mind was blown at how the details of a user could be recovered if they deleted their record by accident. After Raj explained how it worked, it turned out to be such a simple hack. All he used was the * symbol to mark the record. But without that explanation, it seemed an amazing thing to do on the front end.

Coding was not the only thing Raj used his personal computer for. Soon enough, the boys from class switched from their old video games and gravitated entirely to Raj's house to play 3D games like Mortal Kombat and Tomb Raider.

Computers and programming and video games were not for everyone in the class though. Once, during a discussion about the internet in class, China asked innocently, "Guys, can I buy this internet on a floppy drive?"

Enter Sharon

In the 8th grade, boys and girls first started noticing the opposite sex, a bit more than they had done up until then. Secretive glances were stolen, letters exchanged hands and rumors about who liked who ran through the hallways.

Vinay often asked Gajan to switch places with him in the morning assembly line so that he could spend those ten boring minutes every morning ogling a girl from a senior class. In the library period, boys would rush to take those seats from where they could look at the pretty girls from their class. The librarian thought they loved reading books so much. Little did she realize it was all an effort to spend that one hour staring at girls instead of reading books.

Sachin handed his first love letter to a girl in their class who he had a crush on. She promptly handed it to her mother, and Sachin went searching for a rock he could hide under. He was just glad the mother never tried talking to him, and Sachin began to detest the very thought of love letters after that point.

Two other girls in class, Shahzma and Sharon, were seen together all the time. They hung out together more so because they were ostracized by the rest of the class for being 'tom boys.' This was the term given to those girls who dressed and spoke like boys.

One evening, Sharon asked Sachin to meet him outside the school compound and handed him a note. It was a love letter from Shahzma. Sachin was absolutely furious, not just because he never wanted to see another love letter but also because he didn't want the rest of the students to know that one of the 'tom boys' liked him. He called Sharon out to the school compound and yelled at her, "Never, ever give me a note like that again. Just stay out of my life. I will complain to the teachers about both of you if any of the other students get to know about this letter."

It was ironic that while the rest of the class were busy matchmaking, Aishvarya and Raj, who many thought would make the 'first couple' of their class, completely stopped talking to each other. Aishvarya was waiting on Raj to act on the phone number she had written in his Archie comic, but Raj was too caught up with his video games and snooker and drinking and smoking, all of which he knew would certainly not be approved of by Aishvarya, and it seemed much better to avoid her than get around to making that call. Their walks to the Mobile Library the previous year seemed like a distant past. Raj spent all of his time in the company of Thomas, and Aishvarya in the company of her books.

Thomas on the other hand, had his eyes set on Sushmita. He would leave no stone unturned to let her know that he liked her. He would constantly do corny things like popping up next to her at the science lab, placing his burette next to hers, and saying they look good together.

Raj would notice this and make fun of Thomas, calling him a wisecrack. Thomas' persistence paid off though, and he and Sushmita became the official 'first couple' of school.

If you even find yourself outnumbered by the enemy's army, gather your battalion close.

Formation - Closed box style.

Keep the sharpest archers and the heavily armored ground forces on the periphery.

The sickly and not so agile can mock the rest from inside this iron clad boundary.

If you try hard enough, you can laugh off your enemy to an early death...

Like a wise man once said, we have something much more dangerous than sticks and stones. We call it the wisecrack.

Second Act.
2011

Unstable career, three strikes

Thomas was settled in Dubai. He was born in the Emirati city, but his parents sent him to India for schooling. Once he completed school, he moved back to Dubai where he graduated from an engineering college, and then went on to do his MBA, and eventually found a great job, and got married to his b-school batchmate, Sneha. Life couldn't have been better, until he got a call from Raj asking if he could help him find a job in Dubai. The only thing that could have made Thomas' life better in Dubai was to have his best friend over. Or so he thought.

Raj moved to Dubai and hated everything there. He called Dubai, 'The big dusty' and cursed it for going against every principle he believed.

For starters, the company he joined kept his passport. He only gave it to them thinking that it was procedural, but they insisted on returning it only if he were to quit the organization and go back to India.

Raj was a big believer of freedom, liberty and individual rights, essentially all things United States, the country he originally wanted to move to, but he had to settle for Dubai since that was where he could find a job. The fact that his Dubai organization held on to his passport, a representation of his basic identity in a foreign land, infuriated him.

To top that, he did not find his work to be challenging enough. Ever since his early days in school, since the 6th grade, Raj was exceptional at studies, and loved to be challenged by difficult tasks. However, he worked in Supply Chain in Dubai, where you can literally travel from one end of the city to another in a day. Their supply chain barely challenged him.

He was tasked with doing mundane operational work throughout the day like monitoring the truck loading efficiency of his delivery partners, for which he was certain he could write an algorithm, if only the delivery partners took orders from a machine. The boredom at work, coupled with his frustrations towards the state's abject disregard for liberty, created a new hobby for Raj. Finding a new bar that he could visit every night just to get drunk. It was a sort of retribution for him since the state wouldn't even serve alcohol to him as freely as he wanted to. So, this was both a challenge and a resort to vent.

Thomas and Sneha were his only friends in Dubai, and he spent most of his time drinking with them. However, after the first few months, it became difficult for Thomas and Sneha to keep up with not only Raj's drinking but also his incessant bickering. When they started to avoid him, Raj resorted to coercing some of his colleagues to go out drinking with him. Unfortunately for him, they tolerated him even less.

Dubai is a lucrative place to work for most people given their tax-free earnings and plethora of global companies to choose from. A lot of expats therefore found themselves there, and they tend to keep their guard up, at times, even amongst their own people. Raj would often talk unabashedly about work or the government to other Indian colleagues, which to his chagrin, made them very uncomfortable.

Soon enough, he was left with no company to drink with, which was when he began drinking alone.

"Never drink alone. It's how you become an alcoholic," was what Raj would always tell the people he drank with. Come what may, he would force his company to have a drink before getting started himself.

Dubai changed this for him. In the one year he was there, his inner frustration escalated to such an extent that he went against one of his core tenets and began drinking alone. He started to hunt for another job back in India. He couldn't believe he was missing the country he had craved to get out of less than a year ago, after the hellish living experiences he had had in Kolkata and Chennai. But now, all he could think about was getting out of Dubai.

He haaaa…. Alone at last. My entire floor of co-workers has gone to attend a presentation, which I honestly did not know was happening. The whole place is MINE…. Look around…. Ok, getting bored now… start playing music on my comp. Hey, that's a good song… Man… The

Beatles... 'Strawberry fields.' I can seriously picture myself on a boat on the river, days like this make up for the countless other shitty ones. Soon, I will be done working here, very soon say in like 5-6 months. Want to have a lot more fun in my life. Don't get me wrong, this is a pretty good place to work in, but I'm way too young to be working now. Will miss certain things about this place though.... Oh, yes, I will! God, becoming nostalgic about my company... uuugghh... change of music.... Ah, Nightwish... Nymphomaniac Fantasia. Much better, cynical look successfully replaced on face :-)

There was a time when all Raj could think about was moving away from Bangalore. But in the last three years, he had shifted three jobs and lived in three cities, and now all he wanted was to get back to Bangalore. Kolkata, Chennai and Dubai, none of them suited him. After three strikes, he figured being back in Bangalore was probably the best option.

Raj soon landed a job in Bangalore. After barely a year of living in Dubai, he was back in India.

He didn't leave Dubai quietly though. He burnt bridges with his company, his colleagues, and worst of all, with Thomas. He directed all the rage he felt towards the city of Dubai onto Thomas and fought with him endlessly. His departure from Dubai was bitter-sweet for Thomas. He was sad his best friend couldn't enjoy Dubai the way he did, but he was relieved as well because he wouldn't have to deal with his wrath any further.

The day Raj was to fly out of Dubai, Thomas offered to drive him to the airport. Raj accepted, but when Thomas arrived at his house, Raj had already left, leaving behind a note for Thomas which read, "Nostalgia is like a grammar lesson; you find the present tense and the past perfect."

Raj got out of Dubai, leaving everything behind, except for his newfound habit of drinking alone.

Ever feel like the whole goddamn world is spinning too fast?

Every single word you hear makes no sense at all. Removed even from those who are there in that moment with you! Good people surrounded yet looking for a whole lot more. When the laughs just won't come, when the words just don't flow, when you just can't connect. These moments put a nice shine on the concept of loneliness. To be utterly alone, on your own in the middle of wide-open spaces. Just because you are immortalized in that stupid young man's eyes!

Maybe it's just the people....

Maybe.

Chapter 4

Defense Mechanism

First Act.
1996

Master of pranks

Raj's popularity in school continued to grow, and he was always surrounded by people, most of all Thomas. Though Thomas had been going steady with Sushmita for the past year, he would be seen hanging out with Raj more than Sushmita.

Raj had a lot of other friends though. He was like a solitary flame in a jungle that would attract all the flies in the vicinity. One of the reasons for this was his unique ability to engage practically anyone in a conversation. He could speak endlessly with Gajan about football, where he supported Manchester United, and Gajan backed Liverpool in the English Premier League. He could talk about all the latest programming languages and applications and video games with Sachin. And he could speak about music with Thomas.

What made Raj even more appealing were the pranks he was constantly involved in. Once, in the science lab, the teacher had just begun explaining the experiment and asked the students to handle the burette with care. But no sooner had she finished her sentence; a loud clang rang across the lab. The burette on Raj's table broke because he was impatient to wait for all the instructions to start off on his experiment, and promptly made a mistake while handling the equipment.

On his birthday, he took the class out to a restaurant called Tunga for dinner and offered Gajan a plate of rice, saying it was Egg Fried Rice. After the meal, he told Gajan, a staunch vegetarian, that the meal he had was Chicken Fried Rice. That was the first and only time Gajan ever had chicken, and because it was Raj who made him do it, he never said anything, apart from offering quiet prayers to his many gods.

Gajan eventually got his revenge by picking on Raj at the morning assembly line where Gajan oversaw uniform etiquette. If any of the students wore the incorrect socks or unkempt shirts, Gajan would make them run to the school gate and back. He picked on Raj all the time, and made it worse by running after him, throwing stones at a running Raj from behind.

Once, on China's birthday, Raj suggested giving him birthday bumps over a puddle of mud that had been formed by rain the previous day. China was soaked in dirty mud in the middle of the school day, and being the class jester, he simply played along. The teachers were not too impressed though and made all the boys with muddy clothes kneel in front of the entire school. While the boys who were kneeling were stressed out about how serious their punishment might get and wondered if they might even face rustication from the school, Raj was laughing merrily and cracking jokes the entire time. It was as if he knew kneeling was as serious a punishment the school was going to give them, and they were promptly sent back to class after 10 minutes of the kneeling parade.

9th grade was a time of fun and games for the students, but Raj, barely 15, had big ambitions.

Run for public office.

Create a video game.

Learn Magic.

Get Citizen Kane on DVD.

Reach the ripe old age of 50.

Play better poker.

Shave my head and grow a full beard.

Get a dog.

Get a Japanese Tattoo.

Get on the first train I see with a bottle of whiskey for company.

Build a Snowman.

Write a short story.

And many other,

But most of all,

To live without wondering why I exist...

Honnemaradu

Honnemaradu is a little coastal town, an overnight train ride away from Bangalore. The school organized a three-day camp in the town for the 9th graders. This school trip turned out to be a seminal point in their lifelong friendship.

The students were as excited as any group of fifteen-year-olds could be about train journeys. They had an entire train compartment to themselves, and the air inside was charged with energy.

Padmini ma'am traveled with the students and decided to let them choose where they would like to sleep instead of policing them like the assigned seating, she had forced them to adhere to in the 7th grade.

Raj, Thomas, Sachin, China, Vinay, Gajan, Dev, Aishvarya, Sushmita, Sharon and Vivek, found themselves in one section of the train compartment.

Vivek was one of the quietest kids in class. In fact, every time he said something, Raj would scream, "It's alive!" But Vivek was quite popular in class for his paintings. He had a way with the paintbrush that brought incredible landscapes to life on canvas. Every painting of his always had one girl with an abstract face.

Some of the kids speculated that it was a sister he never had. Some of the more mature ones said it was a girl he had a crush on. Vivek would remain his silent self whenever anyone probed him about it and the girl on the canvas remained a mystery for many years.

The group made themselves comfortable and found their seats. Sharon had started to mingle with more students in 9th grade, instead of only hanging out with Shahzma and found herself seated next to Raj on the side upper berth.

Sharon was still a bit of a tom boy, preferring shorts to jeans, unlike the rest of the girls. Raj found this oddly attractive. If Betty from the Archie comics could come to life, Sharon would be it. But he was too uncomfortable to acknowledge her presence and decided that avoiding eye contact was the best course of action.

The group was busy laughing and chatting and making so much noise that Padmini ma'am had to warn them that the racket they were creating would not go down well with the ticket collector.

"We will keep quiet when he comes, ma'am," the students told her.

In a while, the ticket collector did appear in the compartment, and the students immediately pretended to be asleep.

Raj and Sharon, who were occupying the same berth, ended up lying next to each other. The next few minutes felt like hours for Raj. He was trying hard not to breathe, not just for the ticket collector to believe they were asleep, but also to avoid brushing up his body against Sharon's.

The moment the ticket collector left, they got up and moved to different berths. The rest of the kids resumed their laughter and chatter, which continued well into the night.

The next day, the class reached Honnemaradu and checked into the dormitory. The first task of the day was to learn how to swim. They were taken in tiny round boats called coracles a little distance into the beach and simply asked to jump off and swim to the shore.

The students were harnessed with lifejackets and taken offshore in batches with just a few instructions on how to swim. Sachin and China found themselves on the first batch. Sachin was one of the few students who already knew how to swim, and when he saw China struggling, he decided to go towards him and assist him. But the moment he came close, China grabbed him and dunked him underwater, as if to use him as a lifeboat.

Sachin had to kick himself out of China's grip and swim away, letting him figure out how to swim back to the shore on his own. When Sachin reached the shore, he relayed the story to Raj who was scheduled to go in one of the next few batches. On hearing Sachin's brush with China, Raj decided to skip the activity. He quietly removed his life jacket and slid over to the side of the students returning from the activity to make it seem like he had already completed his, with none of the organizers any wiser.

At night, the students had to pitch their own tent to sleep in. There was one large one for the boys and one for the girls. The boys continued their random banter in their tent at night and at one-point, Padmini ma'am had to shout from the girl's tent, "Boys, we can hear everything you are saying. Can you please shut that nonsense!"

The next day morning, Gajan was the first in his tent to wake up. He stepped outside to see Padmini ma'am doing yoga.

"I'm surprised you've woken up so early after that ruckus last night," she said.

"If you don't wake up early, you've already missed the bus," Gajan replied, facing the sun and performing a Surya Namaskar himself.

Soon the rest of the boys were awake, and they were taken to a hill and asked to do their business anywhere on it. Raj decided to climb as high as possible and finally reached a spot from where he could see both Gajan and Vinay, who had started off before him, behind different trees, but with their backs to him while they did their business.

Raj avoided looking their way and was simply glad that there was at least nobody behind him. Just then China screams from behind him, "Hi Raj!"

After the awkward outdoor potty, the activity for the day was to learn how to coracle. Raj and Sharon found themselves on the same coracle. Once again, Raj awkwardly avoided eye contact.

When they were in the water, the instructor on the coracle suddenly noticed a hole, with the water seeping in fast. He asked the students on the coracle to pedal faster to the shore before they sunk their vessel.

Raj and Sharon looked at each other directly for the first time on the trip, and their eyes spelt fright in the exact same way. They quickly began to paddle with all their might and managed to make it to the shore right before the coracle capsized.

On the beach, Raj and Sharon looked at each other between labored breaths and broke into a smile. They were literally in a life-threatening situation and somehow managed to save each other's lives.

The students had one last night in Honnemaradu and were asked to trek to a location where they would set a campfire and sleep around it. This was a night trek where the students had to rely on flashlights and handholding.

As luck would have it, there weren't enough flashlights to go around and the available few were distributed among select students who would assist the rest. Gajan oversaw one flashlight and throughout the trek he kept turning the light on and off just to trouble the rest of them.

As they ambled along in the dark, it so happened that Raj and Aishvarya found themselves next to each other at a point where they had to climb a little hill in the dark. The organizers instructed the students to hold hands for that stretch and Raj and Aishvarya held hands. It was the first, and only time they did.

When they reached their destination, there was enough ambient light, saving them from relying on Gajan and his intermittent flashlight. Raj and Aishvarya continued to hold hands though.

This didn't go unnoticed, and Vinay crept up behind them and loudly said, "Guys, you can let go of each other's hands now," which made each immediately release the other's hand and blush, while the rest of the class watched on and giggled.

The students had to prepare their own campfire, and Dev went about collecting some of the biggest logs for the fire. The girls were offered a makeshift tent nearby to sleep in and the boys were asked to sleep outside.

Just when the boys were beginning to act all macho and took up the sleeping stations outside, they heard a blood curdling scream in the distance. It dawned on them that they were, after all, in a forest.

However, there were no alternative sleeping arrangements nor any explanations for the scream they had heard. And soon, the boys were falling over each other to ensure they were sleeping in the middle and not on the sides, lest a wild animal decided to pick one of them from the edge of the group.

It so happened that China was left sleeping on one corner, and the next day morning, he woke up to find a monkey seated next to him, admiring him peacefully.

In the morning, the students trekked back to the train station to begin their journey back home. Raj, Thomas, Sachin, China, Vinay, Gajan, Dev, Aishvarya, Sushmita, Sharon and Vivek, all occupied one section of the train compartment once again.

This time around they were much quieter though. The fatigue from the previous few days, coupled with the fact that all the fun was coming to an end turned the mood somber.

China was the one who finally broke the silence and said, "We will remain friends forever. Let's call ourselves the Bus Stop crew." He named the group after the play 'Bus Stop' that Padmini ma'am had staged last year, since he felt their specific group consisted of people from different walks of life, now gathered at one Bus Stop about to embark on a common journey together. The rest of the class was not sure if he had thought it through so much, but the name was unique, so it stuck.

Second Act.
2012

Sarcasm as a fabulous defense mechanism

My dearest Bus Stop crew, the day has finally arrived!

I am getting married, and nothing would make me happier than seeing you all at my wedding.

Aishvarya weds someone-who-isn't-Raj

Venue: Some temple in Coorg

Time: 4pm to the next day's morning

Aishvarya's wedding card was sent to everyone in the Bus Stop crew. She was the second person from the crew to get married. Thomas got married the previous year, but his wedding was in Dubai, and it was too far for anyone from the Bus Stop crew to travel. Aishvarya's wedding was in Coorg, which was still feasible to travel. The excitement was palpable among the crew with plans being hatched to make the trip from Bangalore to Coorg.

A few days before the wedding, Aishvarya decided it was time for her to get some closure.

Raj, I think it's time I told you how I felt. It seems like yesterday when we were all at school, so happy, so loved – always surrounded by friends who I knew I could always count on – Sushmita, Sachin, Gajan, Thomas. I could talk to them about my deepest thoughts. I think of you often when I stay up at night – memories and flashes of your face, expressions from sixteen years ago when we were in high school, and then in college. You looking at me ever so often with those intense eyes of yours – and me having no idea what was going on in your mind. You smoking near the chai shops in college, looking at me thoughtfully while I had my chocolate-milk and Gajan stuffing his face with bun-samosa which of course you'd have paid for. You annoying me by calling my 2 best friends pee-chuth, mee-chuth – that was your idea of impressing me? Something deep inside tells me you still liked me. But then, I'm sure you were always conflicted – too many women all around, always interested in your best friends' girlfriends – Sharon, Sushmita, Nitya and so on.

When I used to watch you in school moving around with your best friends, your arms around their shoulders, theirs around yours, bowling (always that black watch and tongue in cheek, and body in the air, ball in hand, swinging), riding past on your bike – smiling, happy – I'll take these images of you to my death-bed. Yeah, I watched you a lot, admiring, from a distance, wishing I was your girlfriend. I could write a book of admiration for you – it would read like 'Bridges of Madison County'. You were the cowboy to my inner-Francesca (smiling sadly). You were my first love, and I wonder if I would ever be able to love anyone with the passion, with the persistence I loved you – without judgement, without expectation, unconditionally.

How did all this change? For the last few years, there has been something dark I could not pull you out of. I needed to meet you face to face, but you refused to meet for anything but a drink. I could not encourage that drinking habit which became your undoing.

In my next life, I want to be your girlfriend and I want you to hold my hand, and I want to sit across from you and talk to you for hours, days, years. And when I'm convinced you have eyes for no one else, I might kiss you.

It was a note she never shared with Raj. Just something to give her closure as she moved on to the next chapter of her life. As was customary though, she invited all her friends. And all of them came, including Raj.

There is a custom in the Coorgi wedding where the people from the bride's side dance right in front of the bride as she walks to the alter, jokingly denying the 'handing over' of the bride from one family to the other. Raj danced right in front of everyone. It was a combination of head-banging and jumping, as if he were at a rock concert. It didn't seem much like dancing, but he was at it. And he danced so much that he was drenched in sweat by the end of it. It was the only time Raj danced, or did whatever he was doing, without anyone forcing him to.

The rest of the Bus Stop crew joined along, and they danced for hours. Aishvarya's father had to plead with them at one point to make way for her to pass and get on with the wedding.

"The wedding band is probably getting paid by the hour," Raj said in a snarky tone to his friends.

"Let's go back to our hotel and continue partying," he egged them.

The rest agreed as the wedding morphed into a boring ceremony that would go on for hours once the dancing ended.

Back at the hotel, Raj ordered beer for everyone, and they stayed up late, drinking and talking. It was almost daybreak when they decided to call it a day and get some sleep.

Raj arranged all the empty beer cans in the form of a pyramid.

"There, we've even created a temple right here. We're not missing the wedding at all."

Raj seemed mighty pleased with his creation.

In the years to come, the rest of the Bus Stop crew got married, and Raj did not attend any of their weddings.

Aishvarya's wedding would remain the first and the last he attended.

So, she is going to get married....

It's now time to give her my impassioned, well-reasoned speech. Her eyes are going to well up with tears as I make a list of my favorite things about her. She's then going to run into my arms, flinging herself to me with a fervor I wouldn't expect her to have. Her smile burns the bitterness from my deepest unplumbed depths and happy tears begin streaming from these cheeks too.

We kiss. Passionately, with ardor and without affect. I lift her into my arms and carry her over to my car, which I left running. THE ENVIRONMENT BE DAMNED, THIS IS TRUE LOVE. We hop in, glance at one another conspiratorially, and laugh with reckless abandon. Her hand in my hand. I shake my head at her. This is a standard – don't be silly, honey. Switch into reverse, back out quickly, switch into 1st, then burn rubber out of there as the wedding party's mental gears are only now clicking into place with the enormity of what's just happened.

But we couldn't care about that. True fuckin' love, bro. They wasted a few bucks booking a venue, hiring a DJ, all that jazz, big tossocks, eh. There's an open bar, they'll make the best of it.

We're driving now and doing that thing the movies always do where you address her directly and establish firm eye contact yet somehow don't crash. We couldn't help but do otherwise – the love for her is too strong to take my eyes off her. This is my time now. You don't have to go through all the grunt work of relationship-building; you just came into the World of Wifery at level 80 prepared to rock out with your cock out?

Everything's going to be perfect. and we both know it. Belle and Sebastian plays, or maybe some shit on a toy piano as someone with a reedy voice talk-sings incoherent nothings into the ether. The orchestra swells, and it's clear to all of us watching at home that we've got ourselves a happy ending, That's pretty much all folks.... The long happy forever....

Sure, her fiancé's probably given her thousands of backrubs, accompanied her on shopping trips he had little interest in, sat through bad movies, met relatives he could have done without, held her while she cried and held back when she screamed. All of that without ever questioning if he really does love her.

Or maybe, I had my chance. I should wish them both well, act my age, try to look good in a suit and not get too loaded and make an ass of myself!

Just cheer them good health and keep drinking... and make sure I choose better movies for the next weekend....

Chapter 5

Lack of Empathy

First Act.
1997

Change of heart

Raj had been mesmerized by Aishvarya's beauty since the first day he saw her and was always drawn to her, be it on the walks to Mobile library in the 7th grade or the trip to Honnemaradu in the 9th grade. But every time Raj got close to Aishvarya, he would lose his nerve and swing the opposite way, ignoring her for months after. They had a lot of similar interests, like reading books or listening to old English bands. But Raj would intentionally bring up books like Russian or Swedish literature, which he knew would be too much on the dark and philosophical side for Aishvarya's liking or deviate to heavy metal when he liked The Beatles and The Rolling Stones just as much as Aishvarya.

He couldn't figure out what it was. There was something about Aishvarya that made him feel naked. It was as if she knew exactly who he was and who he was risking becoming, and that terrified him. He was scared to face the demons he thought existed in him and preferred to keep his brain distracted with things like music, books and video games. But when he was with Aishvarya, she saw through him, which made him see through him, and he didn't like it.

The Bus Stop crew had entered the 10th grade, the year of the board exams. In these exams, the students from all schools competed for a coveted spot in the Computer Science or Biology streams of the 11th grade where the resident consensus was that students passing out from here held better jobs than if you were to pass from an Arts or Commerce college.

While passing the exams was predominantly on everyone's minds, the boys had one other topic that interested them: Sharon. Over the last year, Sharon had completely transformed. She still sported short hair and preferred to wear shorts. But her breasts bloomed pretty much overnight and that made every boy in school give her a second look.

While most boys spent their time talking about Sharon, Raj scoffed at them for being so juvenile.

Secretly, though, Sharon caught his fancy as well. He always found all the things that made her a 'tom boy' attractive, and it went beyond just a physical attraction. Sharon liked the same music and video games Raj liked, but more importantly, Raj felt he could have a simpler conversation with her.

For the first time, Raj felt like doing something about a girl.

What is love?

Baby don't hurt me, no more?

Of all the inane songs and quotes on love I've come by, these one sticks, "Love is giving someone the power to destroy you but trusting they won't."

That is the jumping without looking I can relate with.

At the risk of coming off kid,

I love it too now.

It never gets boring, actually everything else does,

No matter how imperfect the love, you just know,

It's better than before her?

Actually, yup Mitchell and Webb,

It probably is.

Two people who are a little bit deluded in each other's favor?

It's enough,

It's more than I ever deserved for my happy.

Board exams

The board exams were a huge ordeal for all the students. Of all their exams, the Chemistry practical exam was the toughest. The students were given different experiments to perform in the lab, wherein they had to study numerous chemical reactions and be precise in following the procedures for the experiment to be successful.

Not more than two or three students in the group of thirty in the science lab received the same experiment. It was therefore very difficult to cheat, even if one wanted to.

For his experiment, Raj had to prepare soap. If done properly, the final product would appear like Pear's soap, indicating the experiment's success.

Raj knew the procedure well and went about doing his experiment. The last step was to cool down the glycerin mix till it got the signature Pears soap color. Raj left it on the stand and went on to write some notes while the mix cooled down.

A little while later, when he went to pick up his mix, he found that it was missing. He was completely alarmed and started looking around, till he spotted Sharon with the same mix. He approached her and upon closer inspection, realized that it was indeed his experiment.

Just when he was about to complain, he noticed the look in Sharon's eyes. They were screaming an apology. Raj figured she had the same experiment as his and probably couldn't complete it. Since there was enough time on the clock and Raj was confident with the experiment, he quickly set out to repeat the entire process.

He managed to finish just in time. When he got out, he spotted Sharon with her friends. Her eyes once again told him what he wanted to know. They were filled with gratitude this time, and Raj broke into a smile, glad that he could help her, and no harm caused in the process.

Party at Gajan's house

After the board exams were over, the students decided to meet at Gajan's house for a party. There was talk of music and disco lights and dancing. At the mention of dancing, Raj decided to skip the party. He would never be seen dancing!

When the rest of the students met up at Gajan's, Sharon was the talk of town again. She was wearing a sleeveless yellow top, a floral skirt, and brown wedge heeled shoes. It was the first time anyone had seen her in a skirt. She looked gorgeous.

As the party wore on, Sachin asked Gajan to move everyone to another room so that he could have some alone time with Sharon. Gajan pushed everyone to the next room, and the dance floor, teeming with people only moments ago, was deserted.

Sharon stood in the middle of the floor, wondering where everyone was going, when she saw Sachin approach her.

He came close, and as the disco lights sparkled around the room, their eyes met. It was the first they were seeing each other since the time Sachin shouted at Sharon outside the school two years back. But this time, Sachin blurted something very different and said, "I love you."

Sharon's eyebrows shot up, "What!"

Sachin continued to stare into her eyes and followed his proclamation with, "I would like to go out with you."

A million thoughts raced through Sharon's mind, but she figured that the only way out of this eye lock was to blurt out, "Um… ok."

Sachin's story

Just like every other boy in class, Sachin also found Sharon's transformation incredibly attractive. He knew she was the toast of the town and was only a matter of time before she was asked out by someone, so Sachin hurriedly decided to be first in line.

Only, he had never proposed to anyone before and thought the only way to do it was to say, "I love you." These words were cheap back then.

A few days after the party at Gajan's, Sachin asked Sharon out on their first date. They walked around a colony nearby and Sharon told him that she would be visiting Vizag, her hometown, for the upcoming two-month-long summer holidays.

Sachin was bummed out that they could not spend much time together in the summer but promised to keep in touch with her.

Just before they parted ways, Sharon landed a quick peck on his cheek before running off to her house.

It was the first time a girl had kissed him, even if it was on the cheek.

Sachin and Sharon spent the next few weeks exchanging letters with each other. It was the only form of communication, outside of 'trunk' calls to speak to someone in a different city.

A few weeks before Sharon was to return to Bangalore, the letters stopped coming.

Sachin started to worry when Sharon didn't call him after an entire week had passed since the date Sharon was scheduled to return to Bangalore.

One fine day, he received a call from Raj.

"I think you should stop seeing her," Raj told Sachin.

Sachin wondered what Raj had to do with his relationship with Sharon. Fearing something terrible, he went to Sharon's house to see if she had returned to the city.

Sharon had indeed come back on the date she was supposed to, but with Sachin standing on her porch, she figured it was best to clear things up with him before school reopened.

They went out for a walk, and she told him that she felt differently now. Her time in Vizag made her rethink their relationship. She did not want to go out with him any longer.

Sachin was confused, but strangely, felt as little as he did on the day he proposed to Sharon. He didn't seek any further clarifications and made peace with their break-up.

Sharon's story

Sharon fell for Sachin the first time she saw him in school in the 8th grade. He was smart, funny and good looking. His only fault was that he was too popular. Between him and Raj, it felt like you had to go through the rest of the class to get to them. That's how much they were perennially surrounded by people.

To make matters worse, Shahzma, her only friend in class, confessed her feelings for Sachin to her. Given she didn't have any other friends in class, Sharon decided to mask her own feelings and supported her friend in her pursuit of Sachin.

That letter incident did not go down well, and she cursed her decision for handing over Shahzma's letter to Sachin. It didn't work for them and made things worse between her and Sachin.

Two years later, when Sharon had all but given up on Sachin, out of the blue, he told her that he loved her. It took her completely by surprise. He also didn't give her any room to process the information. Hence, she decided to just go with it.

However, the day after Sachin proposed, Raj asked her out on a date as well. When it rains, it pours. The most popular boys in school suddenly wanted to be with her.

She was going to Vizag in any case and decided to keep things hanging with both boys till she got back. In the first few weeks at Vizag, she replied to all the letters Sachin wrote to her. It just felt like something a girlfriend should do, and technically, she had agreed to be his girlfriend.

However, the letters to him felt less and less interesting as the days passed by. Writing to Raj may have been one cause for this, because Raj was a gifted writer and she enjoyed reading his letters very much. But more than this, she felt Sachin wasn't being entirely genuine about his feelings for her.

Sharon felt that Sachin only liked the thought of being with her, rather than actually being with her. Though Sachin wrote to her every day, the letters lacked emotion.

Raj, on the other hand, wrote deeply meaningful letters to her. The very fact that she enjoyed reading Raj's letters made her realize she didn't like Sachin the way she used to. She decided to break up with him once she got back to the city.

The day she returned though, she called Raj first, and they went out on their first date.

It turned out to be the perfect date. They walked around the entire day, spent some time at Sharon's house, and later in the evening, visited a park where they sat in the most romantic spot she had ever visited.

It was at the edge of a cliff, where you could see a railway track below and a forest in front of them. There was a little space between the trees in the forest, and right in the middle of that blank space was a full moon.

The entire time they sat there, they saw the moon slowly rise perfectly between the gap in the trees. It was one of those moments that you couldn't capture in a painting or on film. Simply etched in memory forever.

Sharon told him the story of the rabbit on the moon that she heard as a child. A rabbit was trying to escape a lion in the jungle and reached the edge of a pond. The rabbit thought this was the end of her life, until she noticed the reflection of the moon on the surface of the pond. She decided to jump in, thinking the lion would never catch her on the moon. Unfortunately for her, she drowned, but not before leaving a permanent mark of hers that we can see on the moon to this day. The distinct features of the rabbits' head and ears, every single time on the moon. Raj loved the story. It was both a scientific fact since we never see the dark side of the moon from the earth, and an interesting story since the craters on the visible side indeed resembled the contours of a rabbit's ears.

Towards the end of the date, the two gave each other a longing look since they had to get back home. And Raj mustered up all his courage to give Sharon a quick peck on her cheek. She returned it in that same instant with a peck on his cheek.

The next day they went on another date, this time to the movies. The classic 'Grease' had been re-released, and it was the perfect movie since they both loved musicals. Sharon also looked forward to holding Raj's hand during the movie. But Raj didn't seem interested. She found it strange that they had shared a kiss just the previous day, but Raj was being retractive about handholding. Throughout the movie, he sat clutching his can of coke with both hands.

The days that followed got better though and they spent every single one of them together. Things were perfect, until Sachin showed up at her door, pulling her down to reality.

She decided it was best to rip the band-aid off right away instead of deliberating on the matter any further and decided to call it off with Sachin that very moment.

To her surprise, he agreed without seeking an explanation, and worse, without any emotion either. She was right about his being ingenuine about their relationship all along.

Raj's story

Raj did not attend Gajan's party, and given the exams were now over, the students didn't meet in school either. So, there was no way for him to know about the Sachin-Sharon proposal that had occurred.

He asked Sharon out on a date, unbeknownst to the fact that she had just become his friend's girlfriend. The fact that she was traveling to Vizag also fit perfectly, because he loved writing more than talking or even meeting people. And he wrote often to Sharon, most of his writings being whimsical poetry.

Are we searching,

for ourselves?

does it feel cold,

Surrendering?

Our... souls would be an easy rhyme...

but are we surrendering whole?

If I had a wish,

I wish I could write...

Write the Muddy waters which shine blues,

Sprinkle a bit of Miles and all that Jazz,

and top it all off with a decent bass line.

Wish I could write not a rhyme,

but a decent rhythm.

Tell me you will try,

To slip away somehow....

Cause I'm playing the sixties now...

Excuse me while I...

hmmm...average not/sadly never... Jimi?

So, Excuse me, my beautiful instigator,

While I look at a perfect 60's beat filled sky.

When Sharon returned to Bangalore, he decided to take her to the park near his house, and it seemed like the universe had conspired to offer them an unforgettable view.

They shared their first kiss there and the next day, they went out to watch 'Grease'. Raj was running late and tried to take a short cut by climbing a wall near the theatre. To his bad luck, there was a jagged edge on the wall that ripped the underside of his pants. Not wanting to call off the date, he bought a can of coke and covered his pants with it the entire time.

The day after that, Raj was careful to leave his house well in advance, because they were meeting up at Sharon's house.

Raj suggested they play the staring contest where the first person who blinks loses. They played once and Raj lost.

Then they took a break and reminisced about the moment at the park once more. When they got back to the same position, they were in for the staring contest, Raj said, "Ok, let's do it again." He meant the staring contest, but Sharon thought he was talking about their kiss at the park. She leaned forward to kiss him, and before they knew it, their lips were locked; they couldn't stop kissing each other.

The kiss went on and on and Raj only stopped to check the time, given he had a curfew to follow from home. When he saw the time, his eyebrows shot up, not just because he was late, but because he realized they had been kissing for forty-five straight minutes!

The pair of them never shared a kiss like that with anybody else after that. It was the kind of thing that happened only when it happened the very first time.

Great weather today! One of them days which makes Metallica's, "Good day to be alive sir, good day to be alive he said" line sound prophetic. Mornings like this are so beautiful, should start every day with a long walk in the morning. Have a couple of smokes, listen to a couple of good songs and while away the entire day along with a couple of smiles.

I think Cornershop said it best,

Everybody needs a bosom for a pillow,

Everybody needs a bosom,

Mine's on the 45.

Second Act.
2013

Lack of empathy to a cry for help

"Raj, did you see the mail from Vinay?"

"No. Why, what happened?"

"Dude, it's about Sharon. Vinay mailed saying she passed away."

"Oh...."

Sachin called up Raj when he was between lunch with his colleagues in his Bangalore office. Raj paused for a moment once Sachin hung up. He thought about the conversation he had had with Sharon two weeks ago. It was the first time they had spoken in sixteen years. And then, he went right back to the conversation with his colleagues.

Sharon had called Raj out of the blue and asked if she could meet him at the Legends of Rock pub when they had spoken two weeks ago. Raj loved that pub, but on the day, he was to meet Sharon, he was engrossed in a high stakes betting game of pool with his friends at Prime Time and did not show up.

Raj figured it shouldn't matter much. After all, Sharon did the exact same thing when they were dating back in school. One fine day, two months into their relationship, they had planned to watch the movie 'Titanic' together, and Sharon didn't show up.

After the 10th grade board exams, Raj got placed in the school's 11th grade while Sharon didn't make the cut. She had to move to a college that was a fair distance away. They didn't see each other much and the conversation eventually tapered off. Raj, offended at being stood up at the theatre, never called Sharon back after that day. Sharon preferred to let things be the way they were and avoid an unpleasant conversation.

A few weeks later, Raj heard from some common friends that Sharon was seeing someone in her new college. That was how he knew they had broken up.

However, their conversation two weeks ago made the last sixteen years vanish into thin air. They spoke like they were a couple again. They reminisced about the times spent together. They laughed about being such kids back in school. They recollected the time they visited that spot in the park, where they had exchanged kisses – the first for both.

Raj recalled their conversation and wondered if there was more to it than what Sharon was talking about. Just then, his phone rang. It was a number he had forgotten he had on his phone: Shahzma.

She called to talk about Sharon. She had been her best friend for all these years and knew Sharon was going through a tough time. She had lost her dad some time ago and then her brother took to drugs. Eventually, her brother overdosed and passed away. Sharon, unable to cope with the deaths in her family, took to drugs herself, eventually ending up the same way as her brother.

That's when Raj realized what had happened. Sharon knew she was going to do this. And the call she had made to Raj was her way of saying goodbye.

Raj paused for a moment again, pondering over this, and then told Shahzma that he needed to hang up. His favorite club Manchester United was playing, and he didn't want to miss the kick-off.

He didn't think about Sharon again for the rest of the day and passed out on his couch once the match ended. The next morning, he woke up with a start, his head ringing with the final words Sharon had said when they last spoke. "Goodbye, my dear."

Why is it a crime to not save someone who is dying? (It is. 'Willful negligence', that's what they call it.) If not doing evil is not a virtue, why should not being virtuous be considered an evil? I mean nobody pats you on the shoulder for being a decent human being. Or do they?

Is anything ever absolute? Anything under this sun, why are things always open to inference? Why can't there be a book 'Ten simple ways to life your life.' Wouldn't you read that too?

Maybe our lives are just that random. The shit they forget to tell you in moral studies is none of it ever makes sense. The best you can hope for is blissful ignorance. The more you think about your own pitiful existence, the more it falls apart.

Not thinking about your life? The only thing which truly differentiates us from lower lifeforms is our ability to introspect about our 'self'. Maybe we shouldn't do that too. Yup, lets piss-fuck that away and be happy with our opposable thumbs?

When we force ourselves to be perfect strangers with one another, are we trying to be perfect or are we just trying to be strange? (Look ma, I'm oh-so-interesting!)

Maybe there is a secret to life, but even if I figure it out, will it be worth sharing with the world?

Until then, I couldn't care less about people like Sharon and the choices they make with their lives.

Plato was right; the only people who really survive a war are the dead.

(This pisses me off too, why is Plato always so fuckin right?)

Chapter 6

Blatant lies

First Act.
1998

Enter Nitya

11th grade at MK Jnanadhara was a whole new ball game for the students moving up from 10th grade. Fewer subjects, heavier content. The classroom was also filled with a lot of new faces. More than half the students from the previous year had moved to other schools on account of either not meeting the board exam hurdle rate or choosing to follow a different career stream like commerce or arts instead of science offered at MK Jnanadhara.

The Bus Stop crew was largely intact, with only the conspicuous absence of Sharon sticking out like a sore thumb. She was, however, ably and very quickly, replaced by the new eye-candy on the block, Nitya.

Nitya's reputation preceded her. Some of the students heard she was dating Sharon's brother, and that itself was sufficient to make everyone wait in anticipation to meet her. On the first day of class, nobody was disappointed. Nitya was tall, pretty, and had hair like wildfire, sitting untamed on purpose.

All the new students were categorized basis the states of India they came from. The students from Andhra Pradesh were called 'Gults'; Tamil Nadu 'Tams'; Dev from Kolkata was a 'Bong'; and Nitya identified as a 'Ding'.

This was new for many in class who had never met a 'Ding' before. Most didn't even know what it meant. Nitya's mom was British, which made Nitya an offspring of an interracial couple. 'Ding' therefore was short for bi-racials like Anglo-Indians.

Apart from her above average height and fairer-than-usual skin tone, Nitya was as Indian as any other kid. Nevertheless, the students were excited to have a 'Ding' in their class.

Nitya was also great at studies. If there was one person that could have displaced Aishvarya from her coveted first rank, it was Nitya. However, Aishvarya always managed to maintain her pole position.

Nitya was also shy. Her dad was a banker and constantly moved cities across India. Nitya never had the chance to make close friends and preferred being a recluse and in the comfort of her books. She barely spoke with anyone in class and gave tepid responses when anyone tried chatting with her. The only people who managed to hold a conversation with Nitya were Aishvarya and Sushmita.

Enter Shilpa

Another new face in the 11th grade was Shilpa, the diametric opposite of Nitya. She was talkative, loud and treated everyone in her new class like she had known them forever. She was incredibly good at sports and was a state-level athlete in both Basketball and Badminton.

Her arrival at school instantly led to two big changes in the class. First, upon realizing that there was no girls' basketball team in the school yet, she went about setting one up. Second, she introduced her new classmates and friends to Breezers!

Breezers was a drink the makers of Bacardi launched in India to serve consumers who wanted to have a light, refreshing alcoholic drink but didn't like the taste of beer. Especially among the female target group, who were now too grown up to keep having juice, and unfortunately found it harder than their male counterparts to acquire the taste of beer.

Shilpa introduced the girls to Breezers when they would go out, and this leveled the playing field for them, saving them from spending their outing looking at the boys' drink and 'have a nice time' themselves as well.

There was just one thing odd about Shilpa that nobody had an explanation for. She always wore her sweater, full sleeves down, even on the hottest day. Bangalore weather is known to be on the cooler side but donning a sweater every day seemed strange.

Most girls carried their sweaters with them every day. It made them feel more confident, and often wrapped it around their waists when they were on their periods, and they didn't want to risk a bloodstain being noticed. But they hardly ever wore it if it wasn't required. Shilpa, on the other hand, wore her sweater, all day, every day.

Antharganga

The students who had carried forward from the previous years in the same school to the 11th grade started to request an outbound a la Honnemaradu, so that they could get to know the grade's newcomers better.

Besides, Honnemaradu happened when they were in 9th grade, and it had been two years since there had been any outbound. There was none in the 10th grade, given that everyone, parents and teachers that is, expected the students to do nothing apart from study hard for their board exams.

The school acquiesced, and Padmini ma'am, who was the chief class teacher of the 11th grade, was once again given the responsibility of conducting a class trip. Padmini ma'am had become the chief class teacher for this class first in the 7th grade, but since then, she had remained the chief class teacher for this batch of students. It was as if she was graduating each year with the rest of the class. She did this on purpose, since she loved the students of this class and would convince the school administration to let her remain their chief class teacher till they passed out.

The town of Antharganga, which was a lot closer than Honnemaradu from Bangalore, was selected for the class trip. It was just a two-hour bus journey away. Honnemaradu had been a risky trip. She nearly got fined on the train for the racket the students had created during the overnight journey. On top of that, disaster almost struck when one of the coracles in Honnemaradu, manned by Raj and Sharon, nearly capsized. Lastly, the overall feeling of staying in a forest had not been comfortable for many students, and she received a lot of complaints from many parents post that outbound.

Antharganga felt like a relatively safer option. It was located on a small hill that offered a limited set of activities to do. However, little did they know, the worst calamity to occur on a class trip in the history of the school awaited them there.

The journey started off well, with China delivering the laughs during the game of mafia the students were playing on the bus. In one game, China was one of the last three left behind and the group decided to kill him.

"You're all killing me just because I'm the handsomest guy," China protested.

"You are the only guy left. It doesn't say much about your handsomeness," Sushmita retorted.

In another game, China was nominated to be God; he started, "Village, go to sleep, and now God...."

"Dude, you are God!" Raj shouted from behind.

Once they reached their destination, they had to trek up the hill to reach their campsite. Their campsite itself was made up of two levels, with a narrow flight of stairs connecting them. The camp guide gave them a walking tour. There was a forest on the one side to explore and a patch of plain ground on the other where the students could play. These were the only options available to them, and to make things worse, there was no equipment to play any games – not even a ball to throw around.

Antharganga was a far cry from Honnemaradu where they had had everything from lifejackets to coracles to tents. But the students improvised, and the girls decided to go for a trek in the forest while the boys chose the plain grounds to play Kabaddi since it was the only sport they could think of that didn't require any equipment at all.

On one of the Kabaddi raids, Raj and China were in the same team positioned at the 'right corner' and 'right in', which were next to each other at one edge of the court. Vinay was the raider from the opposition, and when he entered, he began with an attack of the left corner. Raj and China from the right started to flank him slowly. With a sudden twist, Vinay swerved to the right to grab Raj.

Being his usual competitive self, Raj jumped back quickly to avoid being touched by Vinay. However, his leap backwards was so wide that he lost control and fell out of the court. The court was set up on the tiny patch reserved for the students to use for play. The patch was edged by a cliff from which led down to a steep fall off the hill.

Raj had fallen outside the court on exactly this side of the patch, and before he could stabilize himself, he was struggling to hang on to the edge of the cliff. Being closest to him, China jumped out of the court to grab Raj. He just about managed to grab Raj's arm as he was about to fall off and pulled him back up.

However, as he was pulling him up, Raj's legs tripped at the edge and his body started to slip downwards. China pulled on his arm and made it rest on a jagged edge of the cliff. Then ran down the narrow flight of stairs connecting the lower level and reached a point mid-way from where he could grab Raj's waist. He barely managed to whisk him on to the stairs before he could slide down any further.

The whole incident happened in a matter of seconds, and by the time the rest of the boys reached the edge to see what had happened, China had managed to drag Raj onto the stairs and rescued him from potentially falling off the cliff.

China had effectively saved Raj's life, made possible by his laser sharp reflexes and an act he had fully committed himself to.

Later at night, when the students came together around the campfire, all they could talk about was how China saved Raj. For all his silly and sometimes bovine responses when they talked, nobody else could have reacted physically at the lightning sharp pace China had done. Everyone agreed that Raj was only alive because of what China did. Not only was he quick, but he put himself in harm's way to save Raj's life.

The entire episode, no matter how entertaining and thrilling, had another fallout. Antharganga was blacklisted as an outbound location for all schools of Bangalore, and for MK Jnanadhara specifically, outbounds to anywhere were permanently banned.

Truth or dare.

The next few days after the class trip, China's heroic act was the talk of the town. The students would often meet at the Defense Colony gardens near their school in the evenings after school to chat. A number of students stayed in the Defense Colony and the rest in surrounding neighborhoods, so it was the most convenient location to hang out in. They would spend this free time talking or playing games like 'Truth or Dare', which was an especially ubiquitous game with their age group, since it allowed the teenagers to say or do things that they might have otherwise felt uncomfortable with. To play the game, the group would sit in a circle—with boys and girls occupying alternate positions—with a bottle placed in the center. The rules of the game were quite simple: spin the bottle and whoever it pointed to when it stopped spinning would have to either answer a question truthfully, that is, if they picked Truth, or do a task if they picked Dare. There was no need for a bailout penalty, since there was always some sort of a response that led to further gossip and chatter. Which was the very purpose of the game.

On one evening, during a game of Truth or Dare, Sachin found himself seated next to Nitya. Before this moment, he hadn't thought of Nitya as anything more than a newcomer. Like everyone else, his interest did somewhat pique when he learnt she dated Sharon's brother, and he may have even considered asking Nitya out simply out of spite, but he didn't. Nitya had been a strangely quiet girl in class, and he barely noticed her.

Seated next to her at the game, he got better acquainted with Nitya's personality and was pleasantly impressed. As the game went on, the bottle soon pointed at Sachin. He chose Truth and was promptly asked who he would consider dating in school, now that he and Sharon were no longer together.

Everyone in school knew about Sachin and Sharon. He didn't have any qualms about hiding the truth. And everyone was curious to know if Sachin would now date someone else, especially with all the new students joining the school that year.

When the question was posed, it felt as if it was a perfect setup for what was to follow. Sachin looked at Nitya and said in an even tone, "I would definitely consider Nitya."

Nitya didn't look at him. Instead, her chin started twitching, which soon turned into a violet quiver. Noticing this, Sachin couldn't help but feel concerned for the girl and even a little guilty for having elicited such a strong reaction to what he thought was a harmless answer. He asked her if she was okay. Without saying a word, Nitya got up and left.

Normally, in this situation, the group would continue to talk and discuss why Sachin said what he said, and why Nitya behaved as she did. But that day, the awkwardness was too strong to continue playing, and everyone agreed to call it a day the moment Nitya left.

Sachin started walking back home and began replaying the incident over and over in his head. As he thought more about it, his pace started to pick up. Before he knew it, he was running as fast as he could towards his house.

The moment he reached home, he called up Aishvarya. Aishvarya was the de facto 'agony aunt' of the class, and the go-to person for Sachin in such times.

He narrated the entire incident to her and when he stopped speaking, Aishvarya said, "Wow, you actually like this girl!".

"Yea, I just found out myself!"

"What do plan to do about it?"

"Nothing, I suppose. I mean, she is supposed to be dating Sharon's brother right! And all I said was that she was worth dating. It's not like I asked her out. I guess I'll just let it be."

The next day, Sushmita pulled Sachin away during recess and asked him the same question.

When Sachin gave her the same response, Sushmita shook her head at Sachin's thick-headedness, and corrected him, "Nitya is not dating Sharon's brother. It just happens that Sharon's brother likes her, but they aren't dating. And after yesterday, she is expecting you to talk to her."

Sachin heaved a big sigh of relief when he found out Nitya was single. He planned to take up Nitya on the conversation she was expecting and decided to do it at the Halloween party Sushmita was going to host at her house.

Enter Juhi

The Halloween party at Sushmita's house was one of the most awaited events of the year. Sushmita lived in a big bungalow right in the middle of the poshest locality of Bangalore, in Indiranagar. She was the only daughter of wealthy parents, and given Halloween fell on Sushmita's birthday, on October 31, every year Sushmita's parents hosted a larger-than-life costume birthday party for her.

This year Halloween fell on a Saturday, making it an even more anticipated event, as curfew times tended to be longer when there was no school the next day. The culture of trick or treating was non-existent in India, but teens loved costumes! And Sushmita's parents provided them the perfect platform to show off their costuming abilities. They would not only invite the students from Sushmita's class, but from other classes as well. Anyone who bore even a remote acquaintance to Sushmita was invited.

The evening before the party, calls were being exchanged with everyone who would be attending the party to find out who was coming as who, with last minute changes being made to ensure nobody was labelled a 'copycat' or a 'twin'. Sachin was in between several such calls when he received a strange call from a girl.

"Can I speak with Sachin please?"

"Yes, Sachin here. Who is this?"

"Why do you want to know?"

"Well, you called me."

"I just want to talk to you."

Sachin could faintly recognize the voice on the line. It sounded like Juhi, Dev's sister. Juhi was a year younger to Dev and joined school that year starting in the 10th grade. She had answered the landline on many occasions when Sachin called Dev, and therefore he had a hunch this was her. However, it seemed risky to risk an incorrect guess given the context.

Moreover, he had never received a call from a girl saying she just wanted to talk to him without at least introducing herself, so he was curious to find out where this was headed.

They continued to chat for half an hour, with the girl on the line often sighing in between. Sachin was not sure if these were exaggerated lovestruck sighs or if she had some breathing issue. In any case, she hung up abruptly and Sachin never heard from her again.

The next day at the Halloween party, there was a déjà vu of sorts, since this time it was Sushmita instead of Gajan clearing out a section of the party space, and it was Nitya in place of Sharon that Sachin was going to talk to.

"Sushmita said you wanted to talk."

"Yes."

"So…?"

"Well, you can't just say something like that and disappear."

"Actually, you were the one who disappeared."

"Maybe, but you could have still reached out to me afterwards to complete what you started."

"Ok. Would you like to go out with me?"

"Yes."

Nitya's chin started twitching again. But this time she continued to look at him, and a smile broke out on her face. Sachin smiled back, mighty pleased that he had handled this a lot more maturely than blurting out, 'I love you'.

When they rejoined the rest of the group, Sachin noticed that Thomas was gesturing for him to choose between a thumbs-up and a thumbs-down sign. Sachin raised a thumbs up and Thomas winked back. Other people enquired in similar discreet manners about how the whole thing went down, which led to much giggling and chatter. In the melee, Sachin noticed Sushmita was huddled in one corner of the room with a group of girls.

He approached the group and called out for Sushmita as he wanted to apprise her of his 'hot off the pan' relationship status.

"Not now, Sachin!" Sushmita snapped back.

That's when Sachin noticed that Sushmita and the other girls were crowded around Juhi, who seemed to be crying profusely.

On Monday, when the students met in class, everyone was busy discussing the events that had transpired at Sushmita's party.

Raj was one of the few students in class who did not go to the party. His interests seemed to diverge from what the rest of his classmates were developing. While meeting in large groups and dancing and partying seemed to be the thing to do, Raj preferred meeting just a few close friends he was comfortable with, and possibly play video games or snooker with them.

At one point, he chided some of the students to get over the party since it had been nearly two days already. While they retorted to ask him why he didn't turn up, Raj walked away. He just wanted to be left alone.

Morrison said it best. People really are strange.

This whole day has been right out of a trash can. I spent most of the day having very uncomfortable conversations about uncomfortable events. Then spent a good two hours on the bed with a blanket over my head wishing the people I knew would just let me be. Not just for the day, not just for the week but forever. I didn't want to explain or understand. All I really wanted was for the world to collectively fuck itself and leave me the fuck alone. (Trust me this is the toned-down version). Like Lester Bangs once said, some of the greatest art in the world sprung from that precise feeling. So, there I was building my fences. Blocking them out. The romantic concept of artistic inspiration clouding the more realistic concept of unbelonging.

Ah, sometimes nothing spoils a good nasty mood as quickly as a genuine friend.

Sorry Mr. Bangs, you may be right, but I will choose happiness for today.

Raj and Sachin were the most popular students in class, but there was one key difference building between the two. Sachin was an open book. The day after he asked Nitya out, the entire class knew about it. Raj on the other hand was a closed book. He began dating Sharon at the end of the board exams the previous academic year and went on to date her for two months, but nobody in their class knew this.

Raj started to become more and more private about his feelings and his thoughts. Somehow, he felt the people around him didn't completely understand things the way he did or appreciate the things that he was interested in. Soon, he would go to the extent of concocting stories to keep things about him private. In the years that followed, Raj's friends found it hard to differentiate between fact and fiction when it came to the stories they heard about him.

Second Act.
2014

Blatant lies about career

Raj's professional life started out with a bang, but since then he felt like a crash test dummy ramming into a wall in slow motion. First, he was posted in Kolkata, which in relative terms was a great posting, because most of his peers started in smaller towns. Staying in a metro, despite it not being his home city of Bangalore, was a big deal. In fact, it was better, because visiting Kolkata had been his dream since the 6th grade. His science-oriented mind wanted to see India's largest bridge and his interest in rock music wanted to explore the rock scene in Kolkata, which was touted as the only other city as evolved as Bangalore in this genre. However, he found himself with deplorable company there, hobnobbing with goons that would give him a Glock for a gift.

After spending a year in Kolkata, he was posted to Chennai. Another metro and another great opportunity for his career. More importantly, he could share an apartment with one of his best friends, Sachin. Yet, the anger at his career only compounded. The general loathing of India's hygiene and living standards, even among its metros, exacerbated by the scorching hot weather of Chennai, drove him to incessant drinking. And drinking to the extent of committing irresponsible acts like burning the house he lived in.

Keen to get out of India, he landed a job in Dubai. A developed economy with another best friend, Thomas. However, matters only took a turn for the worse here. More than anything, good conversations were paramount for Raj, and he had none of it in the apathy-ridden populace of Dubai. He now began drinking in solitude here, which he had earlier sworn to never do. And he also began directing his spite towards his best friends. It's one thing to be in contempt of your colleagues, but a different ball game if that is directed towards your best friends. Because in the case of the former, you can just quit your job, but what happens if you ostracize your best friends?

Raj found himself back in Bangalore after spending the first three years of his post-graduate professional life outside, one each in

Kolkata, Chennai and Dubai. He began to wonder if he was just being handed a raw deal year after year, city after city, or if there was something wrong with him where he just couldn't find 'happiness' or at least what he saw in his friends as 'happiness'. He just felt angry all the time, burning bridges with colleagues, companies and even best friends like Thomas.

He found a small startup to work in Bangalore. It was not as fancy as his previous two MNCs, but he hoped that within the familiarity of his home city and in his parents' house, he could jumpstart his career.

However, after two years of trying to achieve some semblance of professional success, he found himself at the bottom of the same abyss he was plunged into in Kolkata, Chennai and Dubai. He couldn't understand why all his friends got along with their chosen careers, how they could tolerate their shitty jobs, day in and day out. They even got married, starting with Thomas almost three years back, which made it even more dreadful. It nauseated him to think people could simply settle and be content with what he regarded as mediocre jobs and marriages.

Doesn't it seem like everybody is trying so hard to conform, to fit in and basically trying not to offend anybody? This is especially true of my work atmosphere. Talk the same, think the same, look the same… any sign of individuality will not be tolerated. They say that the meek will inherit the earth, but will it be worth inheriting by then? What is so wrong with the way I speak and the way I think? I don't hold classes to ensure that everybody begins and ends each sentence with the F word, so why must everyone else teach me 'values' Fuck that!

Moving cities, moving jobs, and with nothing satisfying him, Raj began to question if this was all there was to life. All those talks back in school about success being defined by how much you've travelled or how much you've earned, Raj had done all of that, repeatedly, and yet found no joy in it. Somehow his friends seemed satisfied, and he just couldn't understand why or how! He would ask them about it and would never be satisfied with the answers he received.

Unable to find an iota of job satisfaction even in the city he loved, he decided to call it quits once more and just stayed home playing video games over more solitary drinking. Social norms dictated he do some job or the other, and there were frequent checks of concern on this regard from his parents and friends. To quell this menace, he decided to create a fake company and a fake job for himself. Thus, began the spate of lies from Raj. He simply wanted to be left alone, and if it was an interesting story that people wanted from him to achieve that, he would feed exactly that to them.

He told everyone that he was setting up a new firm in Bangalore, which would be the Indian extension of the firm he worked with in Dubai. To make this more believable, he brought in Vinay, who worked in a similar industry, to partner him on this venture.

Vinay was himself in between jobs. He had just concluded interviewing with the Alshaya group in Kuwait where he faced six grilling rounds with different people only to be told at the end of it that they had hired someone with local experience. When he met Raj and heard him out, he decided to help him given he had no other interviews lined up for himself. During their initial conversation, Raj was also curious about Vinay's interview process in Kuwait and asked him for a lot of details about the same.

Raj went on to explain the requirement process for his new job. He needed to establish a team in Bangalore for the India rollout of the Dubai-based firm.

They began interviewing junior candidates, many of them from organizations they had both worked at previously. Raj would use this as a platform to vent all the frustration he held against his previous employers. He would bully these juniors and tempt them with 'take it or leave it' on the spot job offers. After a few rounds of interviews, Vinay realized there was something wrong and decided to conduct some background checks of his own.

He soon figured that it was all a hoax, and the Dubai firm had no intentions of creating an Indian extension. This—the job, the interviews, the recruitment process—was all just a story concocted by Raj. He confronted Raj with this information, and it turned into a big fight between the two. At the end of it, Raj lost another friend.

A few months later, Vinay caught up with China and the topic of Raj came up. China had recently met Raj, and since Vinay had not been on talking terms with Raj, he enquired from China about his state.

China told Vinay that Raj had just concluded interviewing with the Alshaya group in Kuwait and didn't get through. He went on to narrate the exact story Vinay had told Raj, word for word!

Pull my eyes out so that I can't see,

And find troubles to devour me.

Whisper in my ear the sounds of a beautiful beach,

And paint the stars to be within my reach.

Help me sprout wings and help me explore your sky,

To be finally free and make the gods wish they were I.

They say God helps those who help themselves…

So, I too will try,

I will sober up,

I will grow up,

I will finally try to be a better human being!

But my sweet lord, in case that doesn't fucking work… refer paragraph 1!

Chapter 7

Developing Agoraphobia

First Act.
1999

The kidnapping

The commencement of the 12th grade marked the beginning of another board exam year. These exams would decide the fate of college placement for the students next year, in the same way the previous 10th grade board exams had decided the fate of 11th grade placement.

The 12th grade was no piece of cake. The students had fewer subjects than when they were in 10th, but the content of their chosen subjects made for some pretty rigorous studying. These exams couldn't be taken lightly because getting good scores wouldn't be so easy.

For students like Raj and Sachin, the new curriculum was a godsend because they only had to study subjects they found interesting, and not subjects like Hindi language, which they considered to be an utter waste of time. Both Raj and Sachin had barely scraped by in their Hindi exam. In fact, they both scored the lowest marks in class. Raj scored 57 and Sachin 56 out of 100. It was a matter of great pride for Raj that he didn't get the lowest rank in class, and he saved his scorecard to prove this point to Sachin years later when they found themselves doing their MBA together in the predominantly Hindi speaking city of Mumbai.

For some others, especially Gajan, the new curriculum was daunting.

In one of the exams, Gajan felt underprepared and risked facing the music at home if he brought back poor scores. Unfortunately, this scenario was more than common among so many Indian households. Raj's parents were probably the only ones who never pressured Raj about his scores. Raj's father was a rocket scientist, and Raj reminded his friends of this repeatedly. Raj's parents seemed a lot more forward thinking on many topics, making them the envy of his classmates.

Gajan couldn't risk failing an exam as that would directly impact his college placement later. And unlike Raj and Sachin, he couldn't simply appear for the exam and scrape by with a passing score. His stress level was apparent to the entire class until the day before the exam. And on the day of the exam, Gajan didn't show up.

The next day, Gajan's parents were in school enquiring about him. It turned out that Gajan had not only missed the exam but had not even come home that night. His parents had filed a missing person's report since he had been missing for over twenty-four hours.

The entire school was thrown into disarray. Thankfully, by the end of the 2nd day, the day after the exam, Gajan returned home. His story was that he was kidnapped the day before the exam and the kidnappers left him unconscious near some construction pipes from where he had to make his way back home on his own.

Not a single person in school believed the kidnapping story. It seemed too convenient a fact that Gajan was kidnapped right before the one exam he didn't want to sit for. Besides, he was kidnapped and yet returned home completely unharmed in a matter of two days. The facts surely didn't add up to the story.

However, that was the story relayed by Gajan's parents to the school and thereafter by the school authorities to the students. Such a somber mood prevailed around the entire topic that the students decided to err on the side of believing the kidnapping story.

It took sixteen years for the real story to come out.

Dandeli

Desperate to get the attention off him, Gajan decided to float the proposal of a self-organized camp to the Bus Stop crew during the mid-term holidays. This was the final year of school, and the mid-term holidays were the last time they would all be free together. Right after the board exams, everyone would get busy with college placements. The school authorities had also made it amply clear that after the Antharganga fiasco, there would be no further trips organized by the school.

Keen to recreate the experiences they had had at Honnemaradu, which Antharganga had completely failed to repeat, the gang decided to go along with Gajan's proposal.

Gajan planned the entire trip to perfection. From booking the train tickets, to securing the luxury tent accommodations at Dandeli—that too, at a great discount—to even organizing an activity for the whole group which none of them had ever done, white-water rafting.

The gang was more than thrilled and looked forward to the trip. However, the journey started on a somber note, with the overnight train ride being nothing like Honnemaradu. A smaller group this time around, the lack of novelty that accompanied similar experiences, and simply having grown up a bit were all good reasons for the sullen mood. But more than any of these, there was no Padmini ma'am for them to irritate – which was most often the primary objective of their naughty behavior.

Upon reaching the destination, the group quickly freshened up, and braced themselves for the first activity of the trip: the highly anticipated white-water rafting.

The crew had to undergo a few hours of training. They were assigned the Class-3 rafting which was meant for intermediate rafters, and there would be a few rapids along the journey they would be expected to maneuver.

Raj was joking around the entire time, sneaking up behind the boys and smacking them between their legs with his oars. According to him, the organizers were making the entire training sound like it was something extremely dangerous, when they would obviously have all possible safety mechanisms in place. There was no way a campsite like this would risk casualties, he thought.

When it was time to raft, no one grabbed on to the side ropes of the raft harder than Raj. His face turned pale at the first sight of the rapids.

The tricky thing about white-water rafting is the stability the raft needs to maintain when going over the rapids. And this required everyone on the boat to play a part. The raft guide would bark instructions from the back of the raft, and these needed to be executed by the rest working the oars.

With Raj's hands tightly gripping the ropes most of the time instead of working the oars, the people next to him had to work harder to maintain the raft's stability. After a grueling half hour on the rapids, the crew reached a section of calm water. The guide offered the rafters to jump into the water and cool off if they wished. Everyone wore life jackets and was tethered by ropes to the boat, so it was completely safe, but once again, Raj refused to cooperate.

Everyone jumped off the raft and Raj and Sachin were the last two remaining on the vessel. Sachin approached Raj to goad him into taking the plunge, but Raj's eyes betrayed his fear and he yelled at Sachin to stay back. He nearly hit Sachin with his oar when he half expected him to physically nudge him overboard.

Through the series of events that led up to boarding the raft, Raj was dismissive of the activity. He treated it as one would a Ferris wheel in an amusement park, where everyone would make a big deal of it, but the ride in itself would not just be safe, but downright slow and boring at times. Raj expected rafting to be a piece of cake, and all the precautionary messages from the organizers were just a way of setting it up to be an exciting adventure.

All of it changed when Raj entered the raft. The crashing waves and the unstable raft—for the first time, Raj experienced something he never had before, a fear for his life. His cocky attitude, his entertaining demeanor and his never-ending ability to talk - all of it ceased.

In every other situation, Raj chose 'Fight', but when rubber hit the road—or bodies hit the water, in this case—Raj's limbic brain chose 'Freeze'. He even put his friends on the raft at risk, when he couldn't comply with the guide's instructions over the rapids. The others were scared too, but they did what they could for themselves and for everyone else around as they knew only a collective effort would see them through this. Raj was the opposite. In his case, he needed to be bailed out. He didn't ask for it, but it was apparent to everyone to help him. This was something that repeated itself in the future. Raj always needed help, and for a time, his friends noticed and did something about it. But it wasn't always to be.

The unlikely girlfriend

When the crew returned from Dandeli, Shilpa called up each one of them because she was curious to learn about the trip. Shilpa hadn't been allowed to travel with them because of her parents. The moment they realized the trip was not being organized by the school and was instead being put together by the students themselves, they forbade Shilpa from even thinking about going.

Shilpa's need to break free and do her own thing was quite evident in her actions. She left no stone unturned when it came to sports or parties or generally hanging out with friends, in as many places as her parents allowed her to, and even in places she successfully hid from them.

Raj and Shilpa had a great conversation about the trip to Dandeli when she called him up. When the call was over, Raj had a strange feeling in his stomach, and chuckled to himself – he might finally have the 'butterflies' people always went on about.

The next day in school, Sushmita accosted him during recess, "Do you have a crush on Shilpa?"

"What? Who told you that!"

"I just know. I saw the look on your face every time she walked by you today."

"It's been less than twenty-four hours since I even harbored that thought, and you're able to guess this already?"

"Like I said, I just know these things."

The fact that Sushmita vocalized his feelings, and didn't have anything negative to say about it, felt like a stamp of approval for Raj. He decided to take some action on the matter.

He approached Shilpa by the end of the day and said, "I didn't complete the Dandeli story, by the way."

"Great! Let's go out for a drink and you can tell me more!"

Raj was just looking to make conversation, but he was relieved Shilpa suggested they go out, and that too, over a drink. Conversations over alcohol were the best kind of conversations.

After school, they went out and Shilpa had her usual Breezers and Raj his beer. The topic of Dandeli never came up. Shilpa figured Raj used it as an excuse while Raj would much rather never discuss the topic for the rest of his life given the events that transpired on the rapids.

The only time Dandeli was mentioned was when Shilpa confided in him about how strict her parents were, which was the reason for her missing out on the trip. In fact, the only reason she was even able to stay out this late with Raj on that day was because her parents were out, and she had some extra time before she had to be back home.

Soon, they took every opportunity to go out. They even went on some double dates with Thomas and Sushmita. Whenever Shilpa had an extended curfew, she would drink a lot more than just Breezers. Raj loved this about her. She would match him drink for drink and they ended up having the best conversations, and more. Sushmita would invite them over to her house and given the size of her house, they would sometimes end up in a room by themselves and could barely keep their hands off—or clothes on—when that happened.

When Raj looked at Shilpa's body, he felt inspired to spin lines of poetry about it. She had 7 little stars tattooed all over her back, which when seen from behind aligned as the constellation of Orion the Hunter. She chose her back for the tattoos so her parents wouldn't get to know as they would certainly never approve. Whenever they got together, Raj did his best to hit all of her erogenous zones—like the nape of her neck, her toes and that one specific spot on her spine that he struggled to find, in spite of Orion's central star positioned right beneath it. Her body was a wonderland, handcrafted by God himself for Raj to enjoy. They did everything short of full-blown sex whenever they met.

Once, while hanging out, taking a break from what they usually did when alone, Shilpa whispered while staring at the ceiling.

"I really like you, Raj."

"I like you too!"

Shilpa smiled, sensing that it was time to take their relationship to the next level.

"I need to tell you something though."

Raj moved his gaze from the ceiling towards Shilpa.

"What is it?"

"You know why I always wear a sweater at school? It's to avoid these scars on my arm."

"I noticed them, but I wasn't sure I should ask."

"That's alright, I think you have a right to know. It was my previous boyfriend."

"He did that to you?"

"No, I did it to myself, when he left me."

Raj froze. Sure, he was having a good time with Shilpa, but the last thing he wanted was for her to do something like that to herself again in case they split up. And splitting up was very possible since Raj never considered a future with her that went beyond binge drinking and making out at Sushmita's house. He was, in fact, certain that they would split up after the 12th grade when everyone would end up in different colleges.

Not wanting to stretch this out any further, Raj stayed sober on their next date and gently let her down. Shilpa took it surprisingly well and stayed out of his hair after that. However, a few weeks later, on Shilpa's birthday, Thomas invited Raj to Sushmita's house where they had planned a quick pre-party with a few friends before heading out to a club. Knowing fully well that Raj would never go to a club, Thomas goaded Raj to at least wish Shilpa at Sushmita's house, saying it would mean a lot to her if he did.

Not wanting to upset Shilpa any further, and assuming a quick catchup before the rest headed out to a club should not hurt much, Raj agreed to make it.

When Raj arrived, there was nobody but the four of them there. It felt like the old days. Thomas assured Raj that more people would soon arrive, and egged Raj to have a few drinks until then.

Sushmita had prepared some sort of fruit punch that packed quite a punch, and soon enough, Raj was drunk. Before he could gather his wits, he was locked in a room with Shilpa where she was taking off her clothes and then his. Too delirious to resist, Raj went along with the flow. They passed out together, and a couple of hours later, Raj was the first to wake up. He noticed Shilpa next to him and felt the same queasy feeling in his stomach again. But this time, it wasn't 'butterflies' but a heady concoction of the alcohol and the raging emotions within him.

He quickly got dressed and stepped out to see Thomas and Sushmita sitting quietly with guilt-ridden faces. That's when he knew he was set up. Raj went back into the room and woke Shilpa up. He was furious, but he spoke in as calm a voice as he could muster. He wanted to let her down slowly. He would not have a scar on Shilpa's hand with his name. He told her he had an amazing time, but it would be best if they didn't see each other. And just before leaving, he turned to her and said, "Happy birthday."

The truly beautiful are always outsiders,

Strangers at the edge of every room,

Beauty as parachutes? to each high-flier, even the gliders,

Heads upon which, only bright clouds were allowed to loom,

The ones who coast, coast to coast,

On charm fueled mile upon mile.

For in a world that always smiles back at your every smile,

You might compile a lifestyle worthwhile?

but one that breeds a disconnect, not just from the servile,

but from the majority, the rank and file... the us.

The faceless also-rans.... The plain.

Beautiful lives to be led in exile as beautiful isles?

But then again, natural order always did decree,

Beautiful to lead, Plain to breed, Unfortunate to bleed?

Still, beauty never does let the bitter run free, in me,

To paraphrase a better Bukowski.

They never do make it,

The truly beautiful that is...

Again, and again beauty will die, always too soon,

Always too young,

Tragic, lovely and brilliant...till the end,

and leave in its place uglier to lead their plain lives?

So, the next time you see a truly beautiful face,

Spare a smile for your eyes,

for what you see, is much more transient than a person,

Like everything magical... true beauty... is but a moment?

Falling in love

Sachin and Nitya had been dating for a year. But during this time, Sachin always felt they hadn't shared a 'real' kiss. It was not for want of trying on Sachin's end, but every time he tried to kiss Nitya, Sachin felt like he was making out with a wall.

In desperate need of guidance, Sachin approached Thomas, who had been dating Sushmita for five years now. Thomas began to laugh when he heard Sachin out. He had faced a similar problem with Sushmita at the start of his relationship, and it was because Sushmita thought she could get pregnant with a kiss!

Sachin pondered over it for a moment before realizing it was ludicrous to think that was the problem in his case. Anyhow, he decided to have an open and honest conversation with Nitya as per Thomas' suggestion.

This turned out to be a life lesson: The best way to break the deadlock in any relationship is to have an open and honest conversation with your partner.

When Sachin asked Nitya what was bothering her, she said she felt like she was not being honest with her mother when she was with Sachin.

"Would it help if I met your mom and introduced myself to her?" Sachin offered.

"Would you do that?"

"Of course, in fact, I would love to meet your mother."

Nitya invited Sachin over to her house one day and he arrived dressed in his best clothes and on his best behavior. He was all prepared to meet both of Nitya's parents and face all the tough questions they had for him. Instead, he met Nitya's mom and her grandmother, two of the nicest ladies on the planet.

They offered him cola and snacks and had a pleasant chat with him. Nitya struggled to conceal her joy the entire time, glad they were getting along so well.

The very next day, the Bus Stop crew met up at Sushmita's house to play some board games, and once they finished, Nitya offered to clear up the area along with Sachin while the rest headed out. The moment the rest left the house, Nitya grabbed Sachin and kissed him.

They sat on the couch and kissed each other passionately, giving relief to their pent-up emotions over the months of dating.

Later that evening, while talking to each other on the phone and recounting the events of the day, Sachin said, "I love you."

Without a moment's hesitation, Nitya replied, "I love you."

"I love you," Sachin said again.

"I love you," Nitya repeated.

Each kept telling the other that they loved them. Saying it out loud felt incredible. Sachin finally meant the words and was glad he had waited until the right moment to say the words to Nitya.

Nitya and Sachin wore their hearts on their sleeves when they were with each other and could always be seen together in school and outside. If anyone could guess, their relationship and love was written on the stars.

Farewell party

When the 12th grade board exams were over, the students wanted nothing short of a big party to celebrate their win. Given it was their last year of school after which they would scatter to different colleges, it made sense to combine the end-of-exams celebration with a farewell party of sorts, which was exactly what the school administration did. They organized a formal event on the very last day of school, where the boys turned up in their dads' oversized suits and the girls in dresses, they had spent a week preparing.

A big hall was rented out for the event, and it was set up with music, disco lights and the works. The stage was set for the students to have their last official school dance.

Being a mandatory school event, and possibly the last time Raj would meet many of his friends there, he reluctantly went for the event. However, the first thing he noticed was Shilpa missing. Raj wondered if he was the reason for her missing out, or just another one of those things Shilpa's parents prohibited her from doing. In any case, he could only hope she wasn't doing anything more drastic than missing the farewell party. And even if she did, it would all be on her. He had got out of the relationship as fast as he could and ensured there were no emotional strings attached, at least on his end. There was literally nothing more he could do.

He spotted a few boys having a conversation in one corner of the hall and joined them, welcoming the distraction. The topic of discussion was 'pub culture' and how it was brandished as 'anti-Indian'.

Lately, there had been a spate of attacks by politically backed hooligans in some of the pubs in Bangalore. These miscreants had 'concerns' over 'uncivilized acts' by the young girls and guys who went to such pubs. The irony was that the uncivilized behavior was not caused by people drinking and socializing inside the pub, but by these hooligans who came in from outside. They didn't even bother to be discreet about their violent attacks and allowed a cameraman present there to catch the entire episode on camera for the whole country to watch. The worst part was that the groups these hooligans belonged to always turned out to be religious. They cited 'protection of religious values' as the motives behind their violent activities.

Raj, furious about these attacks making headlines, set off on a tirade.

"Wasn't the whole point of religion to teach good values so that people behaved like good human beings? Who are these people? Who gave them the right to do God's work? Who defined 'culture' to them? Aren't we living in a land of ironies? I increasingly feel I'm living in a country I can't seem to relate to anymore. It's almost as if I have outgrown my own nation. I feel the country itself has not been able to keep up with me. And I'm just a regular kid, who has in fact never been out of this country. Isn't this the biggest irony of them all - a person who feels at odds with his own nation! I feel saddened by everything that's happening right now in Bangalore. Worse, I feel scared for my life. India was once colonized, but it still doesn't feel like we have any freedom. We're supposed to be a secular country, right? Then why are there people who don't understand or accept each other? There are people who want to drive things down my throat and will even resort to violence to ensure this. I could have very well been one of those people who were attacked in that pub. I can't wait to leave this country. Once I'm through with engineering here, I'm moving to the US. My dad's sister lives there and I'm going to move in with them. Their sports and politics are way more interesting, and more importantly, I can drink when and where I want. I feel like I'm so much more a part of their culture than our own here."

Aishvarya spotted Raj in the corner and fumed at what clearly looked like another debate in the making, when the entire point of the farewell party was to relax and have fun together one last time. She decided to approach him to ask him to dance with her. There was little chance of this happening the other way around, and not knowing when she would see him again, Aishvarya decided to take matters in her own hands.

Raj was about to flat out refuse given how much he detested dancing. But before he could, he spotted Thomas dancing with Sushmita and Sachin with Nitya and decided to humor Aishvarya for a bit. After all, they might never meet again.

They chatted as they danced, a welcome distraction for Raj from his two left feet. Aishvarya then attempted a tango. Raj wondered what she was up to. Aishvarya spun on her heel, picked a rose from a table nearby, and placed it in her mouth and motioned Raj to pick it. Raj assumed this must be part of the dance move, and since he had his heels dug in too deep, decided to play along. He picked the rose from Aishvarya, their cheeks touching momentarily. It was the closest they had ever come to each other since their first meeting seven years ago in 1993, and the closest they would ever be.

At the end of the party, Raj was glad Shilpa hadn't turned up. He may have never danced with Aishvarya if she was there. Raj felt an inexplicable sense of contentment that he shared his last moments of school with the first person that caught his eye in school. His mind started to wander about a possible future with Aishvarya, but he shook it off instantly. It was too heavy. Everything about Aishvarya was too heavy. A level of seriousness he was petrified of harboring a thought, let alone doing something about it. He quickly switched his thoughts to his career and how other things in life would pan out, now that he was done with school.

Ever wonder how life will turn out for you? I don't do this very often, but sure seems like the 'IN' thing to do with almost everybody I know. Even CAT interviews (which are conducted by some of the, if not THE, brightest brains in the country) feature the standard, 'Where do you see yourself five years from now?' question.

You can prepare your 'cleverest' answer, which many do! That's kind of pointless, isn't it? Don't play it safe, say what you really think. If you don't have a clue, say so! Everybody is trying so hard not to fuck up, even in the smallest things. Like when people travel these days. There is always one digital camera, one video camera and one other digital camera (just in case!), and they return with 200 odd snaps and a head full of memories of posing for them and precious else! Try taking ZERO photos. Now that's a trip to remember for a lifetime.

So, where do I see myself five years from now?

Sir, I frankly don't give a shit. Life is not about reaching a destination. The pleasure is in the journey itself. If all you do throughout the ride is strain your eyes to read a bunch of numbers on milestones, you might get there faster but you won't be better off for it. Take a break, slow down, laugh a little. It is not a race; you don't have to get there before all the others. You just have to get there, if you are really lucky you might get there with some of the others!

Second Act.
2015

16 years to anarchy

The last time the entire Bus Stop crew had gathered together was in 1999, sixteen years ago, at their 12th grade farewell party. They now decided to come together for the biggest wedding in the group.

At the wedding venue, Sachin could be seen running around frantically searching for someone.

"There you are!" he said when he spotted Vinay.

"What do you mean there I am? There you are! You're the bridegroom and do you know everyone has been looking for you?" "Yes, I know. I'm late, but I had to give you this," Sachin handed over his phone to Vinay.

"Why is this so urgent?"

"I just called Nitya and she may call back."

"Ok," said Vinay pocketing the phone and giving Sachin a weird look.

Sachin promptly rushed into the ceremony hall where his fiancé, Nikita, was looking at him quizzically for being late. It had been 16 years since Sachin and Nitya had broken up, but he wanted to hear from her one last time before the point of no return.

Sachin and Nikita had met a year back at work and were getting engaged on this day. This was to be followed by separate bachelor's and bachelorette's parties the next day, and a typical big fat Indian wedding on the third.

The entire Bus Stop crew decided to fly in from wherever they were to attend the wedding. Raj and Sachin were the only two remaining members of the gang who weren't married yet, and given Raj's aversion to marriage, Sachin's was likely to be the last wedding in the gang.

Over the last four years, starting with Thomas, everyone else in the Bus Stop crew got married. And apart from Aishvarya's wedding, Raj was missing from every wedding, reunion or any other party since they graduated from school sixteen years ago. His frequent job changes and the curious case of his startup venture the previous year was relayed by Vinay and China to the rest of the crew and they were anxious to meet and talk to him.

Raj promised all the friends who called him asking him to make it, that he would attend the wedding, especially when this one was happening right in Bangalore, and he didn't even have to travel to a place like Coorg which he had done for Aishvarya's wedding.

Meeting Raj and the bachelor's party were the two events the Bus Stop crew looked forward to the most. After all, it was likely to be the last bachelor's party as well within the Bus Stop crew.

Dev bought a Burger King costume from the US, where he now lived, for Sachin to wear. Vinay planned for the alcohol. China attempted to get strippers but decided against it when he found out that they would arrive wearing saris.

The whole gang rented a house where they met up and simply drank and talked to each other the entire night. They were meeting up after so long that it was better for them to just catch up instead of throwing any other typical bachelor party with games and strippers.

It turned out to be an incredible night. So many old stories from school were recounted. Nostalgia ran rife, but more importantly, some long held secrets were revealed.

Gajan capitulated on the kidnapping story and submitted to fabricating the entire episode.

"Yeah, I was terrified of my dad. Back then, it honestly seemed like a better idea to spend the night hidden inside a construction pipe outside school, than face my dad and tell him I flunked an exam.

The day before the exam, I simply went straight to the construction pipe and hid inside it. It started out as a way for me to avoid going home after school. But as I sat there pondering my next step, it became dark outside. I kept thinking of what I was going to do, but nothing came to mind. All I did was sit there till the next day.

Thankfully, it was summer, and the nights weren't too cold. No rains either, so no mosquitos. Just the stray dogs outside, but they didn't bother me. All I had to do was wait it out. The only useful thing I did in that time was figure out the story I would tell when I got out. And honestly the only thing that came to mind was that I had been kidnapped.

So, that's what I said. The kidnappers attacked from behind and drugged me, and the next thing I knew I was lying inside the construction pipe. I don't know how, but somehow my parents bought it. Guess they too found it probable that I would literally be kidnapped than hide from an exam."

The boys were stunned. They couldn't believe what they had just heard. But it was the harsh reality of those days. Parents inflated the consequences of doing poorly in exams and it was only the pressure they put on their children that drove them to take such extreme measures. And the worst part was they didn't even realize it. They would rather believe their kid was kidnapped than go easy with the exam pressure.

It was Vivek's turn next. Everyone wanted to know who the mystery girl in all his paintings was. Vivek revealed it was Sharon. He liked her so much that he would paint her face—albeit in abstract form—in all his paintings. While the rest of the landscape would be near perfect, only the girl's face would be abstract as 'she was too beautiful' to capture on canvas, as he put it.

Sachin was the most shocked by this revelation. They recounted that time at Gajan's house when Sachin asked Sharon out. Vivek had planned to talk to her that very day. But after he noticed Sachin talking to her, he chose to forever keep his peace. And now, it was too late for Sharon to ever know this story.

It was nearly daybreak when the boys realized Raj had ditched them again. They tried to call him at various points in the night, but his phone was switched off. They hoped he would show up for the wedding later in the day at least. Sachin was after all one of his closest friends and they thought he would turn up for him at least.

But just as everyone feared, Raj did not show up. Aishvarya's wedding remained the first and only wedding he ever attended. As the wedding proceeded, in the solitude of his room, Raj opened his diary and wrote:

Anarchy – it's not the law; it's just a good idea!

Chapter 8

Pushing Close Friends Away

First Act.
2000-2004

Engineering begins.

The 12th grade board exams scattered the members of the Bus Stop crew to different engineering colleges. Without a doubt, the four-year-long engineering degree was only the natural step for the crew since they had specialized in science in the 11th and 12th grade. However, which engineering college and which specific engineering stream they specialized in, depended on the performance of the students in the board exams.

Raj, Aishvarya, Nitya and Gajan found themselves at one of Bangalore's best engineering colleges, while Sachin, Sushmita, Dev and China landed at a close counterpart college. Raj's mom was the happiest about Raj's college and would gloat to all her neighbors and give frequent updates to Raj's atthe in the US. Raj knew where all of this was coming from. Just like in a lot of other things, this was his dad's joy that his mom was expressing in words to everyone around.

The rest of the Bus Stop crew was strewn across different colleges, some even away from Bangalore, such as in the case of Thomas who made a solitary move to Mysore.

The Raj-Aishvarya romance that nearly came to an end in school was given a fresh lease of life, now that they were in the same engineering college. Or so thought Aishvarya. She couldn't be further from the truth, because Raj's popularity only grew in college; he was surrounded by even more people, which made him all the more inaccessible.

Raj was glad to have at least a few people continue from his school into the new college. As serendipity would have it, he made an unwitting friend in Nitya.

For the past two years, she was either stuck to the hip with Sachin, or Arcadian with everyone else. However, they took the same bus route to college, while Aishvarya who lived in another part of town, took a different one.

Raj and Nitya started talking during those initial days when they didn't know anyone else in college. First on the bus journey to and from college and then in the evenings over e-mails, which was in vogue with Hotmail and Gmail having just launched.

Sachin had set up Nitya's Gmail account. She was never tech-savvy and had only decided to pursue engineering because everyone else in school was doing it. Besides, she performed so well academically, that it seemed ludicrous to forgo an opportunity to study at one of the best engineering colleges at the time. But if Nitya had her way, she would rather not study or work at all, and instead find herself a knight in shining armor to shower her with love and attention.

Raj, who recognized Nitya's potential and then learnt how careless she was with it, unleashed his gift of gab to wear down Nitya's attitude towards life. This, and soon many other deeply personal topics was what they talked about, blossoming a new friendship between them.

At the other college, Dev's life had completely transformed. For one, he hit the gym the moment the 12th board exams concluded, and underwent a complete physical transformation, converting his lanky frame to a muscular one. Next, he bravely entered the ring of lions, which were hotspots in college that freshers were warned to dodge, lest they fall prey to ragging. Dev allowed himself to get ragged more than anyone else in the first week of college, but by the end of it, he was the favorite fresher among the seniors. So much so, that he would be seen ragging his own batch mates at times, rubbing shoulders with his new senior batch friends.

His ability to mimic, confidence to speak in public, and overall finesse with all thing's theatre, spread beyond the circle of seniors and into the college faculty. Soon, Dev was offered to host all the important cultural events in college. There was little doubt that he was the most popular student in college, all within the first month of stepping into it.

He would flirt with multiple women at the same time using his phone during the days when SMS was the only available mode of chatting.

Of all the girls who fancied Dev, there was one who caught his eye. Renata was tall, beautiful, and matched Dev on every level, from wits to height. To no one's surprise, they soon became a couple and wanted to move in together. However, both Dev and Renata were day scholars and lived with their families in Bangalore. So, they decided to rent a house where they could stay from time to time, while spending the rest of the days at their individual homes with their families.

In order to make the financials work for them, Dev came up with an Airbnb model, long before Airbnb even became a thing. He would rent out his house to anyone in college for the days he and Renata didn't use it. He branded the house Dasarhawaii, because it felt like paradise (Hawaii) on the street (Dasarhalli)the house was located. Given the catchy name and Dev's extensive network, the house rarely went a day vacant, and Dev made more money from his friends staying there than the rent he paid for the house.

Dev was not just creatively inclined but also had an entrepreneurial mind. Along with his friends from school, Sushmita and Sachin, he established Bus Stop Productions, a company that created the college's first in-house magazine, the college's first branded sweatshirt, and most important of all, hosted a series of plays of which the other members of the original Bus Stop crew were also a part. More than anything else, this kept the crew together, and Dev was at the epicenter of this scheme.

Truth or dare, again.

Some of the students continued to meet at the Defense Colony gardens whenever the opportunity presented itself. One such evening, Sachin, Raj and Nitya were part of a group playing 'Truth or dare'. Raj was given the dare to kiss a girl in the group. Normally, when such a dare was given, the girls would reject the guy, or at best give them a quick peck and move on. This time though, Raj moved forward to kiss Nitya, and they kissed passionately for what felt like hours to Sachin. To anyone else in the group who didn't know better, it seemed like Nitya was dating Raj instead of Sachin.

Raj and Nitya surprised themselves and discovered a passion they never even knew existed. Until that point, they had shared great conversations, but little did they know they fostered feelings that went deeper than their words. They stopped kissing awkwardly when they realized they were the cynosure of all eyes there, most of all Sachin's. But the fact that they wanted the kiss to go on forever, in spite of even Sachin sitting right in front of them witnessing the kiss, made them realize how much they wanted to be together.

Sachin felt he had been sucker-punched when he saw the way Nitya kissed Raj. Barely a year ago, she felt uncomfortable kissing Sachin until he had met her mom, and now here she was, kissing Raj so passionately. But in the spirit of sportsmanship, he bit his tongue and forced a smile through all of it.

Later that day, he logged in to Nitya's Gmail account to which he still had access, to arrest that annoying noise at the back of his head. The noise wasn't unwarranted, since he opened her account to pages and pages of conversations with Raj. He couldn't even read beyond the first few mails as he was shaking with rage.

Those endless 'I love you's' over the phone felt like they had happened only yesterday. Now, his girlfriend was two-timing him with one of his closest friends.

He composed a mail to Raj from Nitya's account, with only the subject line that said, "Sachin here."

In a few hours, he received a call from Nitya, just as he expected, and she asked to see him at Sushmita's house.

When Sachin arrived, Sushmita met him at the door and sullenly led him to the living room where Nitya was seated on the couch. The moment Nitya saw Sachin, she broke down. She could barely get any words out and tried explaining in between sobs that she herself didn't understand the feelings she had for Raj. Sachin just sat there staring at her, his blood boiling inside, wondering if he even knew the girl in front of him. There was so much he wanted to say, when he noticed where Nitya was sitting. It was the same couch on which they shared their first kiss, the day after Sachin met Nitya's mom and grandmom. Sachin finally found his voice at that moment and said the first and only thing since meeting her that evening, "It's over."

The cemetery conversation

A little over a month later, Raj received a call from Sachin. He knew the conversation with him was inevitable and only hoped for it to be later than sooner. Sachin and Nitya completely cut off ties with each other. But despite everything that happened, he knew the friendship with him mattered enough to Sachin for them to eventually talk.

Sachin asked Raj to meet him near the Defense Colony Garden from where they could decide where to go. Raj arrived with two bottles of Kingfisher Strong. It was the most potent drink he knew, and figured they needed something strong to have the conversation they were going to. He also suggested sitting at some place outside, because he felt if the conversation got out of hand, it would be easier to handle it in an open space than within the closed confines of a pub.

They went for a walk and spotted a cemetery where they picked a tombstone to sit on. Raj popped open the beers and egged Sachin to take a few swigs first.

Sachin began a post-mortem of his relationship with Nitya. He could not believe that the girl who was so much in love with him only days before was now no longer with him. He started to diagnose what went wrong. He thought it must have been how he started ignoring her once engineering began, given they were in different colleges, and how he was busy getting accustomed to the new life there. They did indeed spend far less time together than back in school. He also recounted the last argument they had had a few weeks back when Nitya called him at his aunt's house. He had been very busy in the first few days of college, and they hadn't met or spoken on the phone for a while. And one day when he was at an aunt's house for her birthday party, he got a call from Nitya there. He was weirded out that she knew his aunt's phone number, let alone the fact that she called him when he was there; it almost felt like she was stalking him. He told her as much and hung up immediately. In hindsight, he wondered if this was when she began to realize her feelings for Raj and wanted to talk about her confused emotions. And instead of talking, he only made it worse by shouting at her.

All this while, Raj sat listening to Sachin's sob story when he had come all prepared for an argument or even a fight. And now with the alcohol kicking in, that was all he wanted to do. Another drunk guy a few tombstones behind him gave him the perfect excuse. That guy was sitting and drinking and having a conversation with himself, not troubling a soul apart from the fictitious ones he created for himself. Raj stood up and yelled at him to shut up. That's the last thing any drunk guy would want to hear; he yelled back at Raj. Pretty soon they got into a heated argument that could just as easily turn into a physical fight. When Sachin tried to placate the situation, Raj turned his attention to Sachin. He started to mock him and called him a pussy. He wanted nothing more than for Sachin to take a swing at him. That is what he had come prepared for. Sachin stood up to face Raj and said, "I came here to have a mature conversation with a friend. All you wanted to do was get drunk and have another argument. I'm leaving."

As Sachin walked away, Raj continued yelling profanities at both him and the other drunk. Too bad they were just losers who wanted to drink and whine. He had better things to do. He got home and opened the mail that Sachin had sent him from Nitya's account and hit reply...

In a quaint little school in the suburbs… there we were… a long, long way from here. Thoughts occupied but all shrunken to just one. We gave it a shot by scribbling on our archenemies. Then came the consecutive winters of our discontent, though this did happen at different times. We left it all behind one day. Got on our different paths with gusto, different paths to the same place. Strangers in a strange land instinctively we gathered, even traveled the same path for a year or so. Then came the pillars. The seemingly resolute pillars on whom we poured most of ourselves. The pillars came, they saw, they conquered and then like so many before, even they did leave. By now the archenemies they had once scribbled on seemed a million miles away. However, fate decreed that a million is way too much; the archenemies were now less than a scribbling distance. Nobody had a pen, and who really has the time to write nowadays (it is so much easier to email!!). They still dueled, though with diminished vigor than before. Then one-day… fate said enough is enough. No more chances for thee. If you can't make your peace in over a month, you probably never will, it ends now. Both accepted meekly, with no regrets, no complaints. With neither sadness nor happiness. In the race for the future, they both had to shed their bags… and so they did.

No matter what we said, no matter what we did, no matter what… you always were and always will be, Henry the first to me… my friend!

The first date

With the weight of Sachin lifted off their shoulders, Raj and Nitya looked forward to their date that they could have together in peace. They decided to meet at a Café Coffee Day near college, and Raj bunked his classes for the day to arrive at the café well in time. He was there at 10:30am for the 11:00am date and found a nice table to sit by the window. He ordered a chai latte, the sole tea option on a page full of cappuccino alternates. He hoped it would suffice for the friendly staff to let him stay a while on a potential revenue earning table. He sipped on the chai slowly, timing it to finish just before 11:00am so that it seemed like he placed his first order with Nitya. However, Nitya did not show up until 11:30am. The friendly staff were getting impatient. Raj ordered another chai. The mild caffeine from the drinks was beginning to kick in, making him stress about things beyond the ticking clock and Nitya's late arrival. He started to wonder if she had changed her mind about him and if she had decided to go back to Sachin. The clock struck 12 – an hour was the maximum grace normally given to Bangalore traffic for being late to any event. Beyond that, the problem didn't lie solely with traffic. Raj decided to push it a bit longer. The friendly staff would have to breathe down his neck before he budged from his seat. And that happened at half past noon, when Raj and the friendly staff had all but given up on Nitya.

Raj settled the tab sans a tip and made his way back home. Later that evening he was wrestling with the phone.

Should I call her? Or should I wait for her to call?

On the one hand, he wanted an explanation for being stood up, on the other, he didn't want to seem desperate. He wanted to give Nitya the opportunity to call and explain. Thankfully, his presence of mind won, and Nitya eventually called.

"I'm so sorry. I had a project that I needed to turn in today and my team hadn't done any of the work they originally promised to. I had to pick up their slack and complete the work."

"That's ok. Shall we meet tomorrow then?"

"No, I have important classes all day tomorrow. I won't be able to bunk them."

"Oh."

"But we can go out tomorrow night!" offered Nitya, allaying Raj's fears about her interest in dating him.

Raj was thrilled. Rarely did dates ever stretch into the night, let alone start at one, and that too a first date.

"That would be most excellent!" Raj replied, imitating Ted from Bill and Ted's Bogus Journey, which clearly fell flat with Nitya.

"The only problem is that we need to figure out a place to stay. I cannot get back home that late and my first visit to your house is certainly not going to be in the middle of the night."

"Well, I think I have a solution for that," said Raj, remembering to pick up Dev on his Airbnb offer.

This time, Nitya was bang on punctual, and they started off by visiting a new bowling alley called Amoeba, which had opened on Brigade Road. The moment they walked in, the song 'Dancing in the moonlight' started playing.

"I love this song," said Nitya.

"Me too. It's also a full moon tonight, by the way," replied Raj.

The song became 'their' song, and for the rest of their lives, every time it played, it reminded them of each other.

A few rounds of bowling and Chinese food later, they headed towards Dasarhawaii. Nitya dozed off in the cab and kept falling over. Raj tried harnessing her seat belt when she suddenly woke up. He hoped she didn't think he was doing something weird. Nitya figured what Raj was trying to do, smiled at him, and went right back to sleep. Raj continued to struggle with the seat belt till he latched it, which helped stabilize Nitya's bobbing head.

When they reached Dasarhawaii, Raj quickly made the bed for Nitya to continue sleeping. She took up the invite and went straight back to sleep. Raj lay next to her, absorbing her beauty. The pale white light of the full moon filtered into the room through the window and rested on her face. She was more beautiful than he'd ever seen her. He wanted to kiss her so badly but wasn't sure if it was appropriate.

Another debate raged in his head.

Should I try to kiss her? Or should I let her sleep?

It was only the first date, but she was lying right next to him on the bed. Against his better judgement, he decided to kiss her on the lips, very softly, just to see how she might react. To his surprise, Nitya kissed him right back. But there was something amiss with the kiss. It felt like a sleepy kiss as opposed to a fully awake one. It almost felt like he was taking advantage of the situation and he stopped himself immediately. Nitya just continued to sleep. She must have kissed him as a reflex, without even realizing what she was doing.

The next morning, as they were getting ready to leave, Raj asked her, "Do you remember what happened on the bed last night?"

"Yes, we kissed."

"You remember that?"

"It was our first kiss. How could I forget?"

"But I thought you were asleep."

"How would I kiss you if I were asleep!"

"Now I feel silly to have stopped."

"Yes, you must"

Their faces broke into smiles at once and they kissed again. This time it felt right. Fully awake kiss.

Later at home, Raj wanted to write so much about the day, but instead, all he had in his head was a tune.

Dancing in the moonlight

Everybody's feeling warm and bright.

It's such a fine and natural sight,

Everybody's dancing in the moonlight.

- Toploader

The 'break-up' trip

Sachin had hit rock bottom after his breakup from Nitya. He called all of his friends on a rotation speed dial. He would call Aishvarya one day, Thomas on another, Dev on the third and so on. He wasn't sure if it was just his love for Nitya, or the loss of both a girlfriend and a best friend. But he couldn't seem to turn his mind off Nitya.

One day, a couple of months after the breakup when the wounds were still sore, Sachin spotted Nitya and Raj together on the streets near their old school, getting out of an auto. They were possibly returning from a date, Sachin guessed. What shook him more than just seeing the two together was the way Raj looked. He was clean shaven, hair well groomed, and was wearing a crisp white shirt – He had never seen Raj look this prim and proper before. Nitya must have been worth the effort. Watching this new, upgraded Raj with his Nitya was the last straw for Sachin. He desperately needed to do something to get his mind off them.

Dev came up with a plan to travel to Pune and visit Dev's grandparents' house. It would be a 'break-up' trip as he called it. They would travel by train from Bangalore to Pune and then spend a week in Pune where Dev could show him his hometown. This was exactly what Sachin wanted, and along with Dev, started putting the pieces together, which included getting China and Gajan to tag along.

Pune turned out to be a treat for the boys where they got to hang out with people their own age. It was a student town where the average age was less than that in the pensioners' city of Bangalore. What made it better was how impeccably well-dressed everyone was. Especially the girls, who seemed to wear outfits that were tailor made for them. This was unlike Bangalore where people usually wore what they were comfortable in, without putting too much thought into their attires. Pune was different. Appearances mattered. And the Bangalore boys were loving every bit of it.

Upon their arrival in Pune, the boys first dropped off their luggage at Dev's grandparents' second house that was under construction, where they intended to stay. Then they went over to the first house where the family currently lived and met with Dev's grandparents and his sister, Juhi who had travelled back from Bangalore to Pune to spend her summer break with her grandparents as well.

They had dinner with Dev's family. Juhi invited one of her friends, Arshiya, so that she had some company as well with Dev's friends. Arshiya was a model-actress who instantly hit it off with the boys at the table.

Dev's grandmom prepared scrumptious parathas which the boys devoured. Gajan couldn't stop eating. He had Dev's grandmom make repeated trips to the kitchen to refill the parathas just for him even when everyone was done.

Great food and even better conversations later, the party of six went out on the terrace, leaving Dev's grandparents downstairs. Arshiya continued to be at the receiving end of conspicuous flirting from the boys. Sachin hoped his friends would back off and let him have Arshiya to himself since the trip was supposed to be his break-up trip. To his dismay, there was only so much eighteen-year-old boys could sacrifice for their grieving friend, especially in the company of a beautiful woman.

The only boy missing in the group was Dev. Partly because he claimed to have a policy against hitting on any of his sister's friends. And partly because his grandmom wanted him back in the kitchen to help her with the dishes. Getting nowhere with the flirting, Sachin decided to occupy himself with something else, and decided to send a mail to his mom back in Bangalore. He asked Juhi if he could use the house computer, and she led him to the study.

There was a bench in place of a chair in front of the computer, and it was strewn with papers all over. Dev's granddad was probably in the middle of some important work, Sachin thought. Juhi made some space on the bench for Sachin to sit. Then she switched on the machine and sat dangerously close to Sachin as it booted up. There was enough space on the bench for two people to sit, but Juhi was too close for comfort, her arm brushing up against Sachin's as she operated the keyboard. When the monitor came alive, another Juhi stared at them from the screen.

"That's a nice picture," said Sachin.

"I have a lot more. I'll mail them to you," quipped Juhi.

"Sure…," Sachin said awkwardly. She was sitting too close to him, and he had to try hard not to turn and face her.

"There you go," Juhi said as she opened a window of Netscape Navigator for Sachin to use.

Sachin wondered if she would continue sitting beside him as he logged in, but Juhi did not have any plans to budge. He proceeded to enter his login details, thinking he could just change his password later. After all, who knew how secure Netscape Navigator was in the first place.

He was in the middle of composing his mail when Juhi suddenly got off the bench and moved a step back. Sachin looked towards Juhi, wondering what had made her jump. The answer to his question walked in through the door the next moment when Dev entered the room. Juhi had heard him coming in and moved away from Sachin just in time.

"Sachin wanted to use your desktop," Juhi said hurriedly to Dev and sauntered out of the room.

The entire episode was super weird for Sachin, to say the least. He was now convinced more than ever that it was indeed Juhi who had made the call to him before the Halloween party three years back. And just maybe, her crying at that party may also have something to do with his proposal to Nitya on that day. But he never got around to confirming his suspicions. It had been a while since that call, and the boys were to leave that night for the second house where they would spend the remainder of their Pune trip and Sachin didn't expect to see Juhi again.

9/11

The boys spent the next few days of their trip exploring all that Pune had to offer. Driving through the gardens of AFMC, a swim in the waters of the Khadakvasala dam, and a trek to the Singhad fort. The boys also planned a two-day trip to Mahabaleshwar, where the Pune millennial scene was on over-drive. There wasn't a single elderly person in sight. At one point, China turned on his camcorder and started filming a 360-degree shot. He was surrounded by beautiful girls and wanted to capture this moment for posterity's sake.

They spent their days traveling and sight-seeing, and their nights drinking. Somehow, no matter the amount of alcohol they guzzled at night, they would still step out and explore the city the next day. They were young and their bodies recuperated quickly.

The week in Pune ended too soon. On the very last day, before their train ride back to Bangalore, the boys visited Dev's grandparents again to bid a quick adieu.

"Have you seen the news?" Juhi shouted the moment she opened the door to them.

"No, what happened?" Dev asked, worried.

"Hurry, go watch the TV now."

The boys rushed into the TV room and stared, with their mouths hanging open, at the Wall Street twin towers on fire.

Dev's granddad filled them in on the events that had transpired until then, and nobody could believe it.

That's when they saw it happen live. One of the buildings came crashing down.

Juhi, who stood next to Sachin, grabbed his arm and hung on to it when she saw the horrific scene on the television. Everyone else was speechless, staring blankly at the screen.

Back in Bangalore, Nitya and Raj watched the exact same scene on TV, like millions of others across the globe. Nitya grabbed Raj's arm and hung on to it. The couple mirrored Juhi and Sachin in Pune, right down to their shocked facial expressions. That dreary incident bonded Nitya and Raj in a unique way, just as it did Sachin and Juhi.

The journey back

The day had arrived for the boys to return to Bangalore. When everyone was busy packing, Sachin decided to check his mail to see if his mom had replied. This time he knew how to access the desktop and went about it on his own. When he opened his mailbox, instead of a mail from his mom, he had received a mail from Juhi. As promised, she sent him all of her photos from her profile photoshoot. Sachin stared at them for a few seconds, absorbing as much as he could, and then logged off before someone caught him in the act.

Dev's grandparents dropped them off at the station, after another scrumptious meal prepared by Dev's grandmom. As soon as they boarded the train, the heavy lunch combined with the familiar rocky motion of the Indian Railway trains, knocked the boys out and they spent the afternoon napping. Sachin spent the last moments before falling asleep recollecting the photos of Juhi, while Dev was busy on his phone exchanging SMSs with Renata who he missed terribly after the week-long trip.

A few hours later, Sachin woke up to see Dev with a puzzled look on his face.

"What happened?" asked Sachin, still groggy.

"I'm quite certain we haven't reached Bangalore yet, but it seems that the rest of our company has deserted us," replied Dev, pointing to the vacant berths where China and Gajan were supposed to be sleeping.

"Their luggage is still here, so they could not have gone far."

"Maybe we should go look for them."

Sachin and Dev started to walk across the length of the train, and after crossing a few compartments, spotted China and Gajan chatting with two girls. Those two were very quick to make the most of even this mundane train journey. The girls introduced themselves to Sachin and Dev as Neha and Disha, who were returning to their colleges in Mysore after visiting their families in Pune, much like the boys themselves.

"It's good you guys also came here. Now we can move their baggage to our compartment in just one trip," said China pointing to the girl's bags.

"We have space in our compartment, so we've decided to hang out together," Gajan offered, completing the picture.

The luggage was shifted, and China and Gajan instantly resumed their conversation with the girls. It so happened that Disha was the cuter of the two, making both China and Gajan focus their attention solely on her. With Dev still caught up in his SMSs to Renata, the two ignored people in the group, Sachin and Neha, began to chat.

As night fell, Sachin and Neha found themselves together on one berth while China, Gajan and Disha on the opposite one. Dev took the upper berth from where he could comfortably continue exchanging SMSs with Renata.

China, Gajan and Disha spent the rest of the night in a weird three-way. There were times when Disha would have her head on Gajan's lap and legs on China's, and then there were times China had his head on Disha's lap while she sat resting her head on Gajan's shoulder. The three explored every possible combination of sleeping positions that night.

Sachin and Neha sat opposite them, and quietly chuckled every time they noticed a change in their position. They were themselves snuggled under a blanket and Sachin made a few unsuccessful attempts to reach her breasts through the multiple layers of clothing. When Neha figured what he was up to, she decided to make it easy for both, and casually took Sachin's hand and slid it under her shirt. Sachin spent the rest of the night fondling her breasts. She may not have been the cuter of the two girls, but Sachin was glad she was the more forthcoming one.

When they reached Bangalore, the boys bade farewell to the girls as they continued their journey onwards to Mysore. Sachin never saw Neha again, while China and Gajan would continue to fight for Disha's attention for months to come. Sachin was glad Dev put this plan together, since it turned out to be the perfect 'breakup' trip. The trip to Pune not only took his mind off things in Bangalore, but also led to some unexpected developments. He developed a crush on Juhi and experienced his first no-strings-attached one-nightstand with Neha.

The turning-point

Back in Bangalore, Raj, Nitya, Thomas and Sushmita had found a rhythm of their own. Every weekend, Thomas would commute down from Mysore to Bangalore, and the four of them would meet at Sushmita's house on Saturday evenings when her parents were off at a club. It was the perfect opportunity for them to have some alone time with each other and they occupied two of the bedrooms in the house for a few hours until Sushmita's parents returned.

Raj and Nitya spent their time hugging and kissing and rolling all over the bed in their room. One evening, while giving it all they had, Nitya's top came off. Raj started to kiss her neck and slowly worked his way down. He had just made it to one of her breasts, when they heard Sushmita knock on the door.

The club Sushmita's parents visited had fixed timings, and the four ensured they vacated the house before they returned. It was probably time to leave, and Raj and Nitya stopped and looked into each other's eyes for a moment. Then Raj looked down and noticed one of Nitya's nipples peeking out of her bra. Nitya looked down, and back at Raj, and they broke into a smile together.

Nitya had never gone beyond kissing Raj or even Sachin before that. Just kissing was so much fun that it never occurred to them to do anything else. But at that moment, she felt strangely excited about her partial nudity. She looked away from Raj as she straightened her clothes, not wanting him to notice her chin that would surely be twitching at maximum pace then.

The next Saturday evening when they were back at Sushmita's house, Nitya's top came off the instant she was alone with Raj. Second base felt out of the world for both of them. Things started to progress from there on, and every time they met, new ways of making out were being discovered.

At one point, when all their clothes were off this time, Raj suddenly froze. He noticed blood on Nitya's thighs, and his face turned white with fear. Nitya looked down at the blood and then back at Raj with a confused expression on her face.

"Is that mine?"

"I think so. It's not mine. Did I hurt you somewhere?"

"I don't know. I don't feel anything, and I cannot be chumming right now."

"Is that… then… the hymen?"

"Must be…."

Nitya couldn't put her feelings into words. All she knew was that every inch of her skin just wanted to be held. Instead of doing that, Raj was freaking out, helping her with her clothes, fixing a juice he found in Sushmita's fridge, and overall, just treating Nitya like an injured patient who had just walked into the emergency ward.

They spent the next week without saying a word to each other. And the next Saturday evening, when they were back at Sushmita's house, Raj was hesitant to make a move on Nitya.

Nitya broke the impasse by grabbing Raj and kissing him. He pulled back and spoke for the first time.

"Are you alright?"

"Of course, I am! What happened was quite normal. Stop worrying about it so much."

"You sure we can do this?"

"Yes, I'm sure. The only thing is, we need to use a condom."

Neither of them had ever bought or even seen a condom until that point. They chalked a plan where Nitya would put on makeup, don a sari, and Raj would take her to a medical store where she would purchase a pack of condoms.

Nitya's logic was that makeup and a sari added years to a girl, and it would therefore be easier if she made the purchase. Raj didn't argue with the logic. He was just glad he wasn't the one buying the condoms.

The condom purchase went off surprisingly smooth. The medical storekeeper didn't bat an eyelid while selling the condoms to Nitya. Encouraged by her, Raj also started purchasing condoms, as they seemed to be running out of them fast at Sushmita's house.

One particular Saturday evening, Sushmita's parents returned earlier than usual. Sushmita heard the garage door opening while they were all still inside. She immediately ran out of her room and knocked on the door of the room Raj and Nitya were in. Raj and Nitya were completely naked, with Raj's spent condom still on his limp penis. When Sushmita whispered through the door that her parents were home, they flung into action and got dressed. By the time they stepped out, they could hear Sushmita's parents getting out of the car, which meant they had parked the car in the garage and would be through the door at any moment. They rushed out of the front door, just as Sushmita's parents entered from the back door.

"Oh my god, that was close," Raj said, almost out of breath, and started laughing the moment they got out.

"Yes, let's go home now," Thomas told Raj in a despondent tone, pointing in the direction of Raj's house where he spent the nights when he visited Bangalore.

"What's up with you?" asked Raj, but before Thomas could respond, Nitya pulled Raj aside.

"Did you throw out the condom before we left?" Nitya whispered to Raj.

"Oh no… I forgot about it."

Nitya pulled Sushmita aside. Her discussion with Sushmita went on for a lot longer than it seemed to require, which made Raj feel tense.

"It's ok, she noticed it while clearing the room and threw it out," Nitya told Raj after talking to Sushmita.

"Oh no, sorry to have put her through that. But what were you guys talking about for so long?"

"I think you should have a talk with Thomas," Nitya told Raj before leaving with Sushmita who had not uttered a word since they made their way out of the house.

Raj and Thomas started walking towards Raj's house.

"What's going on! It's as if all of us are having some sort of a problem today. And why are you so uptight! We got out on time, right?" he asked Thomas.

"Yes, sure."

"What's wrong then? You've been stoic since we left the house."

"Sushmita and I broke up today."

Raj was stunned.

"She just said she's bored of this relationship. After over seven years together and all this effort I put into traveling from Mysore to Bangalore every week, this is what she says."

"Did it have anything to do with… umm… the condom?"

"What condom?"

"Never mind," said Raj, realizing Thomas had no clue what he was talking about, and how impertinent it was given what he must have been going through.

Thomas and Sushmita's breakup changed a lot of things. Thomas stopped visiting Bangalore; Raj and Nitya no longer hung out at Sushmita's house; and worst of it all, it sowed the initial seeds of strain in Raj and Nitya's relationship.

Thomas had become something of a second son to Raj's parents, given he visited them and stayed over every weekend. Moreover, he appreciated the idlis and dosas Raj's mom would cook instead of the Maggi or omelets Raj demanded if he was even home at all for breakfast. Raj's mom adored this about Thomas, and she started to miss his weekly visits and constantly asked Raj what had happened between them.

Without their weekly rendezvous at Sushmita's house, Raj and Nitya had to rely on Dev's Dasarhawaii all over again. However, Nitya no longer liked visiting the place, given how Dev's friends abused the house every time they visited, leaving it unkempt.

Not having a place to share private moments with Nitya, and Thomas not visiting him anymore, the change was all too much for Raj to handle and he would misdirect his frustrations towards Nitya by starting inane arguments with her.

There was once a time they decided to visit Raj's favorite bookstore, but upon reaching there, found it replaced by a swanky new coffee shop. Raj was completely annoyed, and without a word, left Nitya alone on the street and hailed an auto home.

He picked up his diary the moment he got home to try and calm down and articulate his emotions.

Where have all the bookstores gone? Have they gone to the consumerism that's everywhere?

When I was younger, so much younger than today... There used to be this awesome place where we would just sit, listen, and talk for ages. Replace that with harsh lights, pack it up with every 18-20yr old (and his brother!!), serve overpriced Italian coffee and oh-so high brow sounding food and we have the monstrosities known as coffee day and barista. It is THE place to be seen, to socialize… why? Because everybody is doing it. The most important thing you have to remember is to dress well. C'mon, it's Barista! You have to look good!

Where have all the good bookstores gone, now that MTV and McDonalds are everywhere.

Case in point: Landmark. Even I buy some books at landmark (What other choice is there?) Overpriced, spic and span, huge selection of vastly worthless crap YAY!! The real selling point is the sheer depth of utter ignorance the staff so effortlessly seem to possess. Even the clientele is nothing to write home about. Trust me, go to landmark any goddamn day of the week and the aisle, which is the most crowded, is the self-help books aisle. God, if you read self-help books… You really need help (albeit maybe not from yourself)!

Where have all the good music stores gone, gone to boy bands everywhere.

Welcome all to the bottom of the musical cesspit. We hope you stay a while. Led Zep, Hendrix, Maiden, no, no, we don't have a lot of that but see this CD of Britney Spears… now doesn't that seem like a good buy? Call me old-fashioned but I really don't like to mix my porn with music.

Yup, this is the world I know!

The Mysore trip.

Gajan filled Raj in on all the details of their Pune trip during recess one day at college. Raj was obviously not invited to that trip. He and Sachin hadn't spoken since the cemetery, and the trip to Pune was planned by Dev primarily for Sachin. Raj didn't mind skipping the trip but was curious to hear all the details. Especially, the 'Disha' part of the story.

"What are you going to do about her?" Raj asked Gajan.

"I don't know. I really do like her. But so does China. And neither of us knows who she likes!"

"Why don't you just ask her?"

"It's not a conversation to be had on the phone."

"Why can't you meet her?"

"She lives in Mysore."

"Hey, why don't we go on a trip to Mysore then? I would love to meet up with Thomas now that he's stopped visiting Bangalore."

"That would be amazing. We can make another trip out of it. Let's ask the rest of the crew."

"Sure, but make sure you leave out Sachin and China," Raj said with a wink.

Gajan ran the idea by Dev, who once again offered the perfect plan.

"Mysore is just a three-hour drive from Bangalore. Let's drive there," Dev suggested to Gajan.

"A road trip would be perfect. But we don't have a car."

"Leave that to me."

The plan was set. They would drive Friday evening at the end of the college lectures and reach Mysore by nightfall. Raj would go on to meet Thomas, while Dev and Gajan would meet Disha.

On the day of the trip, the clouds opened up, and torrential rain descended on Bangalore. Raj usually avoided the rain. His mom never let him out in the rain since he was a child, worried he would catch a cold if he ever got drenched. She was particularly worried about the season's first rain, as she thought those rains brought down all the impurities in the sky, increasing the probabilities of catching a cold. She would even pin a handkerchief to Raj's shirt at the start of the monsoon season, so that he could easily blow his nose in case he did catch a cold.

Raj noticed some of the college students playing in the rain and wondered how he had never thought of enjoying a downpour before. He suddenly got an urge to step out and get drenched to the bone. He wasn't sure if it was the excitement about traveling to Mysore to meet Thomas, or just in defiance of something his mom made him miss out on his entire childhood, but out he went, facing the sky with his arms stretched out wide.

"You're not going to fall sick this time," Sushmita told a dripping wet Raj when he came out of the rain, as if she had just read the question in his mind.

"How can you be so sure?" Raj asked, surprised once more at Sushmita's supernatural mind-reading ability.

"Because this time, you wanted to get wet. Every other time you were running away from the rain, and that psychologically made you fall sick. This time you were enjoying it. And when you enjoy something, nothing bad can come of it."

As it so happened, Raj didn't fall sick. In fact, he felt the exact opposite, rearing to travel to Mysore.

Ah, then it rains.

Fluttering your large banner across my best-laid plans, free those restraints on your hand. Do the deed you set out for. In the face of any obstacle, you will prevail.

Ah, then it rains.

On your private carousel,

Thoughts that sink of their own accord. Foreign concepts you were not destined to hear,

Nestled in your ear, taking flight while keeping some here.

Ah, still it rains.

Dev arrived on Raj's campus with China, to pick Raj and Gajan from there. He drove in a brand-new gold colored Maruti Zen.

"Woah, where did you get that from?" Gajan nearly squealed with delight when he saw the car.

"Let's just say I have a fan club. This belongs to a girl in my college, and she was more than happy to lend it to me for the weekend."

"Man, you are all sorts of resourceful," said Raj as he checked the car out.

"The only caveat: we need to be careful with the car. Not a single dent or scratch on it."

The boys started on the road trip to Mysore, making one customary stop at Madhur to have the famous Madhur vada that was a must for everyone traveling to and from Bangalore and Mysore. When they reached Mysore, they first dropped Raj off at the house Thomas rented and then Gajan navigated towards Disha's rented house at the address she had given him.

When they reached the location, Disha opened the door, along with a tall, burly Sardar.

"Hey guys, welcome to Mysore!" Disha told Gajan and Dev, and then added looking towards the big guy next to her "Meet Harpreet, my boyfriend,".

With just four words, Disha had cut the ground from underneath Gajan's feet. Here he had come to Mysore to woo Disha but was instead shaking hands with her boyfriend.

"Let me show you guys to your room. We have plenty of space here as we're always entertaining visitors from Bangalore," said Harpreet, welcoming them inside.

"You didn't know she had a boyfriend?" Dev asked Gajan the moment they were out of their hosts' earshot.

"Do I look like I knew?" said Gajan looking both irritated and shocked.

"You never asked her?"

"Why would I? She was very obviously flirting with me. She agreed to host us in her house when I asked her. Never once in all those conversations did this… man-mountain Harpreet come up."

"Well, he's here now. Good luck with whatever it is you plan to do with Disha."

Harpreet was not just a friendly giant, but an ignorant one as well. It didn't look like he had a clue about the ulterior motives behind

Gajan's visit. Instead, he went about making Gajan and Dev feel as comfortable as he could in his house.

Later that evening, Harpreet organized a little party on account of their new guests and invited some of his friends from Mysore to join. They were great company and Harpreet ensured there was enough alcohol for everyone.

At one point late into the night, Dev noticed that Gajan was nowhere to be found. He scanned the living room and noticed that Disha was missing too. He froze, fearing the worst, and scanned the living room once more, slowly this time. The realization of what he had just observed made the back of his hair stand up. He was in the corner towards the back of this house. Between him and the front exit were five guys, all of them the same size as man-mountain Harpreet. This was not a friendly welcome party; this was an ambush.

Dev slowly put his drink down and started walking towards the exit. He got halfway across the living room when Harpreet descended on him.

"Hey, where's your drink?" Harpreet asked Dev.

"Umm… I think I've had enough."

"Nonsense, you don't look drunk at all!"

Why does he want to get me drunk? Dev thought to himself, picturing the worst possible outcome for him at this stranger's house in a strange city. Raj was dropped off earlier at Thomas' house and hadn't made a note of Disha's address. Gajan was therefore the only person who knew his whereabouts, and Gajan was AWOL.

"Oh. It's ok. I think I should go look for Gajan," Dev gathered himself and blurted out.

"He'll be back soon. He's right outside talking to Disha."

He knows! What exactly is it that he knows?

"You do know what is happening right?" Harpreet asked, as if reading Dev's mind.

What is happening! Dev screamed inside his head.

"What is happening?" Dev let out softly.

"Gajan likes Disha and they're talking about it outside."

Dev was completely confused. This was not what he was expecting. Harpreet wasn't as ignorant as he thought he was. Instead, he knew exactly what was happening. In fact, he was letting it happen, with an irritating smile plastered on his face.

"Umm… are you ok with that?" Dev couldn't help but ask.

"Well, what can you do? Disha broke up with me before she left for Pune. Then she came back saying she wanted to get back with me. Now she wants to talk to Gajan. She needs to figure this out for herself."

Dev only got more and more confused. Was Harpreet an ignorant gentle giant or was he genuinely the nicest and most secure guy he had ever met?

Right then, Gajan and Disha walked into the room. Disha moved towards Harpreet and Gajan towards Dev.

"What's going on?" Dev asked Gajan, pulling him aside.

"Nothing, dude. I'll tell you later."

"Bullshit you are. You're telling me right now."

"Disha is Hindu and Harpreet is Sikh. And the specific castes they are from forbid a marriage between the two, as per Disha's family, at least. So, she planned on breaking up with him before things got any more serious, but the trip to Pune and the flirting with me and China only convinced her of how much she loves Harpreet and wants to be with him. That's pretty much it."

"Well, he must be a swell guy," Dev said, looking towards Harpreet who was refilling Disha's glass.

Back at Thomas' house, another intense conversation was underway.

"I will be moving to my parents' in Dubai and completing the rest of my engineering studies at a college there," Thomas told Raj.

"What? It's bad enough you barely visit Bangalore when you're living in Mysore. And now you're going all the way to Dubai?"

"If I stay back here to complete my engineering here, I would either get a job in Bangalore or Mysore, and I can't live in either city. Bangalore reminds me too much of Sushmita, and I don't know a single person in Mysore. I've spent all my time here attending college during the week and then traveling to Bangalore over weekends so that I haven't made a single friend in Mysore. It's best I head to Dubai."

"Man, I'll miss you."

"I'll miss all of you too. All my close friends are in Bangalore, but everything in that city reminds me of Sushmita. I cannot live there."

"What happened with you guys?"

"Religion. She's Muslim and the only way her family will accept me is if I convert."

"And you would obviously never do that."

"Actually, I offered to. But Sushmita didn't believe me. You know how she is. She has instincts like nobody else and figured I wouldn't go through with it. And even if I did, it would only strain our relationship. And maybe she's right."

"This didn't occur to you guys before?"

"It was never this serious before. We were just kids in school having fun. But things are different now… engineering, jobs… just growing up!"

"Man, I'll really miss you."

"Yeah… maybe you'll move to Dubai as well. Who knows!"

"The big dusty? Not a chance."

The biggest problem with religion is the fact that it has too much power over people. Don't get me wrong, I am as religious as the next guy (ok, that depends on the next guy), but faith should never take precedence over reason. At the extreme end of religion, one out of a million fanatics thinks he is the next messiah who will save mankind. There is nothing wrong with this line of thinking if you don't act upon it. It could even be interpreted as having a good self-image. The shit hits the ceiling only when one of these "messiahs" tries to show the world his newfound holiness by vaporizing an entire city. Most often the answer to the question "Why in the name of god would anybody ever want to do something like that?" is unfortunately "Exactly, In the name of god!"

Granted that is the extremum, but even the most levelheaded people can act prickly about religion…. My religious beliefs…. Let's just say that I have lost faith…. at least, it has been diluted. It really is tough for me to believe implicitly in something which has no tangible effect on my life… like. God, work, etc.

As for the latter, even God himself would be bad at it. Why?

The top 5 reasons why God will suck being me…

1. He would have problems accepting my PM as a higher authority.

2. He would stick out like a sore thumb in this version of hell.

3. Due to his extreme inadequacy in the usage of cursive writing, he would have problems making his opinions be known.

4. You can find a kind god, a vengeful god but a mindless one is tough to find.

5. Even he can't figure out the details of the stupid drawing I have been poring over the whole day!!!

Official quote: Which is it: Is man one of God's blunders or is God one of man's? - Friedrich Nietzsche

Second Act.
2016

Distancing from the best friend

Fifteen years had passed since Thomas' relocation to Dubai from India. The first few years in Dubai were painful for him. He missed all his friends in Bangalore, most of all Sushmita. But with his parents' help, he gradually reconstructed his life in Dubai. He studied hard at engineering, and then even harder for the b-school entrance exam. He studied mostly because it was the best way to get his mind off Sushmita. All of his hard work eventually paid off, and he landed a spot at one of Dubai's premier business schools, where he met his future wife, Sneha. On top of that, after graduation, he secured a plush banking job in Dubai.

Thomas thought Sneha was the perfect girl for him. If someone were to ask him what his definition of a perfect wife was, even before he started dating Sushmita, his answer would define Sneha and all of her qualities. Sneha had wild curly hair, like Dharma from the Dharma and Greg show, which Thomas found attractive. Sneha was the smartest girl in her college even. She won every personality contest, debate, elocution, any event that required public speaking. Sneha was the girl who represented her college since she always beat her peers in inter-college fests and competitions. Thomas, who considered himself to be a sapiosexual, found Sneha's wit and intellect to be incredibly attractive. But the thing he liked most about Sneha was how bold she was. She never refrained from taking a stance on something she believed in, and when she did, even the dean of the college thought twice before going against her.

In many ways, Sneha was the quintessential girlfriend, and Thomas couldn't be happier that she agreed to marry him. They got married within a year of passing out from college.

Unfortunately, like they say, marriage changes things. The very quality Thomas adored most in Sneha, became the bane of their relationship. Sneha was a girl with no greys. Everything was either black or white for her. And if Thomas didn't agree with her on something, for Sneha, it automatically meant he was wrong. There was no ground for compromise, which, he argued, was the very foundation of a successful relationship.

The difficulties in their relationship reached an inflection point when Raj moved to Dubai. If Thomas disagreed with Sneha on a few things, Raj was Thomas on steroids. He disagreed with Sneha on so many levels that they fought constantly. So much so, that Thomas had to completely distance them from each other and live separate lives with them.

He couldn't avoid meeting Raj. Not only was he his best friend, but Raj didn't quite manage to make any other friends in Dubai. He abhorred his colleagues from his office and Thomas was the only person he wanted to meet or talk to in Dubai. Trying to split his time between Raj and Sneha only drove the wedge in their marriage deeper.

By the time Raj left Dubai, the damage was irreversible. It was ironic that despite the end of Raj's maniacal third-wheeling, Thomas and Sneha could never get back to the relationship they once had. They completely stopped talking. Thomas found comfort in a girl from his office while Sneha moved in with her parents. Thomas reached a crossroad in life where he had to decide what he needed to do. He didn't want to leave Sneha as he didn't want to be known as the guy who failed to make it work with 'Ms. Perfect'. Thomas couldn't fathom facing any of his friends or family about this failure. At the same time, the girl from his office wanted him to choose between her and his wife, as she was tired of living as the other woman.

Thomas felt that the only person he could speak to about his situation was the person who got him there in the first place: Raj. But this was not a conversation he could have over the phone. He needed to meet Raj. And fifteen years after leaving, he went back to Bangalore.

Despite the fact that Raj hated Sneha with a passion, Thomas knew he was the only one who understood him enough to give him the right advice. And if not advice, he could at least spend some time again with his best friend.

Thomas made the trip to the city he swore never to come back to, for the sole purpose of meeting Raj, to talk to him. When they met, they spent the entire night talking. Raj, as usual, spoke a lot but said very little. After realizing that he was no closer to solving his problem after the first night they spoke, Thomas asked to meet Raj again. This time though, Sachin found out that Thomas was in Bangalore and insisted on including more members of the Bus Stop crew to the plan. Despite Thomas' refusal, as he wanted time alone with Raj, and despite Raj's discomfort with large gatherings, it was difficult for Thomas to deny Sachin and his other good friends from Bangalore. Besides, only China was available to meet them on such short notice, so Thomas and Raj decided to go along.

The four of them met up at a pub on Brigade Road, and after guzzling a few drinks, Raj got chatty again.

"Have you guys heard about Thomas' concubine?" Raj asked Sachin and China who quizzically looked at an exasperated Thomas.

Raj went on to narrate everything Thomas had told him the previous night, despite Thomas' protests, denials, and frequent attempts at digressing from the topic at hand.

Thomas was devastated. He had traveled across the continent just to meet this guy, and here Raj sat making a mockery of his marital problems. Raj had done exactly this when he stomped out of Dubai five years ago, embarrassing Thomas in front of his colleagues and friends since he was the one who had vouched for Raj in Dubai. Now, Raj was doing the same thing. Showing scant regard for the feelings of someone who adored, and even revered him.

Thomas was one of the most dedicated friends to Raj. He had stood by him on so many occasions in the past. They shared so much together during the times they double-dated Nitya and Sushmita. But all Raj did was disrespect Thomas and show callous disregard for his feelings.

Thomas got up in the middle of Raj's diatribe, wished him well, and left Bangalore, swearing for the second time, never to return.

"Oh, fuck him! That's one less person I have to put up with," said Raj gulping his drink down and ordering two more for himself, as Sachin and China sat speechless at what they had just witnessed.

A long time ago in a town by the sea, there were two people. They had spent most of their lives without knowing each other, They used to go to the same places, saw each other in passing, were blissfully unaware of each other. Then one day they met, it made sense, it seemed right. Then things changed. Then they started living their own lives, each one more spectacular than the other, dreams to achieve, people to love, a life to lead to its fullest. Not a thought was shared between them. Perfect strangers they remained till the end. One perfect, one strange.

Chapter 9

Losing Money

First Act.
2005

Best friends at Strawberry Fields

Sachin had stopped talking to Raj ever since his breakup with Nitya. Thomas had moved to Dubai. But Raj's life couldn't be getting more exciting.

College was over and with that, he could now call himself a certified engineer. Placement season had not yet started, making it that perfect phase of his college life for maximum fun, which was exactly what Raj did, and he was never short of company to do it with.

Strawberry Fields was Bangalore's own version of Woodstock, where lots of small bands performed for twenty-four hours straight, and concertgoers lay wasted on open grounds, with all the alcohol that was on offer.

Raj, China, Gajan and Vinay landed at Strawberry Fields on two bikes and with the music and ambience, were drunk in no time. Raj was so intoxicated that he lay flat on the ground and was even trying to get comfortable there. He tried to make a small pillow out of the mud under him, to rest his head on. He would also throw up every half hour.

Every time he threw up, China had to move him so that he didn't roll around in his own puke. Raj would set about making another pillow in the new location and sleep for another half hour before he threw up again, when China would once again move him.

The routine went on for the entire night until they decided they had had enough of Strawberry Fields and just wanted to get home. They ambled along to the bike park, with Raj the most drunk of the lot, and Gajan not far behind. China and Vinay found themselves supporting their two friends all the way to the parking.

When they reached the bike park, they set Raj and Gajan down in front of their bikes. China proceeded to mount his bike from one side and instantly fell over the other side. That's when he realized he was fairly drunk himself and didn't have a lot of motor control. He lay on the ground, hoping one of the others would pick him up.

"Dude, I think China just fell down," Raj said to Gajan.

"Oh yeah, he's lying on the ground there," Gajan replied.

"Maybe we should help him?"

"Yes, we should."

Raj and Gajan continued to sit and stare at China. That was all the help they could offer him.

Vinay, the most sober of the lot, picked China up and set him properly on the bike.

"You really think you can ride?" Vinay asked China.

"I don't know. Let me try riding a short distance and we'll see," said China and started up his bike. He had barely moved ten feet, when he fell off the bike again.

"Dude, I think China just fell down," Raj said to Gajan again.

"Oh yeah, he's lying on the ground there," Gajan replied.

"Maybe we should help him?"

"Yes, we should."

They didn't move a muscle yet again, and Vinay rushed over to pick up China.

"Are you ok?"

"Yeah, thankfully, I was riding slow. But I think I should rest on the bike for a bit before we start again."

"Yes, let's do that."

Vinay came back to join Raj and Gajan, and the three of them sat there and watched China lay down on his bike. Nobody knew how much time had passed, but soon they saw China standing in front of them.

"Ok guys let's do this," China announced to them.

Gajan was in a deep sleep, so they decided to first help him sit behind Vinay on his bike, wrapping his arms tightly around Vinay. Vinay stooped forward so that Gajan could be more comfortable and tried riding his bike a little and figured he could manage the awkward position.

China helped Raj, who had sobered up a little, and attempted another test ride. This time he figured he could manage, and they set off towards their homes.

En-route, a police car started to tail them. China and Vinay were sure to get fined for drunk riding but kept it together and continued riding straight. The car came up along next to them.

"Hey, the guy behind you is sleeping," one of the cops yelled at Vinay.

"Yes sir, I know. He's not well and I'm taking him home."

"Ok, as long as you know that he is asleep. Take care," said the cop and they drove past the two bikes.

"Wow, a cop who looked out for us? When has that ever happened!" China told Vinay once the police car was gone.

"I know! Hey, by the way, whose house are we going to? I don't think we can take Raj or Gajan to their houses given how drunk they are, and I cannot take them to mine either," Vinay told China.

"You're right! What do we do now?" China replied, realizing they hadn't thought their destination through before they started.

"I have an idea, follow me."

Vinay rode to the Bangalore City train station, and they parked their bike in the parking lot.

"What are we doing here?" China asked Vinay confused.

"I've seen people sleep at the station, so let's just sleep here till morning."

With that, the four boys walked into the station, and found a spot next to a bunch of other people who were fast asleep. They decided it was best to sleep with them, so it looked like they were part of a bigger group.

At daybreak, Raj was woken up by a kick to his butt. He immediately sat up to yell at the person who had kicked him, but then saw China, Gajan and Vinay already sitting up and staring at him with their hands caressing their butts.

Raj looked around, confused, and realized quickly that they were surrounded by army jawans.

The group they had decided to sleep next to the previous night turned out to be a bunch of army jawans, probably on their way to some training camp. When the jawans woke up and saw four silly civilians sleeping alongside, they figured that a kick to the butt was probably the mildest form of punishment they could offer.

"Sir, as I already told you, it was too dark, and we didn't realize where we were sleeping," Vinay pleaded with one of the jawans who seemed to be in charge.

"Just get out of here," he barked at Vinay.

"Yes sir," said the boys in unison and scooted out of the train station.

When they reached their bikes, they burst out laughing together.

I don't have the remotest doubt about anything I do. I know that my life will be spectacular, things always have had a strange way of working out for me. Often, I'm considered cocky. Maybe even a touch arrogant. Equipped with my sailor's tongue and a crew of equally brash buddies, I sail un-relentless into all waters, no matter how troubled. The archetypal existence of a slightly rich, very aimless, relatively young and habitually intoxicated guy fresh out of college. Note that I'm just commenting, not complaining in any which way. I love my life, the things I do just describe a facet of it, for I still try to have a substantial amount of those pursuits, which are considered 'productive' – whatever that means. My dreams are by no means unconventional. I'm humdrum and ordinary in most of the things I really want from life.

Just do a lot of things, which in retrospect may not have been among the best ideas I will have. Like getting hammered and pissing over the divider of the busiest road in this city. It is tough to zip up your fly while running. Like trying to take a turn at 120KMPH on the highway just to impress on others my point, that if the car is low enough, the separation of the stream lines in the turbulent region of airflow is lesser, though drag is higher at higher speeds, thus the chances of swerving from the initial curve are lesser compared to a 80-90 KMPH speed turn...... The score so far..... Me 0, Physics 1.... My dad –19000RS. But these are, by no means, things I regret. My partners-in-crimes and I talk about these and countless other similar incidents. I laugh uncomfortably and then change the topic (It was 19000RS, did you expect no repercussions? I'm sorry but I really can't smile about that!).

The thing is, no matter how injudicious my actions seem, at least I always knew what I was doing. Though some days, a select few, I have no clue, and even worse I'm scared shitless!

Official quote: Experience is that marvelous thing that enables you to recognize a mistake when you make it again - Franklin P Jones

Foam party

Strawberry Fields was just one of many events Raj went to with his friends. Nitya was starting to get flustered for missing out as she craved a bit of fun herself. She too had graduated from college, after all, and had as much free time.

She came across a concept called the 'foam party', and asked Raj to accompany her to one. The concept had been borrowed from some clubs in Brazil and was happening for the first time in Bangalore.

The idea was to dance in a discotheque, where along with the music and lights, there would also be foam descending on the partygoers. Raj abhorred the very thought of it. As if a discotheque wasn't bad enough, they had to add some dingy soap water to it! There was no way he was going to do it.

But Nitya turned up the emotional volume and coerced Raj into taking her. Much to his chagrin, he went along with it, half hoping the organizers would screw up and run out of foam halfway through the party.

However, as bad as Bangalore was in fixing its highways, it was the exact opposite when it came to parties. The 'foam party' turned out to be better than fake Woodstock.

Not only was there plenty of foam, but the discotheque was one of the largest they had ever been to, with an incredible sound and light set-up. Copious amounts of foam flowed through make-shift vents in the ceiling the entire night.

Nitya had brought some of her friends along—people Raj never got along with. He downed a couple of whiskeys to make the company and ambience palatable, and then stepped on the dance floor, giving in to the requests of a persistent Nitya.

Nitya loved every bit of the foam party. Getting soaked to the bone, and then seeking out the warmth from Raj's body by hugging him tight. Soft foam falling over them and snaking its way down their bodies. Psychedelic music and lights that looked even better through their foam-soaked vision. The entire experience was more intoxicating than any amount of alcohol she could have consumed.

Every time they stepped off the dance floor for a drink, Nitya wanted to get right back in. It was colder off it, and the falling foam somehow seemed to keep them warm. It was the best time Nitya had had with Raj since they started dating. She wanted the 'foam party' to go on forever.

Raj, on the other hand, was trying his best to fake it for Nitya's sake. There was something about a club that invoked this primal feeling of dislike in him. It felt like a bunch of people trying too hard to be cool and have a good time. This evening was the perfect example. All the ingredients were present. The guys were well-dressed, looked smart and were even slightly intoxicated and thus much less inhibited. The girls were good looking and in good spirits. Three hours later, soaking wet with the industrial strength nozzles forcing soapy water at nearly supersonic speeds on unsuspecting, young, nubile bodies pressed up together, was probably what the holocaust felt like, Raj thought.

He was so bored with the whole evening, that he craved to get back to his real friends, have a couple of drinks and play on his PS2.

Color me boring if you will, but I shall skip the next one. You know the one, which has the huge billboard saying, 'Be there or be square!' I really do prefer to have a boring time with people I find interesting to an interesting time with people I find boring. If that is being square, so be it. Reminds me of 'Le Dejeuner des Canotiers' by Renoir, the girl in the middle of the painting, the one staring into space... tired of the party, just unadulterated longing to escape to a more comfortable place.

Placement season

All good things come to an end, and so did their post-college holiday. Companies started announcing their recruitment schedules, and the new graduates began to prepare for it.

The entire Bus Stop crew heavily discussed which companies they would apply to and how they would go about preparing for the recruitment process. Raj remained nonchalant through the entire placement process. He did not apply to any of the companies, and his friends began to worry.

One evening, Gajan, Vinay and China decided to catch up with Raj to discuss his career plans. They met at Jags, a bar originally named 'Jagadish Bar', which was their go-to place for having heavy discussions such as this.

"I'm waiting for Infosys. That's the only company I will join," Raj explained to them.

"But how do you know they will select you?" Gajan asked.

"Have you seen how Infosys arrives on campus? They come with a truck! They recruit forty to fifty students from each college and there is no way I wouldn't make the cut from ours."

"But some of these other companies pay better," chipped in China.

"That's a sham. They show you a CTC that makes it look like they are better paymasters, but I've done the math. The take-home salary you get from Infosys is as good as any other company coming to campus."

"But is it your dream company?" Vinay enquired.

"Actually, it is. Your best chance of getting an offsite role is with Infosys. I want to get out of this shithole country as soon as I can!"

"If you dislike being in India so much, how come you never considered university abroad?"

"My atthe in the US offered me an opportunity as well earlier, but it's a bit mental to study in an American University. It's all rat eat rat out there. I figured it's better to get an education here and then get sent to the US or some other place with a job and salary that I can enjoy with. And now, my best shot at that happening is if I join Infosys."

There was no arguing with Raj. As always, it seemed that he was better informed, and more importantly, preconceived to a notion he wouldn't budge from.

And true to his prediction, Infosys recruited fifty people from campus, and Raj was one of them. He got placed in the only company he applied to. Once again, he ensured maximum output with minimal effort. He went to a pub to celebrate the best way he could: catching the Champions League finals with friends.

What a match! Liverpool Champions of Europe!! Being the most pig-headed Man U fan that I am, usually this would have pissed me off, but nothing beats the experience of watching them win with a stupid red jersey wearing, face painted Liverpool NUT!

Milan 1-Liv 0: Frown appears on red face....

Milan 2- Liv 0: Red paint dripping from face from a splendid display of waterworks...Starts drinking water to rehydrate....

Milan 3-Liv 0: Throws in the towel along with the water bottle at the TV. Sulks alone and doesn't respond to my sympathetic mutterings.

Half time: Responses limited to the occasional, 'I don't want to talk about it,' 'Life is not fair,' and 'Why god why??'

Milan3 – Liv 1: Grunts appreciation but frown remains on red (with anger) face.

Milan3-Liv2: Leaps up, starts chanting, 'C'mon boys, one more,' like an LSD laden monkey.

Milan 3-Liv3: Unable to express his joy verbally, starts pulling jersey so hard that it rips...Feels really cold bare-chested...Finds replacement jersey, one which is 2 yrs. old and 5 sizes too small.

ET: Our boy is bursting at the seams with joy at Scheva's miss, maybe it was because of the shirt...

PENALTIES: Scheva's misses last penalty, Gerard Lifts cup...We sleep 2 hours later thanks to, 'I took a kg of steroids in the morning that's the reason for my shirt' boy.

Man, one more year to CL...but what a way to end this one. I still can't believe they won against AC Milan from 3 down...Gives me a lot of hope though...Maybe anything IS possible.

Official quote: You've gotta have hope. Without hope life is meaningless. Without hope life is meaning less and less.

Enter Aishvarya. Mysore orientation.

As part of the orientation process, all the new recruits were sent to Infosys' plush HQ in Mysore. On the first day at the new office in Mysore, Raj stumbled upon Aishvarya.

"What are you doing here?"

"Don't worry, I'm not stalking you," Aishvarya replied.

"Ha Ha!" Raj mocked.

"I've also joined Infosys, of course."

"That's amazing! I didn't know there were others from our group who made it here. Why didn't you say anything?"

"My name was very much on the list, if you bothered looking."

"Ah, who's gonna go through a list of fifty odd people! I'm glad you are here though!"

"Why? What difference will it make?"

"Well, there's someone we know here, for starters."

"Please, Raj. You will make new friends before the day is out, and you will never talk to me again. Just as you did in our four years together at engineering, and even in school before that."

"Yeah, but this is Mysore! I came here once to meet Thomas and blew my brains out with boredom. There is nothing to do in this city. It's a good thing we have each other for company here."

"Ok sure, let's see how long this will last."

Raj and Aishvarya had lunch together in their new office, and then walked around, exploring the campus. The office building was huge, with long, winding corridors leading from one research lab to another. In one of the corridors, there were photos of the famous people who had visited the campus. They saw Presidents from Western countries, sports stars, and even Bollywood celebrities. While nearing the end of the corridor, Raj turned to Aishvarya and said, "You know whose photo will be last? Jesus!"

Aishvarya enjoyed her walk of the Infosys campus with Raj. It was the last she saw of him in Mysore. Raj's roommate, assigned to him at Infosys, had a contact at the army canteen from where you could get alcohol at dirt cheap rates. That was the endgame for Raj. The only way he could put up with the city of Mysore was by orienting himself with alcohol meant for the nation's frontline defense.

My perfect love is no longer perfect. She is flawless enough not to embrace my flaws. She is sane enough to classify insanity. Should I dream of what I can be with no regard to its actual probability? Should I tell you that the world is fair, that people are good and almost everything I see still holds wonder for me. Embracing I shall be. Empathy I shall learn? I shall no longer want to be myself. Me as a different person? Unrecognizable to self. Happier, loving and wanting.

She is for better or for worse, like everybody else.

I'm not what you want. I'm miserable, unhappy, utterly depressed and still have clever happy lines for almost everything. You fell in love with what I showed you. I'm sorry for that and only that.

I really cannot join in your eternal search for happiness.

I love the misery that I find sometimes. So, I will let you be, if only you let me wallow.

For I can never belong with you. For I can never be as them.

There I finally said the words you've been longing for!

For I'm no longer going to waste beautiful days in a city like this on people like you.

Official quote: City Life is millions of people being lonesome together - Henry David Thoreau

Enter Sarah

ICQ was voyeurism for the employees of IT companies before Facebook introduced it to the rest of the world. They didn't even try to cover up the app name when it literally read 'I seek you'. Everyone at Infosys used it to identify people they could chat with. This was where Raj met Sarah.

Sarah worked in the translation department, which was strangely over-indexed with beautiful girls, making them the department that everyone at Infosys wanted to be friends with.

Raj had noticed Sarah with her coterie of beautiful friends many times on campus. She was hard to miss since she was tall—a bit too tall—and had these freckles on her face and neck that gave her an enduring charm. But Raj made no effort to talk to her. He was lazy, shy, and dating Nitya, his girlfriend of four years.

His only interest at Infosys was in doing his work well so that a prospective client would eventually notice and offer him a role abroad. And then spend the rest of the time in Mysore by getting back home as quickly as possible for all the cheap alcohol that waited for him with his roommate. He was not interested in socializing or making any new friends at work. He was just plugged into his headphones listening to music and focused on his coding. In typical IT parlance, coding stood lower in the food chain, after Research and Design, and preceded only the Testing stage. RDCT it was called. The 'thinking' part of the work was done in the 'Research' and 'Design' stage. 'Coding' was all about writing the piece of code that the 'Design' stage developed, and 'Testing' was simply to test if the code functioned the way it was supposed to.

Raj's job, like most other employees of the Indian IT setup, was to code. They would be handed down notes from the 'Design' engineers who typically sat out of client offices in the US, and the IT workforce from companies like Infosys converted the notes to code, earning them the moniker of 'code monkey'. One day, having completed his coding tasks the previous day itself, which was often the case given how proficient he was at coding, Raj decided to capture in words how he saw a regular day at work.

7:45 am: Windfall arrives, Monkey very pleased, though not as pleased as most monkeys, due to copious usage of loss of pay leaves. After considerable (No Math monkey this one) calculations, monkey justifies windfall (i.e., the lack of) to the last rupee. Monkey's faith in the system restored. Monkey smiles!

8.20 am: Smile wiped off monkey's face. Boredom kicks in.

9.15 am: All quiet in the Serengeti, Monkey peers over the cubicle. Movement noticed, oddly familiar shape.... crap Big Boss Man! Monkey retracts probing head. Starts banging on keys furiously and hence blending effortlessly into the surroundings. Plan works, Big Boss Man passes by harmlessly. Monkey's faith and smile restored.

10 am: Propelled by unbearable boredom, Monkey becomes pro-active and searches for Big Boss Man, finds him at his cubicle playing chess on his computer. Engrossed in this classic match-up between Artificial intelligence and Natural dickhead, monkey waits. Big boss Man orders monkey to sit patiently till 1 or 2 PM. Gods willing, the availability of a 16yr old virgin and a couple of sheep, monkey might have some work then. Return to cubicle, caught up in the Serengeti scene, start scratching to kill time. People stare....

11.05 am: High-level meeting called impromptu. Monkey called personally. After wetting pants twice and cleaning up, hesitantly approach Big Boss Man and team. Project deadlines specified. Monkey has forty-two days for final submission. Monkey wets himself again.

12 Noon: Monkey getting hungry, needs food urgently to sustain the looking busy act. Big Boss Man seems to notice the strange sounds emanating from stomach, commands him to cease making funny noises. Monkey stops doing light saber sounds with telephone receiver in hand. Appalled at his obvious intolerance for the freedom of self-expression, Monkey defiantly troops out for lunch, with tribe in tow.

1.40 pm: No rest after lunch. Monkey called for meeting in 30 min with Big Boss Man and the two Wise men. Feels very lost and starts doubting his own measly understanding of the problem. To cope with the stress, starts to scratch again, but by mistake misses his head and finds Big Boss Man's. Asked to stop. Stops, after a careful search, finds own head. People stare again.

5.20 pm: Monkey back after 3hr session with Big Boss Man and two wise men. Monkey feels much better about state of work. Things were very well explained by Big Boss Man. Monkey participation limited to nodding and the occasional grunt. Wise men offer cough tablet after one intense session of grunting. Monkey accepts gratefully to keep mouth occupied.

6.19 pm: The sun is setting. The day is almost over. Successfully survived one more day in the jungle with the minimum possible effort. Monkey prepares for long bus ride back home, feeling of bliss envelopes monkey, quickly relives himself.

Raj found writing code to be boring and listening to music while coding helped him enormously. He had a huge collection of songs on his desktop, but somehow always found himself short of music when he coded. Streaming services like Spotify had not yet been invented.

Raj noticed that some of his colleagues who sat next to him shared his habit of listening to music while coding. Soon enough, they started sharing the music they owned with each other. This increased the collection on each person's individual desktop but slowed down the performance of the machine, what with all the storage space occupied by music.

This was when Raj stumbled upon the idea of Napster, long before Napster even became a thing. Raj wrote a piece of code that created a common shared folder, comprising of all the songs on each person's desktop. This way, Raj and the colleagues who wanted to listen to music had access to all the songs each of them owned, without having to copy the songs onto their own desktops.

Everyone loved the idea, and the group that initially comprised of only the colleagues who sat next to Raj expanded to everyone in the organization who liked listening to music while coding, including some folks from their client companies in the US.

Raj became an overnight sensation. The group named themselves STH, after Led Zeppelin's 'Stairway to Heaven' that everyone agreed was the best song of all time. They also decided it was best to remain covert. Most of the songs people owned were pirated to begin with and sharing it with each other only made it worse, ethically speaking. Listening to songs off each other's desktops also slowed down the overall network from conducting other important tasks, which the Infosys admin would not look upon kindly. Therefore, in order to ensure STH continued functioning, they had to be extremely cautious about who they let into the group. This was a shared responsibility within the STH group, and all of them played an active role in screening new entrants. Moreover, Raj was the only person with access to the source code, so any new entrant had to be manually entered into the database he created.

STH grew into something of an underground organization, with Raj presiding over it as some sort of Don. This was when his ICQ pinged with Sarah.

Sarah had heard about STH from some of her colleagues and she wanted in. Raj was a little hesitant at the start, because she was from translations and not coding, and therefore doubted if she shared the same frustrations as the rest of the STH members. However, he decided to give her a shot and was floored by her knowledge of music.

Not only could she quote all the big names in classic rock but was also the lead singer in her college rock band before joining Infosys. He agreed to add Sarah to the STH network, and the foundations of a new relationship were laid.

Sarah passed a lot of hints to Raj, but when he seemed to not be picking up on any of them, directly asked him out on a date. Raj was hesitant at first, but then thought why the heck not, since he was in Mysore while Nitya was all the way in Bangalore. What she didn't know about wouldn't harm her.

Sarah and Raj went to a pub known for its rock music and sat down for a drink. Before they had even finished the first drink, Sarah motioned for Raj to sit closer next to her. Raj appreciated her forthcoming nature up to the point of asking him out, but this seemed a bit overboard. However, Sarah kept it up until he eventually gave in. The moment he sat closer to her, Sarah moved forward and began kissing him. Shocked, Raj returned the kiss initially before pulling back.

"We're in a pub!" Raj exclaimed.

"Who cares! It's too dark and nobody will notice," Sarah said and continued to make out with him.

"Maybe we should leave," Raj said after pulling back again.

Sarah moved back, embarrassed by Raj's negative reaction.

"I'm sorry, you're right. Let's leave."

Raj felt terrible. He would have anyway never kissed her, let alone ask her out. And given she did all the hard work, all he did was deflate the mood.

"I'm sorry."

"No, you're right. Let's go."

As they walked back from the pub, they came across a tiny section of the forest, where Raj grabbed Sarah and kissed her. To his relief, given he thought he had offended her earlier, Sarah kissed back. It no longer mattered if there was anyone else around who might have seen them.

"I'd like to see you again later today," Raj messaged Sarah the next day on ICQ.

"Yeah, sure. Where do you want to go?"

"My place. My roommate is not home today."

"I see. I'll let you know by evening."

Raj was too excited to work all day and just waited for the clock to strike five.

"Shall we leave?" Raj messaged Sarah at five.

"I'll let you know."

Raj waited half an hour and messaged her again, only to receive the same reply.

This went on till seven.

"It's really late. Can we go now?" Raj messaged her again.

"I don't know yet."

"Fuck!"

"Yes, we will. But I need to finish something first."

That was enough for Raj. He could wait the entire night for Sarah if he had to. Thankfully, Sarah didn't take too long after that, and they left the office at half past seven for Raj's house.

The moment they entered the house, they started to make out. Soon, they were on Raj's bed without a stitch of clothing between the two of them.

Sarah pinned him down and straddled him. This was new to Raj. Nitya was always on the bed with Raj always on top. He didn't know a girl could also be on top, at least not the way Sarah did it, because what followed blew Raj's mind to bits.

Sarah sat on top of him with her feet planted firmly on the bed. Every time she lowered her body, she would bang into Raj's with a loud thud. Raj never knew sex could be pleasurable in so many more ways. Just as he was about to come, he held himself back and looked up at Sarah.

"Have you finished?"

"Many times, already," Sarah replied, out of breath.

This was all Raj wanted to hear before posturing himself for a big release.

The moment he was done, he removed the condom to throw it out. Sarah stopped him, took the condom and tied the end before throwing it out. Raj had never thought of this before; it was obviously the more hygienic way of disposing of it. Sarah was clearly good at this.

She slipped directly into her trousers, wrapping her damp underwear inside a polythene that she pulled out from her purse.

"I'm going commando," she said to a puzzled Raj.

Raj raised his eyebrows. Sarah was turning him on when he hadn't even recovered from his last orgasm.

Once she left, Raj retreated to his room, unsure of what to do for the rest of the evening. He had looked forward to being with Sarah the entire day, but after the sex, which was no doubt the best he had ever had, he felt a little disgusted with himself. Oddly, it had little to do with Nitya. He just felt queasy about having sex with someone he was certain would never commit to him.

The rest of the evening, Raj decided to be by himself. No Nitya, no Sarah, no roommate.

Later tonight, when no one gets to see my side,

Take me for a ride, help me make this slide.

Pull me up; pull me out from inside.

Take me by the hand and help me see,

All that I forgot. Show me your happiness. Spare me some glee.

Sad songs and sad thoughts; pull me out from inside.

Cigarettes, tea and my portrait of Dorian Gray,

Drag me away, sit me down and have your say.

Cause I'm already starting to change my mind.

Every time I got tongue-tied, I lied.

When I could speak, helped you to push me aside.

Now my knees are on the floor, finally alone with my sadness.

If you must know where I am,

I'm still searching through my sadness. Yes, I'm still here.

Finding loneliness... and everything I used to fear.

Moving back to Bangalore

As the first year of orientation at Mysore was coming to an end, Raj's relationship with his tutor, the Big Boss Man, could not have been worse...

Big Boss Man: Hello, how are the calculations going?

Me: They are going all right; I just don't know where…

Big Boss Man: I think we should have a meeting in the afternoon, so that we can tie up all the loose ends.

Me: Can I tie you up?

Big Boss Man: We also have to comply with the naming conventions for the delivery report.

Me: I have two or three name choices for it ……

Big Boss Man: You might have to work a bit longer the next week…

Me: Wha... (Translation: Wha…)

Big Boss Man: It is because your work is lagging behind.

Me: Excuse me (Translation: The fuck I care)

Big Boss Man: Might have to come on weekends.

Me: Excuse me, SIR (Translation: The fuck I care, dip shit)

Big Boss Man: Is this weekend comfortable for you?

Me: About as comfortable as you are with your transvestite tendencies.

Big Boss Man: So, see you Saturday.

Big Boss Man: Oh, btw you are coming for the project party, right?

Me: I so wish I could, I really have to go drinking tonight so that I can reduce my IQ to an such an amoebic level that I can understand tomorrow's meeting.

Big Boss Man: Oh, that's fine but make sure you send a mail notifying me about your non-involvement. Remember to keep the language professional, I have it to forward it to the Big Boss Man on top.

Me: God??

Big Boss Man: No, you dimwit, the delivery manager. Now where is that mail??

-----Original Message-----

From: under_paid_monkey_No17

To: Big Boss Man@hell_hole.com

Subject: United Monkeys protest to personal degradation

Respected Sir, (Translation: You stupid dip shit)

I am deeply disgusted about your proposed employee (sex) orientation project party. Even the expected participation for the proposed undertaking seems to lie on the incorrect side of the previously calculated figure, which was extremely agreeable to all the proponents of the aforementioned venture.

We propose sweeping revisions in the planning of the project to make it more accessible to all the parties. Non-compliance with this suggestion will surely lead to lack of participation in the venture.

ADDENDUM: On a more personal note, any further derogatory comments about an individual's inclinations, namely his/her lack of motivation and consumption of alcoholic beverages during office hours, will be met with a swift and equally scathing response. Many of these responses may involve a multitude of expletives. Considering your despotic institution's severe restrictions on the freedom of speech, these may never reach their destination, which might provoke us to deliver them personally at the risk of grievous physical impairment considering your previous history of violent behavior, which we attribute as a direct outcome of your simian cerebral development.

Thanking you

Under paid monkey no 17

Big Boss Man: Ok I just got your mail; the language is okay overall, but you should not thank me at the end.

Me: I really shouldn't sir, I really shouldn't...

Once, the orientation at Mysore concluded, the new recruits were offered positions in the company. There were broadly two functions that people were placed in: Platform teams and Customer teams.

Customer teams were the most vied for roles as the members of these teams got a chance to visit the Customers, who were typically based in the US. Without a doubt, Raj wanted to be in a Customer team. To his dismay, he was given a Platform role.

Raj was furious. He knew he was one of the best coders in his batch, and if anything, deserved the best Customer job there was. However, as it turned out, Raj's dislike for his tutor was a two-way street and his shenanigans both in and outside the company didn't go unnoticed.

There were days his breath reeked of alcohol in the mornings when he arrived in the office. He barely spoke to anyone at work, and if ever he did, it was to those employees who were also considered to be derelicts. There were a group of employees that appeared as misfits to the organization leadership because they only spoke amongst themselves and wore headphones that blared out loud music throughout the workday. They were least interested in aligning with the culture and values of the wider organization, and Raj was one of them. Needless to say, none of the senior management appreciated this.

To top it off, there were frequent complaints of suspicious network activity from his domain. The admin was never able to figure out the root cause, which was a source of embarrassment for them, but they were sure Raj was doing more than just code on his desktop.

Adding all of this up, Raj was given a PIP, or a Performance Improvement Plan. It was the worst thing to happen to an employee, next only to being fired. The management knew he was at least good at coding and therefore chose to give him another shot at a less critical job like Platforms. When it came to Customer teams, the stakes were a lot higher, and they didn't want a rebel like Raj jeopardizing corporate relationships with the Customers.

This didn't go down well with Raj. He knew he deserved better because the codes he wrote were always rated the highest on efficiency and he never missed a deadline. He was furious and calmed himself down in the only way he knew how: writing some more.

Big Boss Man: Master, I often worry about the completion of events, which although trivial in your eyes, have a very real bearing on my life.

Zen Master: My child, call me by my first name!

Big Boss Man: Ok, Zen.

Zen Master: Much better! Now, my child, the cosmic plan behind our existence is so vague that even an enlightened (i.e., lit up after a few shots) man like myself have trouble assimilating inner worries. We should spend more of our efforts ignoring them, than fruitlessly pondering over their exact nature.

Big Boss Man: Oi, my worries are not vague. They are very well defined. They are defined to the last minute. Look at this activity report!

Zen Master: Ah. You are so innocent, my child. What is time? Can one count the moments of happiness, like the unsaid joy of childhood, the first leaf of spring or the first snow of winter? My son, we are merely the watchers of time, it will roll unrelentingly irrespective of our actions.

Big Boss Man: Why do you keep calling me that?

Zen Master: Calling you what?

Big Boss Man: 'MY CHILD'! I AM forty-two FOR CRYING OUT LOUD!

Zen Master: Hush thyself, do not be so in anger. Maybe your worries stem from an unhappy relationship?

Big Boss Man: Could be Zen, my wife and I have been fighting a lot recently.

Zen Master: You should never do that, my child… eh… you know what they say: Men who go to bed with a problem wake up with the solution in hand.

Big Boss Man: What the hell is that supposed to mean?

Zen Master: All I'm saying is my son, sex is like playing bridge. If you don't have a good partner, you bloody well have a good hand.

Big Boss Man: That is so wise. But master, what do I do about delivery dates and this insane schedule which they have imposed on me.

Zen Master: Don't let work get to you. Consider the bigger picture of this wondrous universe that we are privileged to live in. Often, I just simply stare into space and ponder upon the meaning of my own existence, To the outward eye it may appear as if I'm merely uninterested in work but there is so much more to it.

Big Boss Man: Like what?

Zen Master: eh… you know… stuff.

Big Boss Man: Yeah…. Anyway, better get back to it, Master.

Oh, how fickle this life be, with a casual wave of his hand, the once revered master is reduced to a lowly underpaid monkey again. Ah, how the mighty have fallen….

Raj wanted the role in Customer teams so he could get an offshore opportunity to live abroad. With the role now in Platforms, the chances of that were slim.

He considered approaching some of the senior management to see if they would reverse their decision, but they simply echoed his tutors' sentiments, and decided it wasn't a battle worth fighting. Instead, he would start preparing for his MBA. He could try for an international placement through one of the b-schools, or at the very least, make more money at a job in India than what he was currently getting as a software engineer.

The human ego is a wonderful thing to behold. Some senior people at work questioned the wisdom of selecting someone as young and inexperienced as me for the same role that they had been selected for. How does one find the compromise between experience and potential, granted age does give you wisdom because you learn more from your mistakes? But isn't choosing someone based solely on his or her seniority separatist? Isn't reservation of any kind fundamentally separatist, be it what it may, jobs reserved for women, jobs reserved for the elderly. If you want equality, shouldn't you want it all the way? The corporate environ is so replete with hypocrisy that it is laughable; they tell you that one shouldn't judge other co-workers by their appearance, but they impose a dress code for 'professional' appearance. Basically, it's just a bunch of kids trying to be better than every other kid on the block, albeit in nicer formal wear! I'm kinda tired of this playground; I think I shall go play somewhere else….

As Chili Davis said, growing old is mandatory; growing up is optional.

2005 –The greatest hits

The first year of Raj's professional life was far from what he expected. He barely got any credit for his work, he didn't get the job he wanted, and he felt he wasn't even compensated properly. Just a true code monkey!

The worst part of it all was trying to tell his parents about quitting. Raj's mom frequently checked up on Raj's job at Infosys, and Raj knew this was his dad's doing as his mom barely knew the first thing about IT while his dad was the rocket scientist.

He knew his dad wanted him to succeed at IT. He had done so much in the past to ensure that. Buying him a PC way before it became mainstream in India, sparing no expense to support his move to Mysore for the orientation, he felt like his dad wanted him to follow his footsteps in some way. But instead, he now had to break it to him that he would be quitting IT altogether.

The only saving grace was that Raj knew he would only be conversing with his mom, and even that over telephone. So, he made the call, told his mom that he is quitting for 'higher studies,' which sounded much better, and hung up before she could probe any further.

He then decided to distract himself with some worldly news, in the hopes that they were possibly worse off than what he was going through, and then the theory of relativity would make him feel better.

1) Political move of the year:

January 20 - George W. Bush is inaugurated in Washington, D.C. for his second term as 43rd President of the United States.

Fool me once, shame on you,

Fool me twice?

2) Making money off misery:

April 2 - Pope John Paul II dies, causing widespread grief around the world.

April 19 - Joseph Ratzinger elected Pope Benedict XVI (love the name), causing intensely localized joy in a cubicle.

3) Some more useless information:

April 27 - The Super jumbo jet aircraft Airbus A380 made its first flight from Toulouse. This was very important for some strange reason...I forgot. (Forgot quite easily)

4) Priorities of a lost generation:

On May 17th Kuwaiti women were granted (ah that word should make me popular with the feminists) the right to vote but more importantly (!) on May 19th Star Wars Episode III: Revenge of the Sith was released. It shattered the opening day box-office record with $50,013,859...nobody gave a shit about the Kuwaiti women after that!

5) That's the way the footie crumbled:

a) In May, Arsenal won the F.A. Cup Final, beating Manchester United 5-4 on penalties. Trust me, watch that game and tell me life is still fair. The positive - Viera left. Good riddance to bad rubbish!

b) The Milanese Miracle - Liverpool won the UEFA Champions League by defeating AC Milan 3-2 in a penalty shootout in Istanbul. After being 3 down...against Milan. I swear I'm not making this up!

6) June 13 - Singer Michael Jackson acquitted of all charges of harming children. Of course, he was, of course he was.

July 16 - Harry Potter and the Half-Blood Prince, the sixth book of the Harry Potter saga by the British writer J. K. Rowling, is released. Jackson is seen at bookstores around the world.

7) December 8 - John Lennon died. I really don't consider myself a Lennon fan, I'm a Beatles fan through and through. Even that must be late Beatles (White album, Sgt Pepper onwards). It is impossible to be a Beatles fan without being a Lennon fan, without Lennon you have three guys with bad haircuts who can't play for cock's sake. What made the Beatles THE BEATLES was the lyrics, don't get this wrong - McCartney, Ringo and Harrison were awesome along with Lennon, but that really is true…along with Lennon. Ah, there were some good songs. Granted 'Imagine' must be THE most over-rated song ever but still there were lots of under-rated gems like 'Norwegian wood'. All said and done, the guy seemed to make sense and occasionally even put a smile on my face (Everybody has something to hide except me and my monkey!!).

So, Mr. Lennon, this day is for you. White album on repeat. Like he said - Time you enjoy wasting…

Hoping for another fun-filled 2006

Hush little baby don't you cry, because you know 'The future will be better tomorrow'…

Second Act.
2017

Depleting all forms of wealth

"Good morning, sir, I'm calling from ICICI Bank."

"Can you please stop calling me? I already have a credit card from ICICI Bank."

"We are not calling to offer you another credit card, sir, but to inform you that this is the last chance for you to pay the outstanding dues on your current card."

"How can there be any outstanding dues? My ICICI credit card is linked to my ICICI bank account for auto debit."

"Yes, sir, but your ICICI bank account does not have sufficient funds to meet your due credit card bill."

"What! There is some mistake… I will look into it."

"Thank you, sir. We have mailed you repeatedly about this and also tried calling on numerous occasions. Tomorrow is the last day to make the payment, otherwise we will have to raise a legal case."

Raj usually disconnected numbers he didn't recognize, but this call from ICICI was early in the morning when he groggily picked up half asleep. He was glad he did because the news sounded strange. He immediately logged into his bank's online portal and clicked on the credit card accounts to understand what was going on. His eyes widened when he saw there was indeed a two lakh rupees outstanding amount on his credit card, and his bank account only had a measly three-digit balance. No wonder they had tried calling so many times!

He did a little digging to understand what was going on. He had held an account with ICICI bank ever since he landed his first job. Therefore, he traced the account all the way back ten years. His inflow with his salaries increased every year, and they more than compensated for his outflow, up until two years ago. In the last two years, he seemed to have been spending far more than he earned, which had brought his balance to its current state.

What surprised him even more was that he hadn't received his last month's salary. He had quit the company he was working in, but they still owed him the salary for his final month in office. To sort this out, he decided to call the payroll department of the company.

"Yes, sir, you are right. We withheld your last salary because there is a sexual harassment case against you."

"Yes, there is, because I was the whistleblower."

"That's not the information we have in our records, sir. The internal investigation team has concluded the case with the only penalty against you being withholding your final month's pay. If you would like to appeal this, then you can go to court and make this one-month salary part of your claim there."

"Never mind, you can keep the money," said Raj, and hung up the phone. The effort he would have to put into getting a month's salary was not worth the long and painful wait the bureaucracy of the Indian legal system would surely put him through. Besides, all of his colleagues had warned him about this. He was going up against the founder of the company, and it was not a battle he could win easily. However, Raj couldn't turn a blind eye to the complaint made by a woman in his team against the founder. He had to shake the hornet's nest. It was the right thing to do. But the founder clearly used his equity to steer the matter against him. They probably bought off the woman as well. All that came out of it was Raj losing his job and his final months' pay, which unfortunately coincided with the exact same month that his credit card bill overshot his bank balance.

In a moment of desperation, Raj dialed a number he hadn't called in eleven years, since he left home for his first job at Infosys, Mysore.

"Hi Appa, how are you?"

"Oh, hi Raj. Wait, let me find your Amma."

"No Appa, I wanted to talk to you."

"Oh, is everything alright?"

"I need some money, actually."

"Of course, how much do you need?"

"Two lakhs."

"Yes, sure, Raj. I'll send it over today."

"Ok," said Raj and hung up before his dad could say anything else. He didn't want to have a conversation with his dad, let alone explain why he needed the money.

Being a rocket scientist with the Indian government, his dad was one of the few people who could use the phrase 'It's not rocket science,' legitimately. When Raj was in school, he loved gloating to his friends about the fact that his father worked on rockets. He didn't know much about his dad. They barely spoke. But his dad had never denied him anything. He got him one of the best cycles among his peers, and later a PC with more advanced specifications than his school computer lab had. There were times his friends mocked Raj saying his dad was not just a rocket scientist, but probably owned a bunch of oil wells given the number of gifts he showered Raj with.

However, as he grew up, the weight of his dad's professional success bore down on him. Raj's dad frequently enquired about Raj's progress at Infosys through his mom. But Raj couldn't tell them that he wasn't successful there. Worse, he couldn't even understand why he was unsuccessful or what he was unhappy with at work, let alone explain it to them. So, he started to avoid their calls. He would just have short conversations over long breaks to quickly let his mom know that he had eaten properly, lest she get uncontrollably upset, but completely avoid any other topic of discussion.

After a point, Raj's dad stopped trying to reach out to him, wondering if it was something he was doing that was upsetting Raj. He also tried satisfying himself with the knowledge that at least Raj was healthy.

Raj's phone beeped. His account had just been credited with five lakhs by his dad. This infuriated Raj. He had only asked for two. What was generous to Raj's dad seemed condescending to Raj. He thought about what he should do with the extra money for a minute and then went to work on it.

First, he paid off his credit card balance. Then, he bought the latest iPads for Sachin, China and Sushmita. He sent them each a message saying, "Realized I've never given you a gift before, and I'm making so much money these days that I don't know what to do with it, so here is a little something for you."

Sachin and China believed Raj's story. Throughout school, Raj was always in possession of extravagant things. And lately at work, they assumed Raj was changing so many jobs as he was being offered better opportunities and thereby making more and more money. Little did they realize that Raj was either quitting or being fired from these companies. Sushmita was the only friend that smelled something fishy when the iPad arrived in her mail.

Raj, for his part had reached a stage with no job, no money, and potentially using up the last chance he had of asking his dad for help.

Younger,

I remember listening to other kids,

What their parents got them, what their parents did,

I remember wishing I had those parents...

Wealthy and cool,

I expected expensive birthday gifts,

Instead of that stupid card when I was 12...

"From Amma and Appa,

We love you very much.

Nobody is more important.

Remember that."

Truthfully,

At that moment, I hated that card,

No... I hated them for that card!

I wanted a robot!

Still,

I have that card in my hand now,

For some stupid reason?

Throughout my youth,

I remember being angry at them,

For not letting me go to a concert,

and a million other things,

That I actually don't remember now...

I got over it.

Throughout my young adulthood,

I forgot them.

Easily...

My life was glorious,

Different states, countries, people,

I, Young?

They were still boring to me.

But I was not angry anymore,

I was... indifferent to them,

For they were merely specks in the gloriously new canvas of my life.

Now, maybe too late,

I realize how spoilt I was,

That cocky confidence was always backed,

By their illogical (!) yet unconditional love,

For sans reason,

They decided to always,

Love the asshole I was to them...

Now they are weak.

Every week....

Another hospital...

I don't even think about my leaves,

The doctors and their expensive bills.

All of that is specks now...my canvas is only,

Only, this soul crushing hurt...

Fuck.

Mortality is a funny thing?

Nothing ages you more...

Than seeing the smartest, strongest man you ever knew,

And the most beautiful, caring woman you ever knew,

Looking at your stupid eyes for strength...

Don't cry idiot eyes... please...

Project... pretend strength... please...

REM:

"Amma and Appa,

I just wanted to say,

I always loved you very much.

Nobody is more important.

Remember that!"

Chapter 10

Locked up indoors.

First Act.
2006

Moving back to Bangalore

Raj completed his orientation, accepted the Platforms role offered to him and moved back to Bangalore. He promptly forwarded his resignation letter to the admin and started counting down the days to freedom.

30 days to go.

So tired and bored nowadays at work. Have no drive whatsoever, I gave my formal notice last week, should be out of here by August. Planning to sit and study for a couple of important exams. Been working purely out of courtesy, and some people have been cool to me with the whole STH thing, so don't want to leave on bad terms. This has been the plan for the last year, approximately thirty odd days to go. Simple plans for the next month or so: stay sober, study, attend classes and, most importantly, get focused, the one thing which has been sorely lacking for the past one year. God, just existing can be so tiring. Don't want to spend weeks on end solely waiting for the weekend. Getting up early, wearing a tie, work aimlessly, get by…. It's alright but surely there is more in store for me, surely. At least I'm really going to find out if there is. Ahh… que sera sera, I guess.

10 days to go.

Friends, Romans and countrymen, whatever you do, do NOT lend me your ears. For I know not what I say, not a word they heard could they relate? If only the story was quite clear. Gentle elders of the venerable race talk of days to come when all will be revealed. A new day will dawn, but will you be standing that long? I really don't have anything else left, all I hope for is a pleasant recollection once in a while… oh, one more thing: Hope you enjoyed the ride!

Also, ten working days to go. Messa the office. Messa very happies! Jar Jar leaves the doors ajar one last time. The name is Binks, don't wear it out!

Nice, pleasant evening yesterday. Had gone out with my colleagues. Real good time, good food, lots of drinks and some pretty good company. Somebody else also paid for the entire thing! Good times, ah, just when I had made up mind… they give me small second thoughts. Still the idle Wednesday or Thursday afternoon fills me up with such a sense of wastefulness, it is stifling. In desperate need of wide-open spaces.

AH! Nine more.

Five to One baby!

Aw crap, been too busy to maintain the countdown. Well eight, seven and six have flown by unnoticed. Been SO busy lately. Finally finished most of it. Yup, my dawn is beckoning!

These five fingers will soon make a fist,

All that's missing are some signatures on a list :-)

So.... So, you think you can tell,

Heaven from hell, and did you exchange a walk on part in the world for a lead role in a cage? How I wish, how I wish I was there.

We're just two lost souls swimming in a fishbowl, year after year,

Running over the same old ground. What have you found? The same old fears???

Maybe, will tell you in four more days!

4 days to go.

All in all, it's just another day now. You're falling down. What you gonna do. Standing on top of the world tonight. No one's looking back at you. Stand tall. It's going on. It's going on. It's gonna be just fine. You're holding on. Holding on today....

And Monday and Tuesday. Then I shall be hanging by a moment there with you! And then there were three.

3 days to go.

Three guys+Two men called Jack and Johnnie+8 hours later. Hampi! Man, what an insane trip. Schnappi, Lady looking for the animals, borrowed not returned 'bell-bottom' jeans, One green lassi. Peace and then throw it all away. Ah, something so beautiful about living in the moment.

Life is kinda like this trip. Anything, absolutely anything is possible right here, right now. Sometimes all you must be is a bit braver, other times you just have to be a bit stupid. To do all the right things!

Ah, two more days. Here's to spectacularly stupid times.

Cheers!

2 days to go.

To the lepers in your head, how perfect is this? Today I finish exactly one year of working here and tomorrow, I finish! He haaaa!

We are riding nowhere,

Spending someone else's hard-earned pay?

You and me, Sunday driving,

Not arriving, on our way back home.

We are on our way back home....

One last breath?

Oh, in case I don't see ya, good afternoon, good evening and good night!

D-Day has come. Today I celebrate my Independence Day!

Let there be My life!

The first, and only engagement ring

Raj was finally free from his soul sucking job but didn't feel completely free. The reason was clear: Nitya.

Raj and Nitya had been together for five years and had many ups and downs during that time. But the past one year was particularly strenuous. Their expectations from each other seemed to have forked somewhere down the line.

Raj was frequently distracted with Sarah, was still trying to figure out his career, and was far from making any serious commitments with anyone at the moment. Nitya on the other hand, wanted Raj to take things to the next level. Her parents had started to discuss marriage with her and wanted to introduce her to some prospects they had in mind.

Nitya's arguments that she was just 23 were in vain as her parents were of the opinion that it takes a few years to find someone suitable before deciding to marry, and therefore an early start helps. Because of this, Nitya desperately wanted to introduce Raj to her parents. And a simple boyfriend wouldn't do. Raj would need to be much more. But the thought of anything beyond a simple relationship made Raj very uncomfortable. There were days he thought they were just perfect for each other. Not just finishing each other's sentences, they would sometimes even start each other's sentence the moment they answered the phone. It was as if they knew what the other was going to say, even before they would start to say it. The connection ran deep. But then there were other times when Raj questioned if this was all there was to life. Was Nitya really the companion he would spend the rest of his life with?

The past year was spent with this engagement monkey on their backs. Nitya would keep bringing up the topic and forcing Raj to meet her parents. Raj wouldn't do it and would go as far as breaking up with Nitya when the topic came up. However, every time this happened, they would end up having great sex, and simply trudge along. For all the problems in their relationship, sex was not one of them. Their physical compatibility was as perfect as it could be.

Soon, Raj began considering the possibility that Nitya might be the one. Sarah was great while it lasted in Mysore, but he always knew she would be nothing more than a fling. Nitya, on the other hand, was a smart, beautiful girl, the perfect 'take home package' as some called it. He began telling himself that this is just his noisy brain complicating things for him by concocting scenarios about life that maybe reality just wouldn't match up to. He started to convince himself that he probably would never do better than Nitya.

Armed with that thought, and against his better judgement, he went out and bought an engagement ring. He asked Nitya out for a walk, and they went to the same street, at the back of Nitya's house, where they had spent so many of the initial days of their relationship.

Finally, at one point, he stopped and looked at her.

"I have to tell you something."

"I have to tell you something before that."

"Mine is very important."

"I think mine might be even more important."

Raj had one of those moments when he could figure out Nitya's next sentence before she said it. He hoped he was wrong, and said, "Ok fine, you go first."

"I want to break up with you."

"What!"

Raj clutched the ring inside his pocket, squeezing it hard. He couldn't believe he was hearing this.

"There is more to this, isn't there?"

"That's not important."

"Of course, it is. Who is it?"

"It's not important. You don't even know him."

"So, there is someone. Is it someone at work?"

"Yes, but that is not the reason I am breaking up with you."

"Then, what is it?"

"You know what it is. You've been trying to break up with me for a year now."

"Yes, but we didn't break up, did we?"

"That's beside the point. We cannot manage a long-distance relationship again. You are soon going for your MBA, and though IIM-Bangalore is your dream campus, it's just that one college here, and there is a good chance you may end up outside Bangalore. You really think we can go through another round of long-distance?"

"But there could be another solution than this!"

"What other solution, Raj?"

Raj took out the ring from his pocket. There was a deep, red mark etched inside his palm from clutching the ring too hard.

"We could get married," he said, showing the ring to Nitya.

Nitya's eyes welled up and she looked away.

"I've pictured this moment a thousand times…."

"And?"

"Never once did I think I would say this… no."

"Really? Five years of togetherness and you are leaving me for some guy you met at your office?"

"Please be a little more mature than that. I don't feel the same way I did a year ago. I've been waiting a long time for this moment, but all you wanted to do was break up. It's sweet you bought this ring, but I don't think you mean it. And I cannot keep living this way. I'm sorry, I have to go."

Nitya sped off, wiping the tears flowing down her cheeks.

Raj stood stunned. He watched Nitya's back till she disappeared from the street. Then he looked at the ring in his hand. He had spent a full one-month salary on it, as was customary, and was left wondering what he was to do with it now. The ring went back into his pocket, never to come out of it again.

My very own inner glow on emboss mode,

Kick starting the famed spiel dispenser,

Image manipulation in overload,

Watching someone else in bed with her.

Get her into penetration,

The birth of my salvation.

Go write your wisdom on the whiteboard,

Position her, pin her and watch her squirm.

Go wear your wisdom on your chest.

Smother her scream, a touch gentle… a touch firm.

How long will I let it slide?

The end of time is sticking to my rut,

Shredding my soul, a cancerous child?

A fun filled free spirit of my being a slut.

Refund the dreams that I stole,

The one about breaking out of jail with Jeburk.

I finally saw somebody running free,

Too fucking bad it was on TV!

All the while smelting into the eternal swelter….

In this perfect weather,

Anything will bother me… (this low is gonna be a belter!)

Especially the crazy gods with an undying love for engineering!

Thus, he spoke of a betrayal which broke his heart,

Careful not to let it feel real, careful not to let it hurt,

He lived his life till the very end wrapped in a big fucking lie,

The comfortable, unfeeling lie that he willfully chose!

The final straw that broke this camel's back.

I finally did it today. I removed her number from my phone. Finally, was strong enough to leave behind the only person who ever made sense to me. I really did think that we were going to be, forever. Through our different lives, thought we still had smiles to share. I really don't blame you, how could I? Blame you for living your life the only way you know how! You made my life joyous, gave me my dream, my precious moments of bliss. No more shall I want your shoulder to cry on. My miserable day finally achieved its highpoint.

So, sleep well, sweet dreams and hopefully happy memories.

In the race for the future, I finally, wholeheartedly, want to win.

Desperately.

So here I am,

Shedding my bags and more importantly, my only true friend.

Living and learning, I guess!

Enter Parvathy.

"Hey Sarah, long time! How's it going?"

"Hey Raj, that's a pleasant surprise! Didn't think I would hear from you again since you left Mysore."

"Well, that's exactly why I'm calling. I was planning to make a trip to Mysore, and was wondering if we can meet?"

"I'm not in Mysore right now. I'm in Delhi, on the way to Leh."

"That's amazing! When do you get back?"

"I hope, never. I've quit Infosys and I'm traveling to Leh as part of a charitable course to teach languages to school-going students there."

"That's nice of you. But you don't intend to stay in Leh indefinitely, do you?"

"Nothing is indefinite. But I don't know when I will return from Leh. Right now, I am in Delhi, and I leave for Leh in two days."

"Ok, tell you what. I'll come over to Delhi and see you once before you leave."

"That would be a very long journey for you."

"I'm sure I could find some train to hop on today and see you tomorrow. That would give us at least a day together before you leave."

"If you do make it here tomorrow, then we have a plan!"

"Excellent! I'll keep you posted."

Raj went online and searched for trains. He found a seat on one that was leaving in a few hours. He booked it instantly and got packing. He made it to the station well in time, bought some alcohol to keep him company, promptly gulped it all down the moment the train started, and went off to sleep.

His alarm went off at seven the next morning, half an hour before he was to reach Delhi. He woke up and looked out the window to figure out where he was. He saw the train approaching a station called Panvel. He asked his fellow passengers how far that was to Delhi, and they said they had no clue, since they were only traveling as far as Mumbai.

That didn't make sense. Mumbai should have passed a long time ago. Raj asked a few more people and then it occurred to him that the train was not scheduled to reach Delhi at seven on this day, but on the next day. It was a super slow train, and that was exactly the reason he had managed to find a last-minute seat on it.

There was no point in reaching Delhi a day late, since Sarah would be long gone by then. One option was to disembark at Mumbai and then look for a flight to Delhi. But he had never flown in an airplane before and had heard it was prohibitively expensive. Raj wanted to meet Sarah, but the thought of potentially using up all his savings from Infosys on his maiden flight, didn't seem worth it.

He made peace with the fact that Sarah wasn't going to happen and was probably out of his life for good.

Now, I have broken it all,

Too many a harsh word.

Too many a truth?

Much too often?

Too many a drink?

Yes. That I shall give you, too many a drink.

But sometimes the only way I could survive,

Is to blur my senses…To what we were becoming.

Someday you might find truth in a storm.

See through eyes that never find your calm,

Never in the center but look at the edge.

Then you shall find me.

You will finally know that only a strong wind pulls you astray,

And why it was oh-so-easy to throw it all away.

So, what am I trying to say, I heard you say that too, too often,

OK I'm trying to say this…

Life is a like a dick.

It's not many a wondrous thing,

(Ask almost any guy you know)

But it really is all you have.

(Again, ask any guy you know)

Actually…what I'm really trying to say,

Is sorry sweetheart,

It's just too long till the we way we die,

So, I willfully chose, for today, to say goodbye.

Raj got off the train at Mumbai and plotted his next step. He could find the next train back home to Bangalore, or he could try meeting some friends he knew in Mumbai instead. He picked the latter and set about making calls.

One of them was Parvathy, a girl from his team back at Infosys. She was a Rajput girl who moved to Mumbai after her orientation in Mysore.

Parvathy had a pleasant demeanor, dimpled smile and was friends with everyone at Infosys. People often said she never slept, because if you messaged her on ICQ at any point in the day, pat came her reply. It didn't matter if it was two in the afternoon or two in the morning.

Raj always had a nice time chatting with her on ICQ but could never manage to hold a real conversation with her. It wasn't that she wasn't intelligent. On the contrary, Raj found her to be one of the smartest people at Infosys. It was just that she thought and spoke in Hindi, a language Raj could never get his head around. He barely scraped through the Hindi board exam in his 10th grade, and it seemed to be one of those unfortunate aspects of growing up in Bangalore. You knew about five languages, but none of them were Hindi.

Parvathy, like everyone else, spoke English at the office. But her way of speaking was very different from Raj's. It had to do with the way she articulated sentences in her head. She thought first in Hindi and then translated it to English. Raj could recognize that subtle difference in English speaking, between the people from South India, and the Hindi native speakers from pretty much the rest of country.

Raj wished he knew Hindi better just so he could hold a better conversation with her. But their time at Infosys was spent largely over ICQ, and texting made conversations easier.

"Hey Parvathy, how's it going?"

"Hey Raj, so nice to hear from you. How are you?"

"I'm in your city actually."

"You're in Mumbai?"

"Yeah, in about 15 minutes, I should be there."

"Really? How come?"

"That's a long story. If you have some time today, I could tell you all about it."

"Yea, sure, we can meet today. But you are reaching Mumbai right now? Do you need a place to freshen up?"

"That would be great. I've spent twenty hours in this train and would love a wash."

"Come over to my place then."

"You sure? I don't want to impose. I could find some place near the station itself and meet you peacefully at a café later."

"Not at all. I live all by myself, and you know I barely sleep. So, I'm up already and the house is ready for you."

"That's so nice of you. Cool, give me your address, and I will see you soon."

Raj reached Parvathy's house, which was on the top floor of a building with a separate entrance. He could literally go in and out without anyone noticing. Parvathi gave Raj a tight hug the moment she opened the door. Waiting inside was a full breakfast spread with poha and tea that Parvathi had whipped up in the time it took Raj to reach her place from the station.

"I know you like tea. So, I made some for you along with breakfast. You could use the bathroom there first if you'd like," she said, pointing to a door.

After a wash and breakfast, Raj and Parvathy sat on the bed, sipping tea. He told her all about his train fiasco, carefully leaving out the portions that involved Sarah and making up something else in its place.

Once they were eating, Raj made an excuse to show something on his phone so that he could get closer to Parvathy. Parvathy was very interested in everything Raj was sharing and moved closer, her eyes shining with genuine interest.

If the skin on the arms could speak, Raj felt like Parvathy was asking him to hold her closer. Raj wondered if he could take this to the next level. He had read in a book that the best time to kiss a girl was mid-sentence, when she's talking. That is exactly what he did. At one point, when Parvathi was talking about something, Raj cut her off with a kiss.

Parvathi's mouth was soft, just like everything else about her. Raj was used to a lot more vigor with Nitya and Sarah. He moved over to her neck and continued a combination of kissing and biting. Then he noticed the skin on her neck turn into a strange shade of blue, and immediately stopped.

"Oh my god, I think I hurt you!"

"Did you? I don't feel anything."

"Please have a look. Your neck is shining like Lord Shiva."

Parvathi looked at herself in the mirror and turned back to Raj in shock.

"What have you done?"

"I'm so sorry, I was just giving you a hickey, I swear."

"I'm just pulling your leg. It's fine."

"You mean this is normal?"

"I don't know. This has never happened to me before. But I'm sure it's normal."

"Ok wait, it's changing color. It's turned purple now."

Parvathi looked at herself once more in the mirror, and turned back to face Raj, this time with a twinkle in her eye.

"This is interesting. But listen, I don't feel any pain. Quite the opposite, in fact, so, don't stop?"

They continued to make out, but Raj held back this time. Parvathi was clearly unlike the other girls he had been with. She was far too gentle and tender. Once he paced himself back to kiss her softly, he realized it was so much better.

At one point, Raj slipped a hand into his pocket and searched for the condom he bought for Sarah. He contemplated using it with Parvathi but stopped himself. It just didn't seem right. Besides, he was already having the best make-out session ever, so he decided to keep at it.

A friendship resurrection

Raj returned to Bangalore feeling like he had just been on a trip to heaven and back. He was satiated and ready to enter the next phase of his life: MBA.

He got himself enrolled at a CAT coaching center. On the first day of class, he ran into a familiar face, Sachin.

Raj hadn't met Sachin since the end of Sachin and Nitya's relationship. It was serendipity that he was meeting Sachin after just having broken up with Nitya himself.

Raj and Sachin got along like a house on fire, unaware that in a few years, Raj would set the real house they lived in together on fire.

For the time being, the last five years since Nitya broke up with Sachin seemed to have all but disappeared. Raj and Sachin were friends once again, just the way they were back in school. One day, during a break, Raj and Sachin went to a shop downstairs for a smoke, and as they were chatting, a motorist stopped by them.

"Do you know this address?" he asked, showing them a note with an address scribbled on it.

After a quick glance at the note, Raj nodded.

"You go straight, take the first left and then another left, and you should be there."

"That's great. Thanks so much," said the motorist and sped off.

"Where is the place he was going to?" Sachin asked.

"Who knows! I just told him the same thing I tell anyone when they ask me for directions. Straight, left, left."

"You didn't know the address then?"

"Nope. I just wanted to get rid of him."

"That's super cool. You could have fooled me."

"It's all about confidence, and the secret to being confident, is to act confident."

They met up at Jags later that evening to catch up on the last five years. Raj filled Sachin in on all the details about Nitya, Sarah and Parvathi and Sachin told Raj about Juhi.

"Juhi! She prank-called me once in school. And then we shared a moment when we met in Pune. But the day it all really began was when she joined my office. Just like they say in the movie Casablanca, of all the gin joints in all the world, she walked into mine. Only, instead of gin joints, there were interview cabins in our case. I was part of a speed interview process, interviewing dozens of candidates, and she walked into mine, wearing beige formal trousers and a white formal shirt with the sleeves rolled up. Don't think I have ever seen a girl wear a shirt with rolled up sleeves before. She was the portrait of a girl on a mission to dominate the corporate world, hair tied back and everything. She joined my team after I recruited her and sat right behind me in office. And every time she answered her phone and said 'hello', I would turn back, thinking she was talking to me. And every time that happened, we exchanged a smile that would just make my knees go weak. Everything about her is perfect. Our wavelengths are at the same frequency. You know how they say that there is just one for every person right? She's it for me. She's my one."

"You left out the most important part? Does Dev know any of this?" Raj asked.

"No. He's got these strange scruples about dating any of his sister's friends, so I'm sure he'll have similar or higher expectations from Juhi. So, we've decided to tell him when the time is right. For now, don't breathe a word of this to Dev," Sachin warned.

Raj and Sachin spent the next few months preparing for CAT. After sitting for the exam, along with a few other b-school entrance exams, they had nothing else to do but wait, and decided to call the entire Bus Stop crew for a party together at Jags.

It turned into a night they would remember forever.

In barely an hour into the party, everyone was pitch drunk. There was raucous banter, noisy high fives, and moments of laughter when tears needed to be wiped off cheeks.

When it was time to leave, Raj playfully yanked Sachin's monkey cap, which was all he wore in place of a helmet that wasn't mandated by law and unfortunately 'uncool' for boys their age to wear. Raj knew Sachin could never part with it and sat behind Gajan on the bike and asked him to speed off. Sachin started up his own bike and raced after them, with Dev seated behind him.

They had to cross a small stretch of a highway which at that time of the night was usually overrun by speeding trucks. One such truck drove in front of Sachin as he was riding, and Sachin hit the brakes to slow down. But the brakes didn't work.

Sachin tried again.

Still no luck.

The bike was fast approaching the back of the truck.

Sachin could almost see the big rear wheels that he was uncontrollably racing towards.

He jammed the gears down to slow down the bike.

The bike jerked and slowed down, but it wasn't enough.

Sachin swerved right to avoid a collision with the truck, and then froze up when he saw what lay ahead.

Right in front of him was a yellow barricade that had been set up at night to slow down speeding vehicles.

Sachin glanced at the truck on the left, and the barricade dead ahead of him.

Both were approaching fast. He had to choose one.

He chose the barricade.

BAM!

The bike rammed into the barricade and Sachin and Dev went flying off the bike.

They gathered themselves and were dusting their clothes when Dev looked at Sachin and let out a horrified gasp.

"Dude! Your nose!"

Sachin gingerly felt his nose with a light finger. There was a gash – so deep that his finger could fit in it.

China passed them on his bike. He started to laugh at them for falling off and continued to ride.

Dev immediately dialed China's phone.

"You need to come back. It's serious. Sachin's hurt."

Dev called Gajan as well and told him to come to Sathya hospital, since they planned to take Sachin there.

Sachin sat behind China on his bike, holding his bleeding nose with his handkerchief, while Dev kicked Sachin's bike into shape, enough for him to ride to the hospital. They rushed straight into the emergency ward when they got there.

Sachin was thankfully able to move on his own, with his legs shaking more out of fright than injury.

The doctor inspected his nose and then looked at Dev and China who were standing behind their friend.

"He's lost a chunk of his nose. If you can find it, I can stitch it back."

Dev and China decided to go back to the highway to look for the rest of Sachin's nose.

Meanwhile, the doctor started to stitch a part of Sachin's forehead, which sported a cut as well.

The doctor ran the needle through the skin, and Sachin could see the needle and the black thread that followed, right in front of his eyes.

"Do you feel anything?" the doctor asked him.

"No."

"That's probably the only good thing that's come out of all the alcohol you've had tonight. I don't need to anesthetize you," said the doctor and drove the needle through Sachin's forehead once more.

Right then Sachin's phone started ringing. When he looked at it, he saw it was from Gajan's house, probably his parents calling to know their son's whereabouts. Sachin picked up the call.

"Yes, uncle, Gajan is here," Sachin told an exasperated Gajan's dad.

"Gajan said he was going to meet you, but he was supposed to be home an hour back. Is he ok?"

"Yes, uncle. He's fine. He should be home anytime now."

It wasn't Sachin's first time lying to a friend's parents about their child's whereabouts. He had got plenty of practice in that department, given the company he kept.

Just as Sachin cut the call, Gajan and Raj walked in, worry written on their faces.

"Call your dad," Sachin told Gajan, handing him his phone.

Raj looked at Sachin and was just about to say something when they heard the nurse shouting.

"You cannot throw up here," she warned Gajan, who had started throwing up in the hospital garden.

"I can't handle the sight of blood," he explained to the nurse.

Raj and Sachin broke into a smile when they heard that. Gajan's dad was a veterinarian doctor, and he had seen his fair share of blood in his life. He was just throwing up because he was high.

"Here's your cap," Raj said sheepishly and handed Sachin's cap back to him.

"You're such an ass, man."

"I know. But I do have some news that will cheer you up."

"What is it?"

"Our results are out, and we're going to be classmates in Mumbai.

"Really?"

"Yup, both of us made it through."

"Wow, we're going to leave Bangalore."

"Yes! You're getting a new nose, and we're getting a new life."

Sachin never got a new nose. He didn't even have his old nose sewn back as Dev and China never found it. All Sachin got was a skin graft surgery with a portion of his ear slapped on his nose, leaving a permanently visible reminder to never drunk ride again.

"The world is our oyster, baby!" Raj continued.

"We are never going to be locked up in Bangalore again."

Second Act.
2018

Locked up in Bangalore.

"Rajaaaa…," boomed a voice from the kitchen, through the living room, up the stairs, through a second living room, all the way up to Raj's bedroom.

Raj woke up with a start. It was a voice he could recognize anytime, anywhere. For a moment, he felt like he was a little boy again, listening to his mother's voice echo through the house he had called home for 22 years.

Raj moved back into his parent's house in Bangalore for the first time since he had left home thirteen years ago, when he moved to Mysore as part of his Infosys orientation. In the past thirteen years, he had lived in Mysore, Kolkata, Chennai, Dubai and Mumbai. Though he had returned to Bangalore quite a while back, he always stayed in a rented house, either close to his office or as far from his parents as he could.

But with no job and salary to pay the rent, he moved back in with his parents.

"Raj, you have a friend here to see you," said Raj's mom as he traipsed down the stairs.

"Sushmita!" exclaimed Raj in surprise, when he saw a face he had nearly forgotten.

"Hi Raj, how are you?"

"I'm always great! Come on in!"

Raj invited Sushmita in and they sat down on the sofa to chat as Raj's mom went back to the kitchen.

"How are you, Raj, really?"

"What's with the concern? I'm perfectly fine."

"Why are you living here?" said Sushmita, careful to not let Raj's mom hear that.

"This is my house."

"This is your parents' house, Raj."

"How quaintly western! Who said I cannot live with my parents?"

"You did! Like… every chance you had back in school. All you wanted to do was leave home and travel the world."

"Well, I've had enough of travel. I'm taking a break now."

"You've been on a break for six months now."

"Now, how do you know that!"

"Don't you remember me at all? I just know. I know you have quit six different jobs in the last thirteen years. I know you fought with Thomas. I know you've been drinking too much. The entire time I thought it's just you being the hot-headed Raj you always were. But when I heard you've been living with your parents for the last six months, I knew something wasn't right, and I had to come and see you."

"You know, you reach a certain stage in life when you just want to settle down. I've been working hard, I've made a lot of money, but somehow, I don't know, I just wasn't satisfied with any of it. So, I decided to move back in with my parents and recalibrate my life ahead."

"Ok, that sounds fair. What have you decided to do then?"

"I'm thinking of adopting a kid."

"WHAT!"

"Yeah, Gajan had a baby girl recently and he cannot stop talking about her. In all my conversations with him, I figured that is the only thing that will give my life some meaning. So, I figured, why the hell not?"

"Raj, when people want to settle down, they first find someone nice to get married to."

"I've tried that Sushmita, somehow girls just don't want to be with me."

"You know why that is?"

"Of course! Them be bitches!"

"Stop kidding, Raj. Every relationship needs a bit of compromise, and it is high time you had a taste of that as well."

"Yeah, you can't live with them, can't live without them."

"Are you seeing anyone now?"

"Nope, not interested."

"Hasn't it been too long? Don't you at least miss sex?"

"Ok, you've not heard of Pornhub?"

"Raj, that doesn't even come close to the real thing. You need to be with a real person, and you need to figure out a way to let go of that ego and compromise at least a bit to keep a relationship alive."

"It's just too much effort. I think adopting a kid will be better. And easier."

"You think a kid is going to be easier than a wife? Has Gajan even told you about the effort that goes into having those few moments of joy with his daughter? Besides, there's a stringent vetting process, followed by a three-year waiting period, before you can adopt a child in India. It's certainly not going to be as easy as you think."

"Now how do you know that?"

"Really?"

"Whatever, the one thing I am sure of is that I'm never getting married. Maybe I'll meet another girl to spend some more meaningless time with. But eventually the only true happiness may be with a kid."

"If that is really what you want, can you at least start with a pet? Figure out for yourself if you really have what it takes to be responsible for another life. Start with that! Get a dog, or a cat."

"Haha, a pet! Never thought of that!"

"Figure this out, Raj. Please give me a call if you want to talk sometime. But you need to figure out what you want in life. You cannot be a thirty-five-year-old mooching off his parents!"

With that, Sushmita left Raj's house. Just as she was leaving, she heard a noise from their neighbor's house.

"Pssst…. Come here, ma," said an elderly woman's voice from the house next door to Raj's.

"Hello. Yes, aunty, what is it?"

"Ma, is that boy Raj ok?"

"Yes, he's fine," said Sushmita dismissively as she did not want to encourage neighborhood gossip.

"That's what his mother also tells us. But he is not fine, ma. He has not stepped out of that door in six months. We only see food and alcohol and sometimes even just ice cubes being delivered to the house. Something is wrong with that boy, ma."

"He's fine, aunty. He's just taking a break from work and wants to be with his parents. He is perfectly fine."

Sushmita knew she was lying to herself. After her strange conversation with the neighbor, she was even more worried for Raj. It's one thing to be staying home for six months. It's completely another to be locked up indoors.

Disillusionment is one of the worst things that the human mind could have the misfortune of being able to process. One of the truest defining moments in your life is the one where all your dreams and aspirations get stripped away. It does not make you despondent; it does not enrage you…. It just leaves you numb. What I would give for just a glimmer of inspiration. More than anything, all you truly need is Inspiration, in whatever form, something to strive for, something to occupy your thoughts but most of all, to add some purpose to your existence. Anybody can just exist, how tough is it… the only way to fuck that up is to die! I thought I had that, forced myself to see things a certain way. No more, I have given it my best shot and fallen woefully short. There are times you just accept that what happens to you is so much more than who you are. The amount of control you have over anything is laughable. You can live your life by the best set of rules ever written and still end up with the happiness content of doggie poo. Not that I have always lived like a priest, but then I'm not really into pre-pubescent boys too, so what's the point of living like a priest? Disillusioning, isn't it? I know!

Chapter 11

Psychological Manipulation

First Act.
2007

This is Mumbai!

"This is Mumbai!" Sachin exclaimed with excitement, as he stepped out of the train with Raj at the CST station.

"Yes, including its familiar stench," Raj replied drily.

Raj and Sachin had joined their b-school in Mumbai and traveled there on a Saturday morning, two weeks before the commencement of classes, to find a house they could move into for the next two years.

Their first stop was the college's hostel, just so they could see if there was any possibility of them staying there. One foot inside the dormitory and they both swore never to visit the hostel again. The beds were literally two feet apart. And every bed had a desk right in front of it, which was all the space each person got. Both Raj and Sachin had their own individual rooms in their houses back in Bangalore, and they couldn't fathom living in tight, confined spaces like this.

After their unproductive hostel visit, they went on to meet some brokers who would show them houses. They spent the entire day looking at different houses, and by the end of it, there was only one they liked. However, the monthly rent was seventeen thousand per month when they had decided on a maximum budget of only fifteen thousand per month.

"It's beyond our budget," argued Sachin.

"By just two thousand!" Raj replied.

"Maybe we should look at more houses. This one is too big. It has more space than we need."

"Could we ever have more space?"

It was hard to win an argument with Raj, and besides, Sachin was tired after spending the entire day house hunting. He wanted to settle on one before they caught the evening train back to Bangalore.

They finalized the seventeen thousand per month house and signed a few papers with the broker before setting off to the train station.

That's when they experienced something for the first time that they would grow to become extremely familiar with: Mumbai's peak hour traffic.

They had heard about it before but couldn't have fathomed how bad it could and would get. The same distance that took them twenty minutes in the wee hours of the morning when they reached Mumbai, held them up for two hours in the evening.

Raj and Sachin sat in their auto, helplessly watching the clock tick towards the scheduled departure of their train. The rickshaw driver offered to re-route them to the airport. He knew there were airlines that operated red eye flights that they tended to sell at discounts to fill up the airline in case there were any last-minute vacancies and was only too familiar with newcomers like Raj and Sachin in Mumbai.

The boys decide to give it a shot since they had no alternative, and true to the rickshaw driver's word, they did find an Air India flight that was arriving from overseas and stopping by Mumbai as it flew over to Bangalore. The airline did have spare seats that they were selling at a discount for the Mumbai-Bangalore leg, and Raj and Sachin managed to secure two seats at a marginal premium to the train tickets' rates.

It was their first time on an airplane and for the next few hours, Raj and Sachin were awed by everything they encountered.

The Mumbai airport was the most orderly building they had seen. People waited in a queue there instead of madly rushing into the train when it rolled onto the platform.

There was one friendly old aunty who welcomed them into the airplane. Never had they received such hospitality from any government service before.

The cabin inside had cushioned seats with in-flight entertainment, with all of five channels they could switch between.

And then the grand finale: the airline food. Two slices of cold bread with a colder piece of cheese in between. Delicious!

"Do you think we have to pay for this?" asked Sachin.

"Nope, airlines always offer free food," Raj replied.

"Awesome! And this is delicious," said Sachin, biting into the sandwich.

"Of course, when it's free, it always tastes better," Raj smirked, and gobbled down his sandwich.

Raj and Sachin headed back to Bangalore to pick up their belongings and leave the city they had called home for so long. The next two years of their life would be spent in Mumbai, and who knew where after that!

So, this be it. To the greater unknown, here we go with eager eyes and hopeful hearts. Bigger city dreams filter through these smoke-filled scenes. If this be the end of me and my Bangalore, so be it. Running headlong into my unknown future? My sweet, oh so sweet city.... It's like a rerun of Cheers in my head, where everybody knew my name, fancy times in gilt edged frames and all that shite.

Into this world we choose, we find ourselves thrown. Confused with the constant second guessing? This whole world seems intent... Nah, hell-bent, on moving forward, of leaving their lives behind for the better. When did just standing still go out of fashion, oh wait I know, I know...69 or 77 right? That's the bleeding song, right? The funny thing is unlike the song, I don't particularly want to be a punk rocker. Very content just being in the concert. My motherfuckers, where the fuck art all thou? The bitches who taught me this lifestyle. The beer and the sweet simple times and the Music? The problem with the sweet simple good times is when the simplicity gets over, the sweet stops tasting so sweet you don't feel so good but bastard Dylan keeps on saying the times they keep on a-changing... Is Dylan Le Exception? Aghh, fuck if I know anymore!

I'm stuck in the middle with you. In the land of ambition, the shy, weary traveler finds himself staring into unblinking eyes. Everybody here seems so sure of what they are doing, worse still of who they are. Am I the only lost one? Will it be a Sunday Triple Surprise TM or...? Maybe should jump in? … The interpretation of Random thought? Even Mr. Sigmund couldn't write a book like that now could he!

Mingle, Mix, Smile and Friendly? Networking, connecting with people and fuckin learning. Laughter. Happiness. Abundant, flowing all around. Yup, that seems to be the scene this brush painted. Holding on today, Holding on with a hint of a smile. Lost in a sea of faces. Nothing like being slightly off the median to make you wonder about normalcy. The bitch with normalcy is that it happens to be a viewpoint. What is normal for anybody is what they happen to do. Van Gough was convinced the only "true" way to paint was with rough brush strokes (like him). Get offa me motherfucker, I'm normal…I'm with you Vincent! I feel like that too. Stuck in a post-modern, piccasoist, cubist world and sticking out along with my well used paintbrush. Artistic inspiration in the middle of management class?? Ah, wonders will never cease…. The real problem is that I really do have a sneaky suspicion that sometime during these two years I will cease to wonder!

Random splotches of personalities.

Fit in baby blue, Fit the fuck in NOW!

Erase thy rough edges, erase thyself?

With Creed as my Christ,

On I go, to stand proud alongside the faceless me?

First day of college

On the first day of college, the Student Council invited the new batch to the auditorium and gave a welcome speech. They were introducing things about the college, like the different cells you could participate in, but it was mostly territorial marking by the Student Council, making it amply clear who was going to be really in charge over the next one year before the senior batch graduated. It felt strange to be back in college and both Raj and Sachin had butterflies in their stomachs.

"Did you catch everything they said? I forgot to bring my notebook and couldn't take notes," said Sachin to Raj at the end of the session.

"I wasn't paying any attention at all. I was distracted by all the girls we have in our new college."

There were more girls, who looked prettier, than Raj and Sachin had ever seen congregated at a single place like this before. Not their school, their first jobs and certainly not their engineering college had girls like this. In engineering colleges, the sex ratio could sometimes be as bad as 1 girl to 100 guys, especially in streams like Mechanical.

"It's true. I hadn't noticed," said Sachin, as he scanned the auditorium with a fresh set of eyes.

"You're in love with Juhi!" said Raj, smirking.

Sachin nodded. He was miles away from Juhi, but he couldn't take his mind off her. He pulled out his phone and looked at the last message he received from her.

See you in Mumbai.

Sachin smiled as he read it for the 100th time. He had traveled so far from Juhi to step into an uncertain future, and she didn't say goodbye or good luck. She said See you. As if the distance itself was inconsequential. As if Juhi were right beside him wherever he went. He often thought he saw someone who looked like her or walked past someone who smelled like her in the streets of Mumbai.

"Let's grab some alcohol and get home now," said Raj, snapping Sachin out of his daydream.

"Now?" said Sachin since it was still mid-morning.

"I've had enough of college. It's time to get home and celebrate our new life in Mumbai," announced Raj, beaming with pride.

"Ok, alright," gave in Sachin, as he always did with a Raj plan.

They came upon a liquor store on their way home and decided to try something new.

"Canon 10000!" said Sachin, picking up a bottle of beer he'd never seen before.

"That should pack a punch! Let's get it," offered Raj.

They went home and began drinking the Canon 10000 just as they would drink any other beer. However, this one was as potent as a spirit, and soon, Raj and Sachin were drunk and engaged in a riveting conversation.

"Have you noticed how people get attracted to things they don't understand? 'Curiosity killed the cat' is the very reason we are human and capable of making discoveries and inventions. We always want to solve something we don't understand, and even invented God in this process to explain things we didn't know science could eventually solve. It's all because of the neocortex, where the brain is constantly processing new information and then sending it to the limbic for subconscious and long-term storage, so that it can move on to new things," Raj began.

"You mean like cycling? You focus a lot to get it right initially, and then it becomes part of the limbic where you can do it subconsciously?" Sachin added.

"Exactly! It's what some people call 'flow'. You do something so often, like playing a guitar, that it simply just flows without you having to concentrate on it. Therefore, if your brain is not challenged and you are living off just the limbic part, then time tends to move rapidly. Nothing ever changes. What happened in January is the same as September. The moral of the story is, the more you use your brain for new and different tasks, you can end up with a completely different perception of time.

Here's another one. You tend to choose what is certain for today than uncertain for tomorrow. But, for the very same task, if you can get rewarded today, you would choose that rather than benefits for tomorrow. Let's take relationships. They are sometimes not perfect. But you still know some things for certain, which may be the moments you get to create together, the work you get to do together, and things like that. But what is also a possibility is that there are fundamental differences in the relationship that could make things turn sour at some stage in the future. But then this is the future, which you are uncertain about. And therefore, you tend to choose what is certain today, albeit imperfect, for something you are uncertain about tomorrow.

A better example is smoking. You know you are risking your health in the future. But what is certain is the pleasure it gives you today. So, you take what is certain for today rather than what's uncertain for tomorrow. It's the reason why 'smoking kills' claims on packs never work, and instead do the opposite by getting people to smoke more. It only reinforced what you already knew. The fact that you are putting your life at risk, doing something daring, to get that momentary pleasure, which happens to be certain for today, and you don't have to worry about an uncertain tomorrow." Raj finally paused, taking a long drag from his cigarette.

"You know what's the best way to live life?"

"Not smoking this much, I assume," Raj joked.

"One should live life in such a way that you create as many moments as possible to remember than what average people forget. This is because people only remember highlights, the ups and downs, and forget everything else in their lives. But if you strive to create as many highlight moments as people forget, then that is a life worth living."

Sachin passed out on the couch and the next day, he walked into Raj's room to see if he was doing alright. His jaw dropped to the floor when he saw the wall next to Raj's bed.

Raj had drawn caricatures all over the wall using a black Sharpie.

"Raj! What the hell is this?" screamed Sachin.

"You, giving me a headache," replied Raj, groggily.

"This wall! You know this house isn't ours, right?"

"It's ok. This is the reason why the owner has taken an advance from us."

"You are paying for this Raj, not me. And who knows how much the owner is going to charge for this."

"Yea, yea… fine."

"We are late for class. Are you coming?"

"Na, I'm going to sleep it off today."

"It's the first day of college."

"Exactly why nobody will miss me."

"Suit yourself. I'm off."

"Bye."

"By the way, it's pretty creative," said Sachin, pointing at the wall. It started off as modern art in the form of branches from one end of the wall, progressing as leaves, transforming into buildings, and finally ending in smoke at the other end where the words 'the memory remains' were written.

The lyrics of the Metallica song played in Sachin's head as he read it. Raj had poured out a visual representation of the song on his bedroom wall.

Ash to ash

Dust to dust

Fade to black

Fortune, fame

Mirror, vain

Gone insane,

But the memory remains.

Party is on me

After an intense first week at college, an ad hoc freshers' party was planned by the students of one of the hostels known as Sai Suraj. This was a hostel away from the hostel, where an entire building called Sai Suraj was rented out to the boys of the college who didn't mind paying a premium to the official college hostel's fees. Living conditions were only marginally better here, like splitting the toilets in a ratio of 1:8 to the1:20 at the official hostel.

Raj reluctantly agreed to accompany Sachin to the party, halfway convinced when he learnt there would be copious amounts of free alcohol available there. It turned out to be a good idea as he managed to meet a few people he thought he could have great conversations with.

Overall, the environment at the hostel itself was footloose, as up until now they all only met in class where all everyone seemed to do was outsmart each other.

The scoring system was CGPA or Cumulative Grade Point Average, where the students were given a score from two to four, four being the highest. Therefore, there would always be one student with a two and another with a four and everyone else normalized in between. Hence, one person's success was dependent on another's failure, which explained why the competition was so intense.

The cutthroat competition gave rise to some popular acronyms like CP which stood for Class Participation and referred to students who would speak nonsense in class just to be heard by their peers and the professors. Then there was RG which stood for Relative Grading, which referred to students who would intentionally sabotage another's work, just to get ahead of them on the CGPA score.

All of this was too stressful for the happy-go-lucky Bangalore boys, and at the Sai Suraj party, for the first time since moving to Mumbai, they felt they could let their hair down and have a good time.

Sachin always had trouble holding his drink down, while Raj could easily finish an entire bottle, and then some if the situation permitted.

As the night progressed, Sachin was completely drunk and started making a big scene.

First, he started waving all the money he had in his pocket and screaming, "Party is on me," when he heard they had run out of food. Next, he wanted to take a leak so bad that he did it right on the main road outside the building when they were on a smoke break as he couldn't hold it until they got back in.

The next day, Sachin woke up and found himself in one of the empty beds at Sai Suraj. He had a mysterious cigarette burn on his arm and his money was missing. He had no idea how this had happened. He went looking for Raj and discovered he had promptly ditched him to go and sleep in his own bed at their apartment – as always, the one untrustworthy friend.

Feeling violated and topped with nausea from the alcohol, he groggily started to make his way out of the hostel when he ran into a classmate who immediately started apologizing.

"I'm so sorry, dude. When I was giving you a hug last night, I didn't realize I was holding my cigarette. Is your hand okay now?"

"That explains it!" Sachin replied, relieved to find out his arm wasn't burned on purpose, but just a friendly drunken hug. In an instant, the sense of shame he was beginning to attribute to the burn mark was replaced by pride.

"And here is your money."

"Woah, why did you take this?"

"Well, you were waving it all around saying the party was on you, so I took it to keep it safe till you sobered up."

Sachin was overwhelmed by an incredible sense of joy. He seemed to have found a space where he belonged. New friends he could get drunk with and would look out for him without asking. He wished he could share this with Raj.

Raj on the other hand detested meeting new people. He would make it seem like nobody was interesting enough to deserve his company. But more often than not, he just didn't want people to see who he really was. And therefore, resort to tons of alcohol just to get over his inhibitions before meeting someone new.

He did make a few new friends at the party. But the moment the alcohol ran out, so did his conversations with them. And then things turned so boring that he began having a headache tolerating his new company, and just wanted to get to his bed.

My head hurts! I see trees of green, red roses too.

I see a red door and I want it painted black,

I see skies of blue and clouds of white,

No colors anymore I want them to turn black,

I see them bloom for me and you,

I look inside myself, see my heart is black.

Yeah, my ass it's a wonderful world, lets just paint this

motherfucker black. My head hurts! Thank God for the Stones....

The first placement

"Party is on me!" hollered one of his classmates as Sachin entered class one morning.

"The Sai Suraj party got over last week!" Sachin replied, rolling his eyes.

"Yes, but it's still funny!"

"Party is on me!" boomed another classmate upon seeing Sachin.

Sachin had become an overnight sensation after that party. People couldn't stop talking about his funny antics of the night.

Sachin loved the attention. But he hoped that he would not remain famous just for his drunken behavior. His redemption came in the form of Hindustan Lever Ltd.

"What is HLL?" Sachin asked Raj.

"No clue but I've heard they are an FMCG company."

"What is FMCG?"

"Fast moving consumer goods."

"What does that mean?"

"I'm not sure. I guess they make fast cars like Ferrari?"

Despite how little Raj and Sachin knew about HLL or FMCG, they decided to apply to the company. It was after all the top ranked company to work for in India and was visiting their campus for the first time in the college's history for placement season.

Every other student had the exact same idea, and soon, HLL received the highest number of applications for a single company at the campus.

The application itself was a complicated one, and like most complicated things, was procrastinated on till the 11th hour. As fate would have it, Sachin was at one of his parties on the day of the deadline, where someone prompted a discussion about HLL when he was inebriated.

Sachin panicked when he realized he hadn't yet prepared his application and called up Raj. Fortunately for Sachin, it was one of those rare moments when Raj was sober, and Sachin was drunk.

On most evenings, Raj would be out having a drink with someone. Somehow, he was never short of drinking company. There would always be someone or the other up for a drink on any given day in college.

Sachin, on the other hand, never drank as often. But when he did, could never really figure his limits and almost always outdid himself to syncope.

However, that day, Raj was diligently filling out his application form and remained sober to do it properly. HLL sounded like a great company to work for, but more importantly, was an MNC through which he hoped he may get a chance to go abroad someday.

When Sachin called, Raj decided to extend a rare helping hand and offered to prepare Sachin's application as well.

"You would do that?" Sachin shrieked.

"Yea, well, I'm sober, so why the hell not?"

"That's amazing! Thank you so much, Raj!"

Not only did Raj prepare Sachin's application, but did such an amazing job of it, that Sachin was one among the twenty-four applicants shortlisted out of almost 400 entries.

"Wait, I got shortlisted, and you didn't?" said Sachin, when he received the shortlisting mail from PlaceCom, his college's Placement Cell.

"Honestly, I'm not surprised."

"How is that possible?"

"See, the questions were fairly straightforward, and I copied the contents from your CV directly on to the application. And that's when I noticed, you have pretty incredible credentials. Not only are your grades spectacular, but you top it with all sorts of extra-curriculars. I've heard HLL values those things. I don't have any of those and knew while filling your application, that you've got a pretty good shot at this."

"Wow, man. Nevertheless, you still filled in my application form, and I've only gotten shortlisted because of that. So, I really owe you one."

"Alright, alright, just convert this. Don't blow it."

"Haha…, yeah right! Those other twenty-three shortlisted candidates are the crème-de-la-crème of college. As if I will have a chance with them. I'm still surprised you didn't make it though."

"Hey, don't rub it in. I know you have better grades than me in most subjects, but there's one where I've beat you. Hindi board exam, 10th grade."

"No way!"

"Yes way. I even pulled out our 10th grade score sheet to prove it to you," said Raj, handing over a copy of the class score sheet that he had preserved since the 10th grade, seven years back.

"I cannot believe you kept this."

"Case closed. Now get on with HLL."

When the recruiters from HLL came to campus, the twenty-four shortlisted students were split into three groups of eight each for a group discussion. The best performing students from each of these groups were to be shortlisted for a personal interview.

In Sachin's group, as is the case with most MBA discussion groups, chaos reigned. Everyone wanted to speak and to be heard, so invariably a shouting match prevailed within the group.

Strangely though, every time Sachin spoke, the entire group would go quiet and listen to him. In his head he thought the group was just stunned that the guy who had screamed 'party is on me' was capable of saying something other than his catchphrase. However, it turned out that Sachin was the only one who made any sense at the group discussion, and he ended up being the only person shortlisted from his group for the interview.

The interview immediately followed the group discussion. It was a stress interview, where a panel of three interviewers threw questions at Sachin even before he could finish answering the previous one. At the end of the interview, Sachin rushed outside to meet Raj and some other friends for a smoke. He had had enough stress for one day.

"Sachin! Why is your phone unreachable?" shouted one of the PlaceCom students, rushing towards Sachin at the smoke stall.

"I kept it on silent for the interview and didn't turn it back on. Why, what happened?"

"We have been trying to call you. The HLL panel wants to meet all the shortlisted candidates."

Sachin wondered what this was about. He thought there were only two rounds: the group discussion and the interview. And surely, they could not have decided on who all made it past the interview already.

Sachin rushed towards the meeting room, fixing his tie on the way. Once he entered, he noticed the rest of the shortlisted students were already in the room talking to the panelists. Sachin was the last to enter, which certainly did not look good for him.

"Finally, you are here!" one of the panelists said to Sachin when he entered.

"Sorry, sir, I forgot to turn off the airplane mode on my phone."

"Don't worry about it. We can at least start now that you are all here. Thank you all for your participation today, and we were thoroughly impressed with the quality of students and glad we made the decision to visit your campus this year. However, we are selecting just one student to join us, and that would be Sachin."

If this were a movie, Sachin's jaw would have dropped in the exact same way Jim Carrey's did in The Mask. He couldn't believe that of the 400 incredibly smart people in college, he was the first one to get placed.

After somehow holding his surprise back and smiling through the exchanges of gratitude among the rest of the panelists and the interview shortlists, Sachin came out of the room to a loud applause from the students waiting outside. The folks at PlaceCom had informed them the moment the announcement was made inside.

Sachin looked around for Raj but couldn't find him. A few too many students gathered around for Raj's comfort, he thought.

However, Sachin found Raj at home, eagerly waiting with a bottle of Jack Daniels Red Label.

"Today, we celebrate with good whiskey!" Raj declared when Sachin walked in.

That day onwards, Sachin's life underwent a paradigm shift. Suddenly, he was not just the guy who screamed 'party is on me'; he was the guy who screamed 'party is on me' and bagged the best job on campus.

In addition to increasing his friend circle manifold, Sachin got membership offers from all the important student body committees of college. PlaceCom wanted him as a member. They had a rigorous selection process of their own, since most students wished to join them, but in Sachin's case, they waived those formalities and made him a member automatically.

Sachin, of course, took it up, along with a position in the Dramatics club, the Alumni Cell, and the main governing body of them all, the Student Council. He decided to dip his feet into all of them before picking the ones he really wanted to be associated with. After all, they were offering him positions for nothing, so there was no harm in trying them all out.

Over the next few weeks, the placement season continued. Other companies conducted their recruitment processes, and Raj secured a job at a Retailer MNC based out of Kolkata. Sachin still managed to bag the best job on campus, and Raj couldn't have been prouder for his friend.

I was cheering as loud as anybody else. My king had returned. Amongst the hordes I caught a glimpse of him. He looked every bit the victorious, regal person he was. I cheered him on till I went hoarse. Yes, that is the way it should be. What's the point of having heroes if there is nobody willing to be average enough to admire them?

But that was a hundred years ago. It all changed so quickly. I was taken away from my people and thrown into this bustling city of bright lights.

Now it is a different day and a different place.

On top of the world, I was glancing at my world below. Wasting time while looking at those marvelously tall buildings. They appear almost like giant fingers trying hard to grasp their own private piece of sky. Just a couple of minutes ago I was below them. They seemed so huge, so huge that they blocked out my sun.

Though on top now, I know that I will be looking up at them forever.

Somehow now it all makes sense. They are giants still, but suddenly I don't feel so small.

Kashmir

As Raj and Sachin moved to Mumbai, Gajan moved to Hyderabad. He joined an IT firm there and was biding time till he got a call from one of the universities in the US he had applied to. The moment he cracked one, he called up Raj and Sachin and asked them if they would like to join him on a trip to Kashmir, because he wanted to pray at the Vaishno Devi mandir, before flying out to the US.

Gajan was a man of science, but he also believed in a higher power. In fact, he believed in different higher powers for different things in life. And in this case, it was Vaishno Devi. The temple was dedicated to the Hindu Mother Goddess Vaishno Devi, who is believed to be the bestower of strength to the weak. Gajan had wanted to visit the temple since he was a boy and felt this was the perfect time to seek the Goddess' blessings before leaving India.

Raj and Sachin always wanted to visit Kashmir, and Gajan had a reputation for being a whiz at planning trips. He had done a fabulous job organizing the trip to Dandeli back in school. So, it didn't take much to convince Raj and Sachin, and they decided to head to Hyderabad where they would first meet Gajan, and then the trio would travel to Srinagar together.

Raj and Sachin booked train tickets for Hyderabad. On the day of the journey, they rushed to get to the railway station, still incorrectly estimating Mumbai's peak hour traffic. To top it, the train they boarded stalled for close to three hours in the night because of some engine failure. Raj and Sachin were caught unaware as they had slept through the whole incident. By the time they reached Gajan's studio in Hyderabad, it was too late, and they were too tired to go out exploring the city of Nizams. They decided to stay indoors and have a drink. Gajan opened a bottle of Signature, which soon became Raj's favorite.

As they sat drinking, Sachin observed that apart from a change in location, Mumbai to Hyderabad, nothing else had changed. He was doing the exact same thing with Raj on the days he was home early in Mumbai. Drinking whiskey and having a conversation that tipped on the edge of an argument.

After another swig of whiskey, the trio crashed as they had an early flight the next day to Jammu.

The next day, as the plane descended in Jammu, Raj noticed a signboard saying 'Aircel in Jammu and Kashmir'. Jammu and Kashmir! Raj was suddenly wide awake.

"Guys, we are finally in the famous J&K!" he announced as he shook a groggy Sachin and Gajan awake.

The minute they disembarked from the flight, the cold weather tore through their clothes, freezing them to the bone. The three South Indian boys had never experienced weather like this, and the jumpers they purchased in Bangalore were probably only suitable for the winters there. They were no match for the frosty, cutting winds of Kashmir.

At the first store they found that sold winter clothes at the airport, they bought themselves some fleece coats so that they didn't freeze to death. Then they rented a taxi that would take them from Jammu to Srinagar. The journey was a fascinating one, with the mighty Himalayan range peeping out from a distance, teasing them with glimpses of their snow-covered peaks. And as they got closer, white started to overtake the brown of the mountains. Soon, they were driving in between the snow. It was the first time any of them had seen real snow. They passed a three-kilometer-long tunnel called the 'Jawahar Pass' that cut through a mountain along the way. This was the best part of the drive. When they entered the tunnel from one end, there were just bits and pieces of snow around, but when they came out of the other end, thick white snow engulfed them.

They stopped for lunch at a town called Patnitop, and shoved their hands into mounds of snow, feeling it with their bare hands for the first time. A smile broke out on Raj's face, and he looked over to see Sachin having a similar expression pasted on his face as well. He marveled at the fresh snow that lay on his hands. It was just water, but instead of flowing through his fingers, it lay still, waiting to be squished, eaten, or even flung over at someone.

They continued their journey towards Kulu-Manali, the Rohtang Pass, and finally, Srinagar. They checked in to a hotel called Taimoor, on their driver's recommendation, and went out for dinner with him to try out the mutton sold off the streets that he couldn't stop raving about. The boys weren't too sure about having meat from street vendors, but after taking one bite, they couldn't stop. Hot mutton kababs with cold roti and spicy chutneys, served just as how pani-puri is served in the rest of the country, one by one on small round rotis instead of the puri.

The next day, the boys went out to explore the city of Srinagar and realized that the city didn't get a lot of snowfall. It was just freakishly cold, thanks to the cold winds blowing down from the mountains and channeling themselves into the Srinagar valley. Since the boys wanted to play in the snow, they travelled to a place called Gulmarg, which was two hours from Srinagar and hosted the winter games of India. They found that Gulmarg was a place buzzing with activities for tourists to do. They started with sledging, much like the way Calvin and Hobbes did. They sledged to a point where 'Gondolas' or chair cars took them to a higher altitude, where they tried their hand at skiing. Then got back in the Gondola and sledged back to the base.

They couldn't get enough of the snow and continued to play in it. Creating a snowman, throwing snowballs at each other, drawing angel wings on the snow, the trio effectively tried everything they had seen Calvin do in the comic strips.

The most fascinating aspect of Calvin and Hobbes is the fact that Calvin is not exactly a normal child, He has almost no friends and comfortingly does not find the need for any. Though undeniably adorable he is not without negative traits. He is very anti-social, morally, he is misguided, to say the least, has the ambition of a single-celled organism and his interactions are limited to a large extent to his stuffed tiger. Moreover, he truly believes that Hobbes is alive, and any psychiatrist worth his salt would be smacking his lips at the prospect of Calvin as a patient. Let's face it, the boy is delusional, neurotic and is probably going to grow up to be a lonely, bitter, unemployed bum.

I know, this is not exactly a fan letter so far, is it?

It is actually all these so called 'personality flaws' that got me hooked on to the strip in the first place. After some time, you get tired of watching only the perfect examples of humans prancing around on TV, in literature, the movies and even in comics. Calvin is not perfect; actually, he is far from it.... He is, for better or worse, different from most boys his age. What makes it so readable is the fact that while we mask our differences, petrified about sticking out, he tries to blank out those parts, which contrast his version of the world. That is what courage is all about, isn't it? Maybe it's just me, but I think the fact that I might grow up lonely, bitter and unemployed is a small risk to take as long as I can live my life exactly the way I want.

Ultimately what the strips screams out is the fact that Calvin is different... and that's okay! It really is!

Kashmir continued...

It was Day 3 of the Kashmir trip, and the day began with more winter shopping. Raj picked up a Feren, which were long robes worn by traditional Kashmiris. He wanted to completely blend in with the locals. The Kashmir trip was turning out to be quite an adventure, similar to the books he would read as a kid when his mind transported him to fantasy lands where he felt like one of the characters in the book. Raj wanted to feel like one of the locals in Kashmir. A fantasy trip if you will.

Just as his mind wandered, so did his eyes in the store, and Raj noticed a gun and asked the shopkeeper about it. He told them it was his personal AK-47 and offered Raj to hold it if he wished. Raj held up the gun, and in his Feren, his fantasy was now complete. He felt exactly like one of the bad guy's Hollywood movies loved to annihilate.

Raj safely returned the gun after posing for a few photos that Gajan found too entertaining to miss out on, and the trio decided to check out of their hotel and find a houseboat they could spend their last night of Srinagar in. The houseboats of Dal Lake in Srinagar constantly featured in prominent travel magazines as some of the best places in the world to stay in, which was something they wanted to experience for themselves.

They came across beautifully designed little boats that were accessible from the land via a tiny four-person boat called a Shikara. The houseboats came equipped with every basic amenity. They had electrically heated beds, a bathtub, teak walls that trapped the heat in, and most of all, a dining table fit for a king. Everything was intricately designed, and the woodwork was crafted to perfection.

The boys fell in love with the very first houseboat they saw, and the innkeeper charged them just 900 bucks for a day. The boys were flabbergasted. Barely 300 bucks per person for a slice of paradise? They wasted no time and took up the innkeeper's offer and settled in. They asked the innkeeper to lay out some chairs and a table on the terrace along with something called a Khati, a mini furnace that could be placed on a table to generate heat while out in the open. The boys sat at the table, drinking and eating Kashmiri food prepared by the innkeeper.

They spoke about how amazing the trip was turning out to be, and how it may just be the last time the three of them would hang out this way since Gajan was soon headed to the US. Raj began to overdrink and if not for the cold and fatigue that prompted Sachin and Gajan to retire early, may have gone down as another night of never-ending alcohol and arguments courtesy Raj.

The next day was the start of the pilgrimage to Vaishno Devi, the primary purpose for their visit to Kashmir. The boys left Srinagar behind and started on a long drive to Pahelgam, where they stopped for lunch, and then further to Katra where they reached by dusk. The journey to Katra took a lot longer than planned because of a traffic jam caused by an accident, which had led to a fire. A truck ran over a scooter and then promptly burst into flames.

"Only Indian scooters could be that audacious," Raj commented darkly.

The boys were relieved to hear from some of the passers-by that nobody was hurt too bad. Now, they just had to wait for the traffic to clear.

Once they reached Katra, they checked in to the first hotel they chanced upon and retired early as the climb up the mountain to the Vaishno Devi temple the next day would begin sharp at 6:00 a.m. It was a twenty-six-kilometer trek up and down the holy Vaishno Devi Mountain. Most people usually trekked up the mountain at night to reach the temple by daybreak. But given the hectic drive from Srinagar, the boys wanted to get some rest before the trek. They did just that, and by the time they woke up and got ready to start the trek, it was seven in the morning.

The long climb up was made slower by Raj who took a break every five minutes. The years of alcohol and lack of any form of exercise was beginning to show. Raj was never challenged on anything as physical as this climb he was on, and for the first time, he could feel the toll his habits had taken on his body. He was struggling more than Gajan, who was making the climb barefoot. This was pilgrimage for Gajan, and he wanted it done right, practical arguments against it from Raj and Sachin notwithstanding.

As they trudged their way up the mountain, they kept seeing helicopters flying from the base to the top of the mountain taking passengers who were willing to shell out 2500 rupees. Raj insisted that the money was worth it in place of the arduous trek. But Gajan would have none of it. He wouldn't even take a slightly shorter route that would have saved them two kilometers. He stuck to the original, long path, and traversed it barefoot.

When they finally made it to the mandir, they first washed up and then went inside the cave to see the goddess. They had barely caught a glimpse of her when they were asked to keep moving because of the massive crowd at the temple. Gajan was satisfied though. In fact, he thought the crowd was less than usual, since they had started off a little later than planned. It was nearly noon by the time they got to see Vaishno Devi, and that was supposed to be the peak hour for the pilgrims.

Gajan wanted to climb two more kilometers further up the mountain to another temple called Bhairo mandir. He believed a pilgrimage to Vaishno Devi was incomplete until you visited this second temple. The trouble was, they had a bus to catch at six in the evening and were way too tired to make another grueling climb up the mountain. Not only would it completely exhaust them, but it could also jeopardize making it in time for their bus.

The boys weighed their options. They had just enough money between the three of them to hitch a pony ride to the top. But if they splurged on the ponies, they would only be left with fifty bucks for their climb down and they still needed to have lunch. Raj simplified the decision when he said he simply could not trek any further.

That's how the pony ride began, and it turned out to be a laughing riot for Gajan and Sachin. Sitting on the pony could be a bit scary at the start, because the creatures started galloping the moment you got on, and the path they took was narrow and winding. It was a bit unnerving for a first timer, but you simply needed to trust the instincts of the animal in this case. The ponies obviously don't want to fall off the face of the mountain.

The only way to fall was if you slipped off the pony. Therefore, the one instruction they had to follow was to hold on to the pony for dear life. Gajan and Sachin were enjoying the ride, behaving like cowboys and screaming 'yeehaw' every now and then. Raj, on the other hand, gripped the reins tightly and had a perpetual look of fear painted on his face. He kept shouting at the pony's caretaker to make the pony go slower. His pony was just cantering, and he wanted it to go slower than that. Because of him, Gajan and Sachin couldn't go any faster, which they very much wanted to.

When they finally got off, Raj stomped off, angry at the pony caretaker, both Sachin and Gajan, and of course, the unsuspecting pony as well. A little while later, once he realized he was still alive and his heart started beating normally again, he joined the banter with Sachin and Gajan.

Bhairo mandir was far less crowded, giving Gajan enough time to pray. Then they began the walk downhill, which they expected to be much simpler. There were also stairs at certain places which helped cut the journey short. Gajan continued to take the longer route, since completing the total distance of twenty-six kilometers mattered to him. Raj and Sachin took the stairs at some places, but mostly stuck with Gajan as they were worried if he would suddenly need help. After all, Gajan's feet couldn't have looked worse for wear. Raj and Sachin were themselves starting to hurt in their knees that were taking a bigger beating on the way down. They finally reached the base by five in one piece, took a quick shower, and caught their bus to Delhi. The flight to Srinagar had already busted their budgets, so it was the cost-effective bus back this time.

On the journey back, they couldn't help but reminisce about the memorable trip. They had done a lot of fascinating things like staying in a houseboat, trekking twenty-six kilometers and holding a real AK-47. Raj began to hum Led Zeppelin's Kashmir.

Oh, pilot of the storm who leaves no trace

Like sorts inside a dream

Leave the path that led me to that place

Yellow desert stream

Like Shangri-la beneath the summer moon

I will return again

As the dust that floats find you

We're moving through Kashmir

Holi, the festival of colors, and bhang.

After Kashmir, Raj and Sachin got back to their regular b-school grind in Mumbai. One evening, they decided to take a break and watch a movie. It was a Tuesday, when Hutch, their cellphone provider, ran an offer to get one free ticket with the purchase of one silver class ticket at Fame Adlabs, one of the most expensive multiplexes of Mumbai. Getting a ticket for half price there was almost the same as buying a regular ticket anywhere else. Given they had never visited that multiplex before, and because Hutch was kind enough to honor their loyalty, they decided to make use of the offer and watch a movie.

They landed up at Fame and saw two queues formed. The shorter queue was made up of only about four people while the other snaked its way almost to the vehicle entrance of the multiplex. They asked the guard about the two queues, and he told them that the long one was for the Hutch customers. Clearly, Hutch had a lot of loyal customers.

They joined the long queue anyway and began haranguing about which movie they should watch. They finally settled on one, but it was due to start in five minutes.

The queue, much like any other traffic in Mumbai, took such a long time to inch forward, that by the time they reached the counter, were over twenty minutes late into the movie. Sachin lost interest and decided to turn back. Raj asked him to hold on since they had already invested so much time standing in the queue.

Upon reaching the counter, with a straight face, Raj asked the usher, "Can I have two tickets to the Da Vinci Code, please?" The Usher was a little confused. He checked the system and told them that the movie wasn't running. Raj told him that the posters for the movie were put up outside saying otherwise. The usher got more confused and decided to confer with a fellow usher, who also got confused by Raj's request. Sachin joined in, and both of them insisted on watching only Da Vinci Code, especially when they were extremely loyal Hutch customers who had spent the last half an hour standing in the queue. The usher tried his best to convince them that the movie wasn't running. Finally, when the people behind them in the queue realized what they were up to and started yelling, Raj and Sachin decided to call it quits and leave the place.

They had a good laugh about it and decided to put the 200 bucks they saved on the movie ticket to good use and went to an Italian restaurant very originally called Little Italy. The place turned out to be a good decision, not just because they had Cobra beers and good food and a live band performing, but because there were four hot Italian girls sitting at the table right next to theirs. Three Cobras down and neither could take their eyes off them.

Just as they were running out of money for more beers, their phones pinged at the same time. The boys at the Sai Suraj hostel had sent out invitations for their Holi party. Raj and Sachin decided to join, remembering the amazing time they had had at Sai Suraj at their freshers' party.

In addition to that, they were curious to know how Holi was really celebrated. Back in Bangalore, Holi was rarely celebrated. If anything, a few friends would gather and amicably smear a bit of gulal on each other. Mumbai was a different ball game. They knew that Mumbaikars turned wild on Holi, covered head-to-toe in gulal, going beyond the point of recognition. And at Sai Suraj, the wild factor was taken a few levels higher.

On the day of Holi, the moment Raj and Sachin reached Sai Suraj, they were physically roughed up by some of the boys in a corner and forced to gulp down two glasses of what tasted like milk.

"What is that!" sputtered Raj when he finally managed to get a word in.

"Bhang!" shouted one of the Sai Suraj boys.

"Great! But you didn't have to force me to drink it. I would have happily had it!"

"Haha, most people here have never had bhang before, and if we tell them what they are having, they may refuse. So, we first force them to drink it the moment they enter."

"Ok cool. I don't feel anything though."

"Give it an hour," he said with a knowing smirk.

"Screw that, just give me some more bhang."

The boys obliged happily, and Raj gulped down two more glasses.

"I'll see in an hour if I want any more," Sachin said, once again in awe of Raj's seemingly endless capacity for drink.

"Why do they mix it in milk though! May have worked faster if you just had the real thing directly," Raj said, inspecting his empty glass.

"Maybe for the same reason a new bride gives milk to her husband on the first night after their wedding. It's supposed to be an aphrodisiac and possibly drives up the potency of the bhang," Sachin thought out loud.

"Milk is an aphrodisiac? Man, babies must be so horny all the time," said Raj and broke into a laugh.

Suddenly, the Bangalore boys were pulled from where they were standing and dunked in different colored waters. Just as they were recovering from all the water abuse, somebody tore off their shirt and threw it at a nearby tree. The tree began to look like a piece of art, covered with colored shirts belonging to all the boys at the party.

It seemed quite an achievement that the girls at the party were distinguished from the boys, so that they could keep their shirts on. Holi in Mumbai was maniacal so far.

After the violent first five minutes, Sachin went about exchanging pleasantries with everyone at the party. Raj found a quiet corner with a few people he knew from college and continued drinking more bhang, highly suspicious with its potency by now.

Soon, the group around Raj began to grow bigger, and at one point, a girl joined the group and started to talk to everyone. Somewhere during that conversation, the bhang took its effect on Raj, and he slowly looked around. He saw all these boys standing quietly, in rapt attention of the one girl in the group. He then tried listening to what the girl was saying that was so important, and then waited for a moment when she paused for breath.

"Yak yak yak yak," Raj said loudly to the girl.

All the boys in the group turned to face Raj, including Sachin who had joined the same group, with an expression of horror writ on his face. He couldn't believe Raj could be that openly rude, that too in the middle of so many boys who seemed to vie for that one girl's attention. But as if to quell any fears he harbored, the entire group burst out laughing.

Clearly, the effects of bhang had spread out to the others as well, and they found Raj's antics funny.

Sachin got high as well eventually. It was their first time on bhang, and they had never experienced anything like it. They were fully in control, in fact, a little more than they would have liked. Yet, it gave them a massive buzz and made them do and say silly things, just like regular alcohol did.

After spending some time at the party, Sachin started to feel sleepy and thought it best to head back home this time. He didn't want to pass out once again at this hostel and end up with a cigarette wound or his money missing the way it happened last time around. He went about looking for Raj to check if he would want to get back as well but couldn't find him anywhere.

Assuming Raj had ditched him once again, he left for his house by himself. However, when he reached home, Raj was not there. He was expecting Raj to be waiting with a bottle of whiskey, saying something like, "Now, let's have the real thing." But Raj wasn't home, and Sachin was too high to try and call him and decided to sleep it off. When Sachin woke up the next day in the afternoon, he was surprised to realize he had slept through the morning.

Once awake, he took a shower and stared at the shower's floor where a kaleidoscope of swirling colors was forming with all the Holi colors washing off his body. He then went to Raj's room, and found it was still empty. Sachin realized he had slept for nearly eighteen hours. It was possible that Raj had returned home, slept, and left for college already in that time.

Sachin ambled to college himself, spent what remained of the day listening to the lecturers who made no sense, and returned home to once again find Raj missing. This was completely unlike Raj. He was always home. The effort it took to visit college was too much for Raj. He, at best, spent a few hours outside, either in college or at a bar, and then came straight back home.

Sachin dialed his number, and once again received the 'switched off' notification he had been getting since trying him that afternoon.

Sachin decided to wait a few more hours before raising an alarm. Thankfully, Raj returned late at night.

"Where have you been!?"

"Goa!"

"What?"

"Yeah, that Sai Suraj party was insane. One thing led to another, and soon I was on a trip to Goa with a bunch of guys."

"But why was your phone unreachable?"

"It got wet at that party and stopped working."

"Ok, I was beginning to get worried."

"I'm going to make it up to you!" said Raj, removing a bottle of Signature, his go-to whiskey from his bag.

"Now, let's have the real thing."

I'm not a drinker anymore,

I was. I really was a fun drinker. I was entertaining, I was happy, and I made people around me in the countless pubs I grew up in, pretty happy, if only for a couple of hours.

I'm no longer that person.

I'm no longer a drinker.

I'm a fucking raging alcoholic.

The ordinary day for me involves one full bottle.

750ml of pure, strong and self-destructive whiskey.

Yes, I'm fucking raging alcoholic.

As I write this, its 5:30 in the morning, I have a hangover (God, I no longer even remember waking up without one), it's before dawn, my house is quiet, my roommates are asleep… and I've finally had enough.

I've finally had enough of being the person I've been trying to become.

I'm going to deal with the monotony of life in general and my life like a person.

Like a fucking person…. Like an honest, stable and mature person.

Can I just stop drinking just like that… probably not?

*Can I stop at least for *insert magic number* days… probably not again.*

I will put this up in some days from now.

*So, if you ever read this, I have been sober, happier and bored out of my brain for *insert magic number*days now….*

If you don't read this, none of this really matters…

Because by then I would be well on the way to killing myself… one drink at a time.

Enter Aishvarya. The Suburbs of Mumbai

Aishvarya last met Raj at the Infosys cafeteria in Mysore. Raj promised they would meet there often, but as always, he lied. Raj never once messaged or called her during their time together in Mysore.

Aishvarya continued working with Infosys and had heard about Raj quitting the company to join a b-school in Mumbai. She was glad he was moving far away from her. But as luck would have it, she was now being posted in Mumbai for a few months. She hated how destiny always landed her at the exact same place Raj was, only to be ignored by him.

Mumbai was thankfully much bigger than the Infosys cafeteria, and she hoped to never run into Raj there.

But luck would simply play her again, and she did run into him. Covered in gulal and reeking of bhang.

"Aishvarya! What are you doing here?"

"I was buying some groceries."

"I mean, what are you doing in Mumbai?"

"I live here now. For a few months at least."

"You do? Why didn't you tell me!"

"I wasn't sure where in Mumbai you lived. It's a big city."

Aishvarya knew exactly where Raj lived, and it so happened that the accommodation Infosys provided her in Mumbai was in the very same suburb.

"It IS a big city, so it makes it that much more amazing that we are running into each other this way.'

"Yes, I guess so."

"This party here has been terribly boring. You want to grab a tea or something?"

"Now? You don't even have a shirt on."

Raj was so high on bhang that he hadn't even realized he was walking shirtless through the streets of Mumbai, which was yanked off at the Sai Suraj party. Raj was terribly uncomfortable with nudity. He couldn't even change his shirt in front of another guy. It was the reason he insisted on a bigger house with Sachin while moving to Mumbai, so he could have sufficient space with a separate room to himself.

However, he felt more exposed than just his topless attire. It was that feeling Aishvarya roused in him ever since they were in school. As if she could go beyond his façade and see the Raj deep down. Aishvarya had a way of making him feel naked, and it had just taken on a literal manifestation.

"Hey! Wait!" Aishvarya yelled, as Raj suddenly turned and broke into a jog away from her. It was as if he was ashamed, both at the physical nudity and the person he was being that he didn't want Aishvarya to see.

As he ran, Raj's phone rang.

"Hey dude, where are you?" said one of his friends who noticed Raj had suddenly gone missing from the Sai Suraj party.

"I had to leave man. Something urgent."

"Yeah, this party is bloody juvenile. We were headed to meet some friends who have more fun stuff with them. Given the way you gulped down that bhang, we figured you may be interested in something heavier as well."

A neuron burst in Raj's brain. It was as if the perfect magic words were just spoken. All he wanted to cover himself up with at the moment was more substance.

"Where you guys headed?"

"Will message you the address. Hope to see you soon!"

Just as he hung up, as if on cue, Raj passed a Nike showroom. Nike was one of his favorite brands, more for it being a brand from the US, than for any of its edgy advertising. He decided to purchase a shirt from there, cover up that physical nudity as well while he was at it, and picked out a classic white shirt that had nothing more than the single signature black swoosh on it.

Raj quickly paid, stepped out to find an auto-rickshaw and directed them to the address he received from his friends on his phone. On the way, his brain started nagging him about deserting Aishvarya on the streets. He had done that so often. Every time she came close to him, he would just freak out. He knew he should confront Aishvarya someday. Not for her, but for himself. It was the only way he could confront who he really was. But for the moment, he pushed the nagging thought aside, and decided to focus on doing what he did best: Get high.

He caught up with his friends at the given address, who came up with an impromptu plan to fly to Goa, gamble, and get back in a day. He went along, and in a few hours, was gambling at the casinos on the ships of the Goan coast, only to return home the next day to a worried roommate.

He had all but forgotten about meeting Aishvarya, and she never saw him in Mumbai again.

Goa!

Travel

Crap! Flights delayed. A journey to Goa delayed due to fog! Airports in India always depress me. In any poor country, rich people have this unerring tendency to be dickheads. All the money in the world cannot buy manners. Throw in a few hours of boredom and you get to see the worst in people. Twelve-year-olds (along with richer-than-thou moms and dads) screaming at flight attendants for a fucking fog delay!

Hotel

Thank God the boys booked a cheap ass hotel. Man, this place is an acquired taste though. The receptionist seems to be on acid from 1989! I asked him if they have fresh fruit juice. Very honest answer, 'Sir, we have fruit juice but not fresh!' [They had only canned juice]. That made sense at the time though, a meeting of glazed minds, I guess.

Casino

Can hardly believe the hands I'm getting. Two flushes (dealt), one straight and must have been at least ten blackjacks! Shouldn't have had so much vodka, my head is starting to hurt. Funny places casinos are… 1000 bucks is usually a really good meal, a good movie and a good book. Here it is black chip, useful only when I want to get orange ones or play baccarat. Money has ceased to mean anything to me. Okay then, time to make some more!

Cross shopping

Afternoon. Head hurts like mad. My friend wants to buy a gift for his girlfriend. Ask a taxi guy if he knows the Wills lifestyle showroom. He almost takes us to a cigarette shop!

Shopping at the women's section.

Saleslady: What's her bust size, sir?

Us: Is ample a size?

Beach

Sunset. Good company. Topless women. Golden sands. Five beers. Unlimited laughter. 'Peaceful easy feeling' playing on the iPod. Enough said.

Return

Wooh, that was a blur. Early for my flight. Nicely insulated from the rich people in my smoking cube. They even have alcohol at the airport. Takeoff and landing must be a blast.

Just like any good trip to Goa, I came back home with a sneaking suspicion that I had a really good time. If you come back knowing it, then trust me, you could have had a crazier time. Ah! They say a picture is worth a thousand words. Lucky me… I came back with both!

Second Act.
2019

Taking advantage of someone who cares

"Welcome to yet another WhatsApp group, guys," pinged a message from Gajan to a group titled King James he had just created with Sachin, Raj and Aishvarya.

"You guys are the biggest fans of LeBron James I know, and I thought it would be good to chat amongst ourselves," Gajan continued.

"Wait! Aishvarya watches the NBA?" Sachin quipped.

"I ran into her at the Lakers game last year and she seemed more into the game than me!" messaged Gajan.

Gajan and Aishvarya had been living in the San Francisco Bay Area for quite a while. Gajan moved there for his post-graduation in 2007, and Aishvarya moved to live with her husband shortly after her wedding in 2012.

Having lived in the US for so long, Aishvarya had acquired a few western tastes, NBA being one of them.

Growing up, she wasn't a big fan of sports, but began to appreciate what people enjoyed about it in a country where sports was at its entertaining best.

"That's amazing! So, what do you think LeBron's chances are, now that he's moved to Lakers?" messaged Sachin.

Aishvarya read all the messages but didn't reply to any of them. She was aghast that Gajan created a group with her and Raj in it. But she couldn't blame Gajan, as he barely knew the history between the two of them.

"Hey Aishvarya, how's it going?" came a message from Raj.

That's when Aishvarya realized that even Raj didn't know any of the history between the two of them. He was just as oblivious to it as everyone else in the group. She felt silly about her behavior. It had been years since she had last seen him. Raj, too, had barely acknowledged her presence in all that time. It was time for her to treat Raj as just another friend she knew from school.

"Hi, Raj! Yes, I'm here, and it's nice to see you all," read Aishvarya's message on the group.

While the NBA conversations continued on the WhatsApp group, Raj messaged Aishvarya privately.

"Hey, seriously, how's it going?" messaged Raj.

"It's great! Staying in the US has been a fascinating experience, to say the least."

"I can imagine. It's my favorite country. Always wanted to live there."

"Why didn't you?"

"Life had other plans. I was too busy having too much fun in India."

"As always!"

"How's marriage been?"

"It's alright."

That was it. All Raj needed was a crack to open his plethora of rhetorical questioning and spiraling psychoanalysis. It was what he loved doing more than anything else: having deep discussions about others' problems, effectively distracting him from his own.

But what was an arbitrary time-filler for Raj, especially given that he had managed to oust every other good friend who was willing to lend him an ear until that point, was like sweet nectar for Aishvarya's years of penance.

She longed to have Raj for herself, if not as a boyfriend or a husband, at least as a friend she could talk to. But Raj was never there for her. He repeatedly popped into her life, out of sheer coincidence, but just as quickly walked out, with abject disregard.

Aishvarya was tired of the way Raj treated her and decided to get some closure by pouring her heart out on a letter she never sent him, right before her wedding.

Her objective was to focus solely on her new husband and new life. She was moving to the US and wanted nothing more than a fresh start. However, things did not pan out the way she expected. Her husband barely showed any interest in her. The only things that mattered to him were his work and his family. She tried everything short of procreation but couldn't find a way to break through. Lately she had begun wondering if bringing a child would solve their problems but knew the answer to it only too well. Solving one problem by creating another is a recipe for disaster.

She then started to foster thoughts of calling it quits with her husband, and that's when Raj popped into her life, again. And this time, Raj appeared exactly the way he did when she first met him all those years ago in school. He was interested in her. He wanted to know about her life.

And Aishvarya poured it all out. Every single detail of her life, she bared them all to Raj. And Raj enjoyed talking with Aishvarya. She was his new muse. Someone with a fertile brain to dissect. They went on to have conversations that lasted all night for Aishvarya, spilling over into nighttime for Raj given their time difference.

When they weren't talking, they would text. And irrespective of time of day and whether they spoke or texted, Raj was drunk. Aishvarya was beginning to learn how to measure his level of drunkenness, as his meanness was directly proportional to how drunk he was. And every time he was a bit too mean, Aishvarya knew he had had one too many drinks, and gently suggested they call it a night.

Raj's health was steadily deteriorating. He underwent a full body checkup where the doctor said that along with his fatty liver, he now had an enlarged heart. His drinking was taking a toll on his body, and he needed to cut down his alcohol intake.

Raj, however, could never cut down. He found himself to be relevant only when he was drinking. He would mix his liquor with Red Bull, just to overcome his stomach's protests, and take his brain to a place he felt comfortable in. And he joked about his medical reports and his parents' concern over them. Nothing the doctors or his parents said seemed to shake him from the path he was on.

"Nobody could like you as much as I do," he once told Aishvarya.

"Really? Why is that?"

"Because I have a large heart. And I have a medical report to prove it to you."

Along with a fatty liver, his heart began to grow big. Raj's body was in destruction mode. For most of his life, he was on the over-weight side of the scale. But with failing organs, his body no longer functioned the way it was supposed to, and he started to shed kilos.

"Hey, Raj, I saw you near Raj's CD shop while driving past it the other day. You seem to have lost a lot of weight," Sachin messaged on the King James group.

"Oh, ya, I've started to exercise daily. I go for a run at 6:00 a.m.," Raj replied.

"You? Running?" came replies from both Gajan and Sachin.

"Yea guys, I am planning to get married…."

Raj switched to his private chat with Aishvarya.

"… to you," he messaged.

"Stop joking, Raj."

"I'm not. I'm very serious. I want to marry you."

"We have not even met in the past so many years. We've just been having these conversations on the phone."

"We don't need to meet, Aishvarya. We've known each other since you wore pigtails, and I had a handkerchief pinned to my shirt to wipe my snot."

"Nevertheless, before you say anything else, we should at least meet."

"Absolutely. Just that I cannot travel right now. I've injured my leg."

"What happened?" You said you were running everyday?

"It's nothing serious. Just stubbed my toe at work. So, it's a few days off running. It's just a hairline fracture, but you know how doctors love putting a cast over any little thing."

It was serious. Raj's latest medical diagnosis indicated cirrhosis. The beating his lungs, kidney and heart were taking, was beginning to show on his legs, inflating them and making physical movement difficult.

"Then I will come to India," Aishvarya messaged.

"You can't do that. You're married."

"I'll figure a way out."

Raj tried to dissuade Aishvarya from visiting, but she was insistent. In her head, she knew she wasn't doing the right thing. Raj was playing victim, being manipulative. However, she pressed ahead, and made an elaborate plan to travel from the US to India, fibbing her way through her husband, family and work.

She landed in Bangalore and went straight to Raj's house, only to find him missing.

"He didn't say where he was going, but he left just this morning," his mom said to a stunned Aishvarya.

She had traveled all this way to meet him, and he deserted her on the very day he knew she was coming to see him.

Aishvarya spent the next week trying to reach Raj and repeatedly called and visited his house. But he had gone AWOL.

At the end of the week, Aishvarya needed to return home. She had run out excuses to stay back in India. She couldn't believe that even after all this, Raj did exactly what he always did to her. Build her hopes up and then squash them when she was at her most vulnerable.

She returned to the US, exited the King James WhatsApp group, blocked Raj from her contacts, and swore to never see him again. She never did.

Surprisingly, little has changed. Still totally scared shitless by the only person I can't really have, Still warding off the ones who are trying really hard, Still stuffing this empty life with more things I really don't need (YAY, I got an iPad), Still constantly searching for the 'higher' path, Still discovering good Beatles songs, Still pretending to have a really good time, cause god forbid others find out that I of all people actually have problems, The weird thing is it is always the same problem, is it really so hard to find somebody whom you like who like you back, sure doesn't seem like it. I mean I'm pretty sure it happens all the time; it's all over the movies, magazines and even the newspapers. Nothing makes you feel so old as the thought that maybe life isn't going to turn out the way you thought it would when you were young. Maybe you never will see Paris, maybe you never will fly an airplane, maybe your job will be boring (fine, scratch the maybe for this one) and Maybe. Just Maybe you WILL end up alone.

The only thing that gets me through days like this, is a certain wise friend of mine who keeps saying 'It will all add up, Trust me, It will. I'm just hoping the dude is right. It all must add up someday.

Official quote: When I find myself in trouble, four wise men still sing to me, speaking words of wisdom…. 'Let it be…'

Chapter 12

Reaching out before the Final Act

First Act.
2008

The Lords of college

Raj and Sachin entered their second year of MBA. They had graduated from freshers to seniors and played the role of welcoming, inducting and ragging the freshers. At least Sachin did, since Raj's attendance at college was worsening by the day.

Sachin became the President of the Student Council, the most coveted student position in college. It was the only position that gave a student the same authority as a faculty member, when it came to things like giving attendance to other students. All Sachin had to do was sign a 'pink slip' for a certain date, and the holder of this 'pink slip' received free attendance for all the classes on that date.

Raj got Sachin to sign an entire wad of these 'pink slips', effectively enabling Raj to skip even the minimum number of classes he needed to, in order to be allowed to write the exams for those subjects. Raj would either while away his time at home playing video games or find some company to go out to a bar, sometimes starting as early as midday.

By the evening, when Sachin returned home, Raj would either be sleeping drunk or showing off a new game he'd invented given he had all the time in the world by himself at home. Once he arranged a set of beer bottles at one end of the room, and the idea was to play 'bowling' and knock the bottles off as bowling pins from the other end of the room. On another day, he converted the dining table to play table tennis on.

Then one day, Raj taught Sachin how to box. On one particular evening, when they were sparring, they forgot to latch the main door, and the neighbor barged in to break them up, thinking they were involved in an actual physical fight.

Sachin had to explain that he was simply learning to box, so there was no need to worry.

Sachin spent his days working hard to meet all of the different requirements and responsibilities he had in college, while Raj whiled his time away at home.

One day, PlaceCom approached Sachin for some help with their placement algorithm since summer recruitment for the juniors was coming up and the code had gone buggy. The costs to get the algorithm fixed by a professional were quite high, and Sachin wondered if he could ask Raj to give it a shot. Raj had, after all, been a whiz at programing during their school days.

Raj was more than up for the task, since it gave his idle brain a worthy challenge. More importantly, he could do it from the comfort of home.

Raj not only debugged the faulty code but made it a whole lot better. Now, in real time, placement updates could flash across the different plasma screens in college, irrespective of which room the student had got placed in. Nobody in college had ever seen anything like it, and Raj, whose name was attached to all those codes, became an overnight sensation.

Everyone was eager to know who Raj was, to meet him to congratulate him on the successful placement season. However, Raj was just a name on the code sheet, that none of the juniors ever met, and he only remained faintly recognizable to the senior batch. Sometimes, it seemed the only reason people even believed Raj existed was because Sachin said so. He may as well have been some sort of an advanced AI writing software code for the college.

One day, Raj popped into the council room to take the house keys from Sachin. He had been out drinking during the day with a few classmates and lost his keys at the bar.

But as he was leaving, pocketing the keys Sachin gave him, Sachin said, "Bye, Raj, see you at home." The entire council room that was buzzing with activity with over thirty people crowded in a tiny 200 sq. foot room froze. In unison, all of them craned their necks to look at the enigma that was Raj. The silence was finally broken when one junior said, "Oh! You are Raj!"

The council members forgot what they were doing as they shifted their attention to Raj. A crowd instantly formed around him, with people wanting to talk, exchange contacts, or simply shake his hand.

Both Raj and Sachin, the two most inconspicuous guys who had joined the college about a year ago, were suddenly the two most important students on campus.

Looking around my library. Strewn among the suits, are youthful hearts beating behind ties. We suddenly became seniors while freshers dream of the big buck, but our future minds do not mind their future voices screaming... Just another bunch of future lucky fucks! Our faces look so peaceful, a scene lit by the afterglow of a thousand laptops.

In the sea of faces, I see the girl who liked to drink in the pouring rain, another punk rocker who got lost on her path to be another wall-street broker. She is staring at a guy who liked lesbian porn, who lost Jenna Jameson to her, a mother to his unborn son? A half smile, for the fingers baptized by PlayStation. Next to the wall he sits, my Aristotle... after a bottle, another good hard philosopher, who grabbed what life offered? Is that my goddess of goth, hurriedly making posters for the batch, trying to leave a mark of her passing through?

Still,

There is no beauty in poetry, there is also no poetry about beauty,

What is truly poetic is gargantuan genocide like misery, The massive fuck-all, the stillness after a war, A face shot down mid-smile, a defiant stare in a soldier's eyes, a drop of sweat, over a mask of hate, the slow-motion swoop of a vulture while we decompose. Now that is poetic, now that is poignant...Yes, I still stand by that, the massive fuck-all is the only true poetic thing I know!

So, I will pretend that we were not poetic in that moment,

So, here's to looking at ya, kid.

So, I will still pretend that you did not make me smile!

Enter Priya

Raj became an honorary member of PlaceCom, following the incredible work he did with the code. He was frequently called on to support them in some of the work they did.

One day, a big-shot politician from Mumbai was to visit college, as part of his rally campaign in the city. His agenda was to address the students and deliver one of his standard speeches.

The Student Council was to organize the event and they took help from the other cells, PlaceCom included. The members of PlaceCom called for all hands-on board, and Raj was one of them. Raj's job was to mind the students in the auditorium and ensure they stayed silent during the speech.

Asserting authority in such a way was the last thing Raj would do, but PlaceCom needed all the support they could get, and even offered Raj the last few rows to monitor so that he could even slack off in the middle if he wanted to as the last rows would usually not be too visible or audible to the speaker on stage.

On the day of the event, Raj moved into the position assigned to him at the back of auditorium. At one point, he noticed a group of girls chattering amongst themselves just when the politician was entering the stand.

He decided to interject, now that he had already accepted this responsibility, and tapped the shoulder of a girl from behind who seemed to be the epicenter of the commotion. The girl swung her head rapidly to see who had disturbed her. Her curly hair was waving all through from one side to the other as she turned. Her irate face instantly calmed. She recognized Raj. She was one of the juniors in the Student Council the day Raj had entered there and stunned the entire place to silence.

Her eyes met Raj's, and he smiled at her. Curly hair girl smiled back, understanding instantly what she needed to do, and turned back and motioned to her friends to stop talking. Raj was glad it was that easy. The rest of the politician's speech was uneventful, just as he hoped.

Curly haired girl was Priya, a quintessential Mumbaikar. She was bold and wore whatever she felt comfortable in and went anywhere she pleased at any time of day or night. The daughter of a rich businessman, she lived in a mansion in Bandra—a rare sight in Mumbai—and frequented restaurants and clubs that only allowed exclusive entries.

She thought she was a tad bit plump, which showed more on her face than the rest of her body. She had thick, curly yet smooth hair. Though she was a fresher, she had managed to attract a large coterie of friends around her within the first few days of college.

Priya wanted to be part of the PlaceCom, as she thought they did the most important work on campus, like networking with big companies and managing and organizing the college's placements.

Her application to be a member of the PlaceCom was shortlisted and she was due for an interview: a mock discussion with a company's recruitment lead.

The interviews were scheduled for just the day after the politician's visit, and the shortlisted candidates were sent to a room with a phone from where they had to dial a number given to them beforehand. The call would be answered by an existing PlaceCom member. The objective of the interview was for the interviewee to convince the interviewer to visit their campus for recruitment.

When Priya's turn came, she put on her game face and dialed the number, prepared to knock the interviewer off their feet. The mock interviewers were known to be ruthless and grilling the callers was common. Priya, to her surprise, was on the receiving end of the friendliest 'hello' when her call was answered. The conversation turned out to be one of the best phone conversations she had ever had, largely due to the caller's charm, which managed to completely disarm her.

The interview proceeded without any grilling or snarky comments. The caller asked her good questions to which Priya had even better answers. At the end of the conversation, Priya couldn't contain her curiosity and had to know who she was speaking with.

"I know this is unusual, but I'd like to know who I am speaking with," Priya asked.

"Raj here," came the reply.

Raj was pulled in once again by PlaceCom for one of their errands. Raj accepted this time as he thought it would be a bit of fun to conduct the interviews, especially because interesting conversations were one of the few things he liked to engage in.

Priya froze on hearing Raj's voice. Raj, again?

"Are you there?" Raj asked.

"Sorry, I'm here. I was just wondering if you're the same Raj that organized the junior's placement process."

"The PlaceCom organized it. And I'm part of PlaceCom… sort of…"

"I see. But great job on it though. Congratulations!"

"Thanks! Great job on your interview just now as well. One of the best conversations I've had so far. We'll keep you posted on the results soon."

The next day, during lunch break, Priya went into the canteen with her friends and ordered a juice for herself. Her order came through fast, and she decided to hunt for a table they could sit at while her friends got their food.

The canteen was busy as usual, and she couldn't spot any empty tables. She found a standing table that had just one guy at it who seemed about to finish his meal. She walked up to the table and froze two feet from it. It was Raj again.

Priya had already committed herself to taking over the table, so she decided to go through with it. And introducing herself to one of the most popular seniors shouldn't be too bad in any case, she thought to herself.

Raj was wrapping up another rare visit to college with a bite from the canteen before getting back home when he saw Priya approach his table.

"Hi," Priya said, as she planted herself in front of Raj.

"Oh, hi!" replied Raj, breaking into the same smile he gave her at the auditorium two days back.

He recognized the curly haired girl he had shushed at the auditorium.

"Hey, listen, I'm so sorry about the auditorium," said Raj.

"That's alright. We were indeed a bit too noisy."

"I was just, sort of, doing my job there. Hope you didn't take it too seriously."

"Of course, not!"

"I'm Raj, by the way"

"The same Raj that interviewed me at PlaceCom yesterday?"

"You're Priya? Hey nice to meet you!"

"Likewise! I've heard a lot about you and now it seems I keep running into you."

"Heard good things, I hope! And is that juice all you're having for lunch?"

"I've got the rest of my lunch with me," Priya said and pulled out a lunch box from her bag.

"Oh, you're a day scholar! Lucky you! You get fresh home cooked food every day."

"You can have some if you'd like."

"I really wouldn't mind a bite! I've really been missing home cooked food here in Mumbai."

Priya spent the rest of lunch with Raj, chatting and sharing her food with him. Her friends never found her. She figured they must have occupied another empty table. Secretly, she anyway hoped they didn't come looking for her, as she was having a great conversation with 'mystery-man' Raj.

Once they finished lunch, Raj bid adieu, flashing the same smile again. This time, Priya blushed. Raj had smiled at her now three days in a row.

Long after Raj left, Priya noticed she was still blushing. She found her behavior a bit strange as she had never felt anything like that for any other boy before. She was in a serious relationship with Dinesh, her boyfriend from school, who she was due to marry as soon as she passed out of her MBA.

She had been with Dinesh for so long that it was second nature to disregard advances by any other boy. She would discuss boys with her girlfriends, always having a strong POV on all of them, but never had any of them affected her emotions in any way. Raj was the first boy that broke her clean sheet.

Enter Amit. Party at Poisons.

Everyone wanted to visit a new club that had recently opened in Mumbai, called Poison. Amit, one of Raj and Sachin's friends from college, asked them if they would like to visit the club. He knew one of the bouncers who could get them an entry.

Sachin was always up for a party; Raj was always up for a plan that involved drinking.

The three of them huddled into Amit's Zen—one of the fanciest small cars of the day—and drove to Poison.

The club was packed with incredibly well-dressed and fashionable people. Raj and Sachin wondered if they would even be allowed to enter, given their simple attire, but Amit's bouncer friend seemed to be quite influential.

They found a spot by the bar which had a vantage point of the dance floor and the three sat down to drink. The dance floor was divided into two sections. There was one section that seemed to be for the general public, and another elevated section for which you needed another level of clearance, where possibly celebrities hung out.

Raj and Sachin craned their necks to see if they could spot someone they knew. Amit interrupted them with three beers.

"Drink up, guys!"

Raj and Sachin were only halfway through their beers when Amit looked at them with disdain.

"You guys are slow! Gimme that!"

Amit grabbed the half empty bottles from Raj and Sachin and finished them off in two quick gulps. He went and bought three more beers for them.

This routine continued for a while where Amit constantly bought more beers even before they finished the ones they had. Next, Amit got on to the celebrity dance floor and began dancing, once again thanks to the bouncer friend. He egged Raj and Sachin to join him, but Raj would have none of it. Sachin decided to humor Amit and joined him. Besides, he wanted to be closer to the celebrity spotting action.

Raj took out his phone and opened the app that was lately the talk of town: Facebook. Raj would eventually develop a disdain for social media, but for now, he was curious to find out if the app was worth the hype.

As he scrolled through his feed, he noticed Sarah had checked in to a club in Mumbai, called Banana Bar, which happened to be very close to Poison. Raj took one look at a drunk Amit and Sachin dancing and figured they wouldn't miss him much if he hopped over to Banana Bar to surprise Sarah.

When he reached Banana Bar, he spotted Sarah among a big group of foreigners. Probably her new friends from her stay in Leh, he figured.

He went over to the bar and waved at Sarah. Sarah's eyes widened and she screamed when she saw him. Thankfully the music was loud enough to drown out her scream and Raj was glad to have been spared the embarrassment.

Sarah came over to where Raj was seated, and they got talking. They were both quite drunk and somewhere along the conversation, Sarah said she needed to use the restroom. Raj accompanied her and noticed that Banana Bar was fairly empty compared to Poison. Clearly Poison was where people wanted to party that night.

When they reached the restroom, they noticed there was just one door for a unisex entry. They looked around and didn't see any other options. They looked around again and noticed there was nobody else in sight. Sarah looked at Raj and smiled. He knew what it meant. The next moment, they were in the restroom, making out.

He checked his wallet for a condom and found it. As luck would have it, it was the same condom he had bought all those years ago, when he had wanted to meet Sarah in Delhi. He finally put the condom to use, and they ended up having wild sex. When they were done, Sarah asked if he would like to meet her new friends. But Raj felt the way he did the last time he had sex with her, and just wanted to be left alone.

He made an excuse saying his friends were at Poison and were probably worried about his absence, which may have even been true. He bid her adieu, wondering when and if he would see her again.

Just as he was starting off towards Poison, Raj turned back to see the big bright yellow neon lights of Banana Bar shine brightly behind him. He smiled to himself that the bar was quite aptly named. He never visited it again.

As he neared Poison, he saw Amit and Sachin wobbling out of the club's gate.

"Ok, I need to get home right now," said a visibly drunk Amit.

"Yes, yes, but we need to find your car first," said Sachin, and the three of them started a search for Amit's Zen.

They spent the next half an hour trying to find the car since only Amit knew where he had parked it, and he was too drunk to remember.

When they finally found it, Amit took the shotgun seat and yanked the back rest lower.

"Dude, you need to drive," Sachin said.

"No, you drive," replied Amit, handing his keys over to Sachin.

"Dude, I've been drinking too. I would have held back if I knew I had to drive."

"You are barely drunk. I was having all your beers. I trust you with my car."

In the end, Raj took the backseat and Sachin found himself in the driver's seat. It was his first time in a Zen, and he realized why the car was so popular. Even in his inebriated state, it was extremely intuitive to drive. It was also the first time he was back at the wheel in a drunken state since his bike accident that gave him his nose scar. But with no alternative now, given Amit was drunk and Raj could never seriously drive, Sachin decided to give it a go with a slow and steady pace towards their house.

"Wait, stop!" yelled Amit suddenly.

"We are right on the Juhu main road. There is no place to stop here," Sachin yelled back.

"You have to stop," yelled Amit, "right now."

Sachin spotted a vacant section near the JW Marriott where cars parked till a valet from the five-star hotel came to pick it up and decided to stop there for a second. The moment he stopped though, Amit pushed the door open and stepped out. Before he could say anything, Raj opened the door behind and stepped out as well.

"Guys, we cannot stop here. It's a valet pick-up point. And we are in front of a 5-star hotel for crying out loud," Sachin's warnings fell on deaf ears. Amit and Raj were well on their way to the entrance of the hotel.

Sachin stepped out of the car too to see what was going on. Amit reached the wall and started to throw up on it. Raj stood next to him peeing.

Sachin couldn't believe what he was seeing. He tried protesting but speaking to Raj and Amit was no different from speaking to the wall getting abused by both of them at that moment.

Sachin's thoughts began to spiral into paranoia, thinking someone from the hotel might come out any second. Just when he was about to scream at them again, Amit and Raj started walking back.

"Let's go!" Amit screamed as soon as he took his seat.

Sachin looked back at the hotel. Seemed like no one had spotted them so far. He quickly got into the driver's seat and continued forward.

By the time they reached their house, both Amit and Raj were fast asleep. Sachin parked the car and tried lifting Amit, but he wouldn't budge an inch. Sachin then went to the backseat to wake Raj up. Raj woke up and immediately started marching towards the house, completely ignoring Sachin's calls for help.

The watchman heard Sachin though and decided to help him hoist Amit home. The three of them sauntered home, and when they entered, Raj stood there with his Signature whiskey and three glasses, "It's my turn now, Amit."

Amit had partially woken up due to the walk up the stairs, and now with Raj forcing him to drink, he was wide awake. The three of them began discussing life at college, when it occurred to them that there were so many people in college with the second name Shah. Either a Rohan Shah or a Sapan Shah or a Vidisha Shah… It was a name fertile for jokes, and they began cracking jokes about them for the rest of the night.

What is the quote a Shah remembers after a Faux Pas?

Once bitten, twice Shah.

What does a Shah say when they don't get a 3+ GPA?

That is Shah-cking news!

Why do Shah's work so hard at presentations?

Because they feel they have to make the best Microsoft PowerPoint Slide-Shah.

What does Vidisha Shah say before commencing on a project?

We have to Shah-re our work equally.

And what would happen if you don't Shah're your work equally?

Vidisha Shah will get Shah-ken and emo-Shah-nal

And what happens if you do Shah're your work equally?

Vidisha would say Danke-Shah-on.

Why did Rohan Shah shift from Finance to Marketing specialization?

Finance concepts like Shah-dow accounts totally scared him.

What is Siddharth Shah's favorite time pass?

Window Shah-pping.

What is Sapan Shah's dream profile in an organization?

Shah-ping its Shah-tregy.

Why did Vipul Shah drown in the swimming pool?

He used complex formulae to miscalculate the depth of the pool, and thought it was too Shah-llow.

Why is Sachin in a Shawl with the Shah's in the photo above?

Because he is trying to be Shah-ndy. Shah-ndy in a shawl.

What does Siddharth Shah think about the photo?

Shah-ndar.

Enter Sanjana

"Dude! Wake up! Wake up!" Raj screamed, shaking Sachin violently the next morning.

"My head is throbbing man. Please let me sleep."

"There is a bird inside our house."

"There is a what?"

"A bird! Inside our house."

"This is not funny, dude. My head is hurting from last night, especially with the way you and Amit completely killed my buzz."

"I'm not joking. Amit left the main door open when he left this morning, and a bird flew in."

Sachin groggily headed out to the living room, and lo and behold, a pigeon sat on one end of the curtain rod.

"Ok, can you open the door? I will try shooing the bird out the way it came," Sachin asked Raj.

"I am not going anywhere near that thing," Raj replied, from behind his bedroom door.

"What? You afraid of a pigeon?"

"I don't know what diseases that thing is carrying. I'm not going anywhere near it."

"You talk like some sort of a superhero when you're drunk. And now you see one stupid bird, and you hide behind a door?"

"Exactly, it's a stupid bird, with a sharp beak, and I'm staying away."

Sachin spent the next ten minutes running after the bird with a broom, with just words of encouragement interspersed with laughter as support from Raj.

When he finally managed to shoo the bird out, his headache was gone.

"That is one way to cure a hangover," Sachin remarked, putting the broom away.

"Job well done! Let's go to college now."

"You are going to college? What happened? Important lecture today?"

"No way! I have some work to do in the Council room."

"In my Council room?"

"Your Council room, is it?"

"I mean, are you referring to the Student Council room?"

"Yes, the one and only."

"But what work do you have there?"

"You're not the only one who has to be in the Council room and be a good leader to everyone there."

"Leadership is not about others, it's about you. But I want to know, why do you need to visit the Council room?"

"I'm helping the IT team for Euphoria."

Euphoria was the annual cultural fest of their college, which had earned the distinction of being one of the premier b-school cultural festivals in the country. Students from b-schools across the country traveled to participate in the fest, and the organizers of Euphoria had to once again ensure they outdid their previous year's performance.

Raj had attained celebrity status with the work he did on the PlaceCom code, and a lot of students reached out to him to help with all the IT elements of the festival, like the website setup, logo design, e-mail invites, etc.

It was easier to coordinate all the work when he was physically present with the teams in college. However, this was barely enough motivation for Raj. The real reason he wanted to be physically present in the council room was Priya.

Ever since they shared lunch at the canteen, Raj had started talking to her more and more. He visited college every now and then just to see her in person.

When Raj and Sachin got to college, Sachin got busy with some phone calls with the fest's sponsors, and Raj sat down on the couch with his laptop.

Shortly, he was joined by Sanjana, who sat down awfully close to him.

Sanjana was one of the juniors, with a face that belonged on TV. She had bright pink lips, thick eyelashes, and a jawline you could sharpen a knife on. She was unequivocally the prettiest girl on campus. She was also dating one of her batchmates, a guy also with a face that belonged on TV.

It was common knowledge to never flirt with someone in a very public relationship in college. Raj had no intentions of flirting with Sanjana, but he couldn't avoid the attention he received from her either.

"Hey Raj, can you tell me if this e-mail template works for our invites?" she asked, pointing to a section on her laptop.

As Raj started reading the mail, Sanjana pulled out a lollipop from her bag and began licking it. Raj wondered if the lollipop was the reason for her perpetually pink lips.

"Do you want some?" Sanjana offered the lollipop she was sucking on to Raj.

"Oh, it's ok," replied Raj, part shy, part stupefied.

He wondered if it was normal to be offered a half-eaten lollipop, or if Sanjana was hinting at something else. In any case, he kept his focus on the mail, and helped her make a few corrections.

"Thanks a ton, Raj!" Sanjana said and moved to the couch opposite Raj, with her laptop.

Raj couldn't take his eyes off Sanjana or the lollipop. He decided to message her on G-talk since she had her mail open.

I've figured out why you have bright pink lips all the time.

Haha, you caught me.

I'm wishing I had some of it now.

You still can. Want me to bring it over?

I'm worried someone will notice.

I can give one to you later if you'd like.

How about going out for lunch after this? We can have a lollipop as dessert after that.

That sounds good. Where do you want to go?

You like seafood? There's Gajalee's nearby.

I love their crabs. Let's go.

Raj and Sanjana visited Gajalee, a popular seafood restaurant close by to college, and were offered an apron to wear in case they made a mess of the crabs they ate. Halfway through their lunch, Raj wondered why he came up with Gajalee as an option for a date. Sure, it was fine dining and walking distance from college, but if you're trying to impress a girl and be on your best behavior, crabs are the last thing that will allow you to do it. Raj had crab juice running down the fingers and on to his apron, and he looked an absolute mess in spite of trying as hard as he could to maintain etiquette. The only saving grace was that Sanjana was almost just as messed up as him.

"This was clearly not the best idea," Raj said.

"But it is the only way to have crabs."

"We need to clean up after this. You want to come to my place? Its nearby."

"Sure."

Raj and Sanjana headed towards Raj's house and on the way, he regaled her about the JW Marriott incident the previous night and the pigeon incident that morning.

When they reached the house, Raj was missing his house keys again. He searched all his pockets and realized that in the excitement of shooing the pigeon in the morning, he had forgotten to carry his keys.

He knew the watchman had a pair though, so he could at least let them in.

Once they were in, Raj showed Sanjana the bathroom while he used the kitchen sink to clean up. Sanjana walked out with bright pink lips again.

"How do you do that?"

"What?"

"Those lips!"

"I'm blessed."

"You are! They look simply delicious."

"We need to get back to college now."

"How about one kiss?"

"It never stops at one."

"No, it will. We do have to get back to college."

Sanjana rolled her eyes, and Raj planted a kiss on her lip's mid eyeroll. They stood in the living room, kissing each other for a while.

"Ok, you said one kiss," Sanjana pulled back.

"Yes, I did. Ok, let's go."

Raj opened the door and stepped out and Sanjana followed him. Just as he was about to close the door, he looked at her.

"I don't have the keys. So, once I close this door, there's no going back in. The watchman isn't always here. We just got lucky earlier."

Sanjana rolled her eyes and walked back in. Raj followed and promptly began kissing her again. After a few moments, Sanjana pulled back once more.

"We really need to go."

"Are you sure? We cannot come back in."

"I'm sure. Let's go."

Nobody is ever good to me,

Nobody is ever bad to me,

Sad has been said,

For a life not still made,

My people just being people, the only way they know how,

Today among them I did grow, Put on a show,

Loved the high, forgot the low,

Today I loved being me,

Could this last, that we will see...

Getting ghosted

Ah, that's what I call a sumptuous meal. Would give anything for a nice dessert now. Priya a la crème would be awesome.

Behave! Now please let me try sleeping,

Oh, come on, you sleep so much anyway.

I think good food has intoxicated you. In the past 24 hours, I have slept only for 2. I'm not an owl, so this is definitely not enough. Now shh

Good night... wake up to your vacation.

Good night. Please take care of my Scrooge.

He will be in excellent condition. Don't worry one bit. Just have an absolute blast. Love you.

Love you too.

Raj and Priya returned home from another one of their dates and lay in their respective beds, exchanging messages. Over the past few months, they had become close. Sanjana didn't meet Raj after the Gajalee incident. She did have a boyfriend after all, Raj thought to himself. He was very much in love with Priya now. Nobody else knew about it though. To the world, Priya was going to marry Dinesh, her long-time boyfriend.

They both knew they would need to have the conversation eventually but kept procrastinating it. After all, it was too much fun to spoil what they had with serious discussions.

Priya was leaving for a vacation with her family and Dinesh's family was going to join them. The two families had known each other for a long time, but this was the first time they had planned a holiday together. Priya had an inkling that something big was going to happen, but for now, all she could think of was her evening with Raj.

She had worn her favorite distressed jeans and a short black blouse with the topmost button popped open. Raj looked sharp in his black shirt and trousers. They had dinner at a restaurant right around the corner from college and took a walk through the by lane afterwards. They loved this stretch – the by lane was nearly deserted and they could walk while holding hands without worrying about being seen.

That evening, under the moonlit, star-studded sky, Raj grabbed her just before they stepped out of the lane, pulled her close, and kissed her in a moment of pure ecstasy.

In bed, Priya kept replaying that moment in her head. It was the best kiss she had ever had. She shut her eyes to sleep, wondering if it would be the last kiss she would ever have with Raj.

Raj lay in bed, thinking about the evening as well, when his phone pinged with a message from Sarah.

You feel like doing it?

Raj smiled to himself. Since their encounter at Banana Bar, Sarah often popped up on his phone this way. He had fond feelings for Priya, but Sarah had this way of getting into his brain that he simply couldn't resist.

I'm wearing a sari today…

They regularly had phone sex, driven entirely by the scenarios Sarah painted out for Raj. Every time they spoke, she would come up with something different. Sarah's creativity was boundless.

You there?

Raj thought about Priya and Dinesh. Their relationship was a lot more serious, with families involved, and an impending marriage was on the table. But he was sure he was in love with Priya, and he knew she loved him back as well. It was only a matter of time before he ended it with Sarah for good.

Yes, of course, let me lock the door.

Raj messaged back. The breakup discussion with Sarah could wait, he decided.

A week later, Priya returned from her vacation, and asked Raj to meet her the same day.

"Sure, shall we go for a walk in our favorite lane?"

"No, can you come to my house?"

"Woah, really? What's this about?"

"Nothing serious. There is just no one at home. I thought it's better we meet here."

"Ok sure, I'll leave right away."

Raj traveled to Bandra and met Priya at her house. It was the biggest house in Mumbai he had ever seen. Priya gave him a tour.

The different sections of the house were separated by glass, and the glass was not just any plain glass, but embossed with photographs. The house was not just big, but plush with custom-made interiors.

At the end of the tour, Priya took him to her bedroom. The bedroom was as big as the entire house Raj currently lived in.

"Your walk-in closet is as big as my bedroom," remarked Raj.

Priya watched Raj as he checked out her closet and wondered if she could push him in and lock the door and keep him to herself.

"What are you smiling about?" said Raj, looking at Priya's reflection in the mirror.

"Just thinking if you could stay here instead of going back to your own bedroom."

Raj gave her an amused look. They went back to the dining room and sat down at the dining table, sipping a cola. Priya pulled her chair closer to Raj and kissed him on the lips.

"You sure there is nobody in the house, right? It's a pretty big house! And you have plenty of cupboards!"

"It's just you and me."

Raj closed his eyes and kissed her back.

"This is much better than kissing in our lane."

"Mmm… much better than kissing in an auto as well."

Making out in autos was commonplace in Mumbai. In fact, couples would go on random rides, just so that they could make out in the auto. Space was always an issue in Mumbai, and if it wasn't the streets of Bandstand, it would be the autos.

The autos themselves seemed to be designed in a way that people outside could not see the upper half of the people inside the auto.

The auto drivers also focused their rear-view mirrors to look at the road outside and not the people sitting behind. All of this made autos highly conducive to making out. And when Priya and Raj were not kissing in the lane next to college, they would be kissing in an auto. Somehow, those were the only moments he had with Priya. Every time he invited her to his place, she came up with an excuse. He wondered if they would ever go beyond just kissing, until this point.

"But I must admit, the autos are more comfortable than these chairs."

"We can go into my bedroom, if you want."

Priya took Raj's hand and led him to her bedroom.

When Raj sat on the bed, Priya straddled him, and they continued making out. One thing led to another, and soon enough, all of their clothes were off. They lay next to each other, and Priya began stroking Raj's penis. He seemed to be enjoying it, so she went faster and faster.

Suddenly, Raj let out a scream and hugged her.

Did he come already!

Raj was breathing heavily and holding Priya tightly in his arms. She held him back. Soon, his breathing stabilized, and he broke the hug to lay on the bed.

Priya looked down; he had indeed come. She quietly slipped off the bed and went into her shower.

Was that it? All this effort to send the servants away just so that I could have him one last time, and that was it?

Raj had put his clothes back on and moved to hug Priya as she was stepping out of the shower.

"Not now," Priya said curtly.

"Oh, ok."

"The servants may be coming back any time now."

"Oh, should I head back then?"

"Yes"

Raj put on his clothes, stepped outside, and hailed an auto. On the way back home, his phone beeped. It was a message from Priya.

We cannot see each other again.

What? Did I do something wrong?

No, I did something wrong… I'm sorry. I wanted something… but… I guess it was never meant to be.

Listen, can we talk?

Priya didn't reply. She ghosted Raj for the next month, avoiding all his calls and messages.

It finally happened, Bruce,

Whatever I never wanted to surrender,

The world has finally stripped away.

Dreaming of the girl I can never have. Way, way out of my league (man, hurts admitting that sometimes). The smallest touch of her hand blows my thoughts for a day. A small smile, any smart comment takes residence inside my head along the Houses of the Holy. Still rational enough to see the futility of my infatuation. God, I thought I was smarter than this, a stupid schoolboy crush (Why me, God? Why?) …She is everything I'm not.… Popular, happy, genuine and so easy to fall slit-your-own-throat in love with. They say that opposites attract… sure. Ma look at me, just a human being given to fly… sure.

Clothing a lack of style with my carefully crafted denial! Never ever going to happen, in your dreams baby blue…that's what they all tell me. Well, at least my dreams are my own. As long as I have my private fantasy… this is to hoping, singing and needing. Eh, I'll drink to that!

Till then, the plan is: (don't argue, people, this is the way it's gonna be!)

1. Craving for a little human touch.

2. Not asking for too much.

3. Just wanting something to hold on to.

Life is so confusing sometimes. Surprising understanding spoils a good nasty mood. Like the Stones said… I really can't always get what I want, but just sometimes I get what I need!

You almost made me forget her,

Thanks, my oh-so faithful minions!

Thank you kindly.

Euphoria

The grand cultural festival had kicked off and the student council was buzzing with activity. Sachin was at the center of all the action, making welcome speeches, hobnobbing with the visiting dignitaries – the works. Raj was occupied with all the technical elements of the fest. Dressed in a formal white shirt, black trousers, even a tie, he looked like the picture of someone taking his job a bit too seriously, especially when he rolled up his sleeves.

"It's good to see you here," Sachin remarked at Raj, and meant it. He hadn't seen Raj this involved in anything since their first day in Mumbai when they had to find the house they lived in.

The grand event was spread across three days with activities planned from the wee hours of the morning, well into midnight. The marquee events were reserved for the evenings. These were the most fun parts of the day, when alcohol flowed in abundance and participants and the audience were in wild spirits.

On the 2nd day of the fest, a personality contest was held, which Raj found incredibly boring.

He was quite drunk, and yet, could derive no enjoyment from the banal answers given by the participants. He decided to head to the Council room to take some print outs for a debate event he was overseeing the next morning. That was an event more to his liking.

When he reached the Council room, he was surprised to find it vacant – the Council room was never vacant. There was always someone doing something there. But at that time, it seemed like everyone was downstairs at the open auditorium, ogling at the personality contest participants.

Raj got to work, firing up the printer and getting his prints.

"Oh, I didn't expect anyone to be here," said a familiar high-pitched voice from behind him.

Raj turned around to find Sanjana at the entrance to the council room.

"Yeah, I just needed some print outs."

"Now? Personality contest not really your cup of tea huh?"

"You caught me. What brings you here?"

"Came to collect my bag I left here earlier. But honestly, same reason as you. Couldn't stand that sham of a personality contest for a second longer."

"Well, this is the place to be then. Strangely, the one place that is always buzzing, is the quietest place on campus tonight."

"I didn't even realize there was a piano in this room," said Sanjana, noticing the vintage set in one corner that was usually covered with stacks of paper, but seemed like someone finally put the effort to tidy it up.

Sanjana pulled up a chair and sat in front of it.

Raj hadn't noticed it either and was just about to say something about it being more furniture than instrument, when Sanjana started playing it.

"Wow, it actually works!"

"Seems like it. You want to play something with me?"

"I don't know the first thing about pianos. Or any musical instrument for that matter."

"That's alright, I can show you. Come here," she offered, patting the seat next to her on a stool that was barely large enough for her, let alone two people.

Raj sat down, a bit hesitantly, and observed the keys Sanjana was tapping. She showed him some sequences he could play on the low notes of the keyboard. Raj tried it out a bit and realized he had to concentrate way too hard for it. It was killing his buzz which was the last thing he wanted. He stopped and looked at her. Her lips were bright pink as always, and he remembered how they tasted. He felt like kissing her again. It was certainly the better thing to do than learn to play the piano. He moved his head forward to kiss her and suddenly stopped himself and looked away.

'What am I doing, I'm trying to work it out with Priya now!', he thought to himself.

"Are you ok?" asked Sanjana, looking at him expectantly.

Raj turned to face her, and their eyes met.

'Those lips…,' Raj thought.

He moved forward again to kiss her. She moved towards him as well. As their lips locked, the Council room door swung open, and at the entrance stood Priya.

Sanjana instantly got up and left, making her way out of the Council with the little space between Priya and the door. Raj stood up to face Priya, his expressions switching from confusion to apology and even a drunken smirk.

Slap!

Priya slapped Raj hard across his face. Before Raj could turn to face her, she was gone.

Raj wanted to run after her, but his legs were frozen. His body was still trying to make sense of what had happened in the past five seconds.

Raj never saw Sanjana again. And this time, Priya ghosted him for posterity.

He had heard about Euphoria being a festival that was infamous for events like this, and he had just experienced it for himself.

Raj took his prints and walked slowly downstairs. Strangely, he was in no mood to drink any more. That almost never happened. By the time he got back to the auditorium, the personality contest had concluded, and the DJ had started playing his music which would last for as long as people stayed on the dance floor.

"Let's go home," Sachin said to Raj when he saw him.

"You don't want to stay back and party?" Raj asked with a surprised look on his face.

"Not tonight."

"All ok?" Raj asked, expressing genuine concern, as he thought he saw a shade of grief on Sachin's face.

"Not really. Can we talk about it at home?"

Sachin had received a rather unfortunate call from Juhi earlier in the day. She had called to tell him that she wanted to break up with him. Long distance had taken its toll. They had been together for three years, most of it spent in long distance. First Juhi was in Pune when Sachin was in Bangalore. And just as she moved to Bangalore to work at the same place as Sachin, he had to move to Mumbai for his MBA. Juhi simply couldn't go through with it anymore. She was very serious about the breakup. And Sachin wanted nothing more than to just go home to some peace and quiet.

Raj was reliable on a few things, conversations over alcohol was one of them. The two spent the rest of the night talking about girls.

"The one good thing that came out of this breakup is that you don't have to deal with Dev. But it's tough. Girls! Can't live with them, can't live without them," said Raj.

"I need a break after this," replied Sachin.

"I have a plan. Why don't we travel to the US?"

"Seriously?"

"Why not? I've always wanted to go there and my atthe has been calling me repeatedly of late. Euphoria is done, our placements are done. The next challenge is our final exams, and after that we have a short break before we begin work. Once that starts, who knows when we will meet again. The break after our exams may just be the last opportunity for us to travel together."

"Dev and Gajan are also there. They just moved there for their post-graduation and stay at opposite ends of the country. We could cover both the coasts by catching up with them." Sachin thought about it for a moment before saying, "Alright dude, let's do it."

Later at night, Raj couldn't get any sleep. He wasn't sure what exactly happened after the closet incident, but always hoped Priya would eventually get around to talking to him. But now, he was certain there was no chance of it happening. He twisted and turned in bed, thinking about how majorly he had messed up with Priya.

You see her from behind, against the blue of the sea. With the blowing the wind, long hair and a frilly summer frock. You see her from behind. No matter how hard you try, she still has no face. You know what she is thinking. You want to stop it. You know that you can't. You were never meant to be a part of this story. This stage is hers.

The very moment you know this,

she knows it too.

She purposefully picks up those stones. Puts them in her pockets. Now it is suicide. Now you panic. Still, you know you can't move, move and you will ruin everything. So, you stand silently and force yourself to watch.

You stand and you watch.

You stand and you watch.

She goes into the sea without a sound. No last looks, no doubts. Quiet and faceless. Deeper and deeper. You realize why she wanted to remain faceless. You realize if you had a face to paint on a pain like this, you would have stopped her. It would have no longer been surreal, it would have been human. Too human, yes, you would have stopped her.

And ruined everything.

Now it's your turn in the line. Now it is your feet in the sea. Now it's your pockets with stones. So, you look at that sea, you look at that blue. You don't look back, careful not to ruin it for the person watching you from behind.

The story is the same, the stage is the same.

Now it is your stage, now it is you.

You stand and you watch that blue. There will be no change after it swallows you. No change at all.

Still, now it is your turn in the line.

Now it is you.

Now you walk.

Then, it ends.

USA Trip

"Dude, we're actually going?"

"Dude, we're actually going."

"It's finally happening?"

"Finally."

Raj and Sachin boarded their Emirates flight in Chennai, embarking on their maiden international trip. They decided to take the flight from Chennai, as it was working out much cheaper to travel by train from Bangalore to Chennai and then board the flight there, than taking a flight out of Bangalore itself.

The flight turned out to be an experience to remember. The one from Chennai to Dubai was like any Full Cost Carrier of India, but the one from Dubai to JFL was a mind-blowing A380, the double-decker dream liner from Airbus. It was spacious, comfortable, and offered the best in-flight entertainment and service Raj and Sachin ever thought possible. They watched a ton of movies—Revolutionary Road, Transporter 3, Max Payne—tried out whiskeys they had never heard of, like Famous Grouse. When they stepped out at JFK, despite the thirteen-hour flight, they were completely relaxed, had a slight buzz, and almost sad that the flight had come to an end.

The only disappointing part of the journey was that they couldn't get to go to the upper deck as it was cordoned off for the Economy passengers. Sachin tried convincing an airhostess, but she sweetly denied, and offered another Famous Grouse to shut him up.

After making their way through baggage claim, the two got out of the airport. While waiting for Dev to pick them up, they decided to hit a bar called Avion that was right outside the airport. The drinks were ridiculously expensive given Raj and Sachin were converting everything from Dollars to Rupees. They later realized that $8 for a drink was pretty much the norm and they were wasting their time converting currencies. They needed to simply switch their mindset to spending in Dollars. Dev caught up with them soon and Raj was surprised to find he had lost weight, since according to him, every American was a Fat Bastard. Watching Dev drive on the opposite side of the road, guided by a female voice out of the GPS console was a culture shock. But then, they drove to Times Square.

Raj and Sachin had seen Times Square hundreds of times on TV, but the real thing was something else. The bright lights, the people, the energy – it almost felt as if they had stepped out of their mundane lives, right into a Hollywood movie.

All sorts of things were happening on the streets. Drunken bachelorette parties, Elvis wannabes, and a million tourists taking photos of the million billboards on display. Off the streets, supercars roared through the roads. They were totally in awe of the place. First, Dev took them to Planet Hollywood, then to the 'original' Hard Rock, though Raj debated that the 'original original' was in London.

They went to an Irish bar called Caravas, with an overly friendly Irish lady serving drinks. The boys sat at the bar, drinking, chatting and catching up. Then they hit another bar, then another, and finally decided to head back to Caravas since they had the most fun there. This time, they decided to order the most popular drink at the bar: the Jager bomb.

Sachin had attended the launch party of Jägermeister at a club in Bangalore, and he saw so many people smashed out solid at the end of the party, that he had decided never to have the drink. But, now in the US, he ended up doing the opposite and downed Jager bomb after Jager bomb, with Dev and Raj coming a close second.

Finally, when it was time to leave, they asked for a drink on the house. The friendly Irish lady obliged and poured each of them a shot of 87% vodka, potent enough to knock out a horse. When that wasn't enough, she promptly set it on fire. The three boys looked at each other, and they knew none of them were going to stop at that point. So, they downed the drink, and a big burly African American man sitting next to them gave them a fist bump saying, "Respect."

Raj caught on to that and went about shouting 'RESPECT' to everything on the street, from the Transformers type garbage truck to the Fast and Furious type cop cars. Sachin took photographs of everything, and when he was about to take one of the cop cars, Dev dragged him back, saying those things tended to 'shoot back'.

The night was still young, so they decided to hit yet another bar: a hole in the wall that went by the name Suzanne's, named after the waitress there. The boys drank Jack and Coke till four in the morning at Suzanne's. When it was time to leave, Raj asked Dev if he was sober enough to drive. Dev then revealed the biggest surprise of the night yet. He pointed to the house they were staying at, which was right above Suzanne's. Dev had pulled enough strings to find a friend who lent them his studio, right in the heart of Times Square.

"I could honestly kiss you right now," Raj told Dev, as they headed towards the house to finally get some shut eye after a long day of flying, drinking and partying.

The next day, Raj woke up before any of the others and headed out to buy breakfast. Back in India, he was never the first to wake up in the morning, let alone do something nice like buy food for the others. But being in the US had a transformative effect on him. He seemed to have left the lazy, drunk, argumentative monster in him back in India.

They spent the day sight-seeing NYC. Walking around Wall Street, visiting the Met, eating the city's famous hot dogs while listening to a band playing at the park near the ferry terminal to the Statue of Liberty – it was the classic New York experience. Raj and Sachin were fast falling in love with the city.

Later in the day, they walked towards ground zero. Raj and Sachin stood looking at what was now a construction site for a new single tower World Trade Center that was coming up at the spot. They found themselves transported back to the moment they saw the crash on TV, Raj holding Nitya and Sachin holding Juhi in two different cities halfway across the world, in much the same way as so many people around the world may have witnessed that event.

Next, they went to Central Park, which Raj was disappointed to find was an actual park, and not the café from the show 'Friends'. The minute Sachin stepped into Central Park he threw up.

"Damn, I'm disappointed too, but not that much," Raj said, looking at him.

"All those Jager bombs and Jack and Cokes from last night are finally getting rejected," Sachin replied, in between coughs.

Raj and Dev decided to drop him back to the studio to recover and headed out to visit some more bars. Sachin lay down in bed and tried to get some shut eye and to get over his nausea, but just couldn't bear the thought of being in Manhattan and wasting his time sleeping.

So, within minutes of the other two leaving, Sachin called them and asked where they were. After some haranguing by both Raj and Dev on the other end, they directed him to a bar called Jekyll and Hyde. It was a concept bar where the waiters were dressed up as characters from the eponymous novel turned movie. The entire bar was full of weird funky things like flickering chandeliers, skeletons falling out of the walls, and even a creature that came out of a Swedish cuckoo clock talking in a Marlon Brando voice. At one point, a big section of the roof came crashing down, which held a coffin in it from which popped out a Frankenstein marionette.

Sachin ordered French Onion Soup, given his rumbling and upset stomach. The rest of them ordered normal drinks. One of the waiters in a pirate's costume came up to Sachin and told him in a raspy voice that no one would come close to him now, because he was having the smelly Onion Soup.

They continued barhopping again, and visited a place called Fat Cat, which was a sports bar. After playing a bunch of games like 8 ball pool and Foosball there, the three of them decided to once again visit Suzanne's. Some of Dev's friends, including his girlfriend Renata, joined them there. They got drunk and decided to play "Never have I ever…" where each of them took turns to make a statement, and all those for whom the statement didn't ring true would have to take a sip of their drink.

Dev gave an example and said that if he held up his glass and said, "Never have I ever used a flavored condom," all those who had used one would have to take a sip of their drink. The game was a riot. There was one time when one of Renata's friends said, "Never have I ever done it in college." While everyone else remained still, Dev and Renata looked at each other for confirmation, nodded in unison, and proceeded to take sips of their drinks.

Another one of Dev's friends said, "Never have I ever done it in a car." Once again, Dev and Renata took a sip together and then told Sachin that it was in his car. Everyone burst out laughing. When it was Renata's turn, she said, "Never have I ever done it with Dev." While nobody else on the table drank, Dev cheered loudly and downed his entire drink.

The next day, everyone had work to do, so Raj and Sachin decided to visit the Statue of Liberty by themselves. It began to rain that day, and combined with the wind, the ferry ride was a pain with the freezing cold of the Hudson River. Raj only got tickets that provided them with audio sets that described the entire place, without permission to go inside the statue. Thus, they were stranded outside in the biting cold. Before boarding the ferry to head back, Raj told Sachin, "Dude, get me big pork!" Sachin bought a double patty pork sandwich, topped with extra bacon for him. Five minutes later, Raj winced, "Dude, no more pork!"

Raj was so stuffed with the sandwich, that he had to sit down for a bit. Sachin kept telling him that the ferry was about to leave, but Raj wouldn't budge. Suddenly, the ferry blew its horn, and Raj got up with a start and made a run for it. Sachin ran after him, laughing his guts out. They took a ferry from Manhattan to Liberty Island, and then another ferry from there to Jersey.

The second they reached Jersey, it felt like they were in a totally different place. Jersey was just across the Hudson River, yet Jersey and New York were miles apart in how they looked. "No wonder people call Jersey the armpit of the US," Raj remarked.

The people of Jersey were a lot friendlier though. An elderly bus driver got out of the bus and explained directions on a map to Raj and Sachin when they stood looking lost. Nobody in New York would have done that given how they always seemed to be late for something. They reached a hotel in Jersey that Dev had booked for them for the night, and as soon as they entered, Sachin slid under the covers and went to sleep. Raj went to check out Jersey and brought some hot chicken soup back to the hotel for Sachin.

"I love the effect the US has had on you, dude," Sachin said, sipping on the soup and popping some medicines Dev had given him while they were in NYC. He proceeded to sleep for twelve hours straight, getting over his jet lag.

The next day, they planned to visit Niagara Falls, and stood waiting at the Jersey station for the train. But at the last minute, Raj decided to go to Philadelphia instead. Sachin knew better than to argue with Raj, and pleasantly surprised with his impetuousness, decided to go ahead. They crossed over to the opposite terminal, and instead of going to Niagara, went to Philly.

Dev had told them to visit a place called the Comcast center that was near the station. So, once they got off the train, Sachin asked a Security Guard where Comcast was, but he just could not understand what he was saying. Finally, it occurred to him, and he said, "Oh Khaham-Khahast?" And Raj repeated, "Yeah, Khaham-Khahast!" rolling his eyes at the difference in accents.

The Philly Comcast Center was their version of NYC's Wall St. Tall buildings, long straight roads, and lots of people who looked like they had stepped right out of an episode of the 'Apprentice' show. Raj and Sachin went looking for a place to catch a football game since Man U was playing and found a pretty neat bar showing the game. But apart from Raj and one other guy at the bar, nobody else was interested in the game. EPL was clearly not much of a thing on this side of the Atlantic.

The two of them then planned to visit the Art Museum of Philly as this was where Rocky ran up the flight of stairs in the movie Rocky. They hailed a cab and Raj tried to explain to the driver the place they wanted to go. When the driver didn't get it, Raj started humming the Rocky tune. The driver started singing back and laughed, finally understanding what Raj was saying.

Once they reached the historic flight of stairs, Raj asked Sachin to go up the stairs first and then film Raj, since he wanted to recreate Sylvester Stallone's iconic scene. Sachin went up and signaled Raj to start running. He did the entire act, including the gloves in the air dance when he got to the top, when Sachin noticed he hadn't pushed the record button.

Raj went back down to repeat the entire thing, but this time, about a hundred children got out of two big buses, wanting to do the exact same thing as Raj. Sachin managed to record this time, and it seemed like Raj was racing against an army of little humans.

After a great trip to the Statue of Liberty and Philly, Raj and Sachin regrouped with Dev and decided to play some mini golf the next day. At the mini golf course, Raj started drinking early and only managed to score four in the entire 18-hole game.

The next day, Dev insisted that they visit Niagara Falls and the trio drove to the famous waterfall. The drive was worth it, as Raj and Sachin had never seen anything like it. They couldn't believe they were so close to one of nature's fiercest spectacles.

Boston was next on their East Coast itinerary. The first pub they visited in Boston had a live band playing "Shipping off to Boston", the soundtrack from the movie The Departed, solely on violins. The memorable performance was the perfect way to kick off their trip to Boston. Later, they walked around and chanced upon a pub called Cheers. Raj was excited to see this place, because it looked just like the one in the TV show, which was one of the shows he enjoyed watching. He was most kicked when he got to know the bar had come first and the show later, rather than the other way around. Never would he have thought an actual bar inspired that show, which then went on to create an award-winning spin-off with Frasier.

The boys spent the rest of their time in Boston visiting Harvard and MIT, and on their way back to NYC, they experienced a flash rain. They were peacefully driving on the highway, and suddenly some water from the opposite side of the road splashed on their windshield. However, the splash didn't stop; it kept coming down. Dev, who was at the wheel, hit the brakes hard. As they slowed down, they could see the cars all around them coming to a halt. It was a miracle that nobody banged into each other. It took a mere second on a highway like that with fast cars and sudden rain to cause a traffic pile up.

They spent their last night on the East Coast quietly in Dev's apartment, taking a short break before the next leg of their journey.

The next morning, Dev drove them to the Syracuse airport for their 6:10 a.m. flight. When they reached the airport, Raj remembered they forgot one of Gajan's bags that his mom had given to Raj to hand deliver to Gajan. Dev suggested he drop the two of them at the airport before rushing back to pick up the luggage and return to the airport. Raj continued to check in and tried to stall the flight with the authorities. Sachin stood at the parking lot, eagerly waiting for Dev to return with the bag. The moment he did, Sachin grabbed the bag and ran in for his security check. Thankfully, Raj had taken the rest of the luggage inside, and the airport was small enough for Sachin to quickly whizz through. The moment the security cleared Sachin, he picked up Gajan's bag and ran all the way to the gate and then to his seat inside the plane! When they entered, it was 6:05 a.m.! With five minutes left for the flight to take off, everybody in the plane stared daggers at Raj and Sachin, for holding up the entire flight.

"You are just full of surprises here," Sachin remarked yet again to Raj, for successfully holding up an entire flight so that Sachin could make it.

Once they reached LAX, Gajan picked them up and showed them around LA. They visited the Hollywood Boulevard, the Wax Museum and the Guinness Book of Records Showroom. For lunch, they went to a place called U-Wink where you could order food using screens installed on every table. It was all very new for Raj and Sachin, who had never seen anything like it before. By the evening, they drove past Beverly Hills, making one quick stop at Mulholland Drive from where one could see a fascinating view of LA.

The next day, since Gajan was busy with work, Raj decided to pay his atthe a visit. His atthe was thrilled at the news and organized a trip to

Disneyland in the day before the boys would come over to her house to spend the night.

Sachin was not sure if visiting Disneyland would be fun for people their age, but Raj insisted that it was the 'Happiest place on Earth' for everyone. He turned out to be right. From the moment they stepped into Disneyland till the moment they left, they couldn't stop smiling.

Raj's atthe brought her son and daughter along to Disneyland, and along with Raj and Sachin, treated them all as little kids in a play store, or more appropriately, kids in Disneyland!

She introduced them to all the cartoon characters they had seen at some point of time in life. Then she took them on the rides. The four of them covered twelve of the best rides and even did the Pirates of the Caribbean ride twice.

"There's a reason why Pirates of the Caribbean is one of the most popular rides at Disneyland," Raj explained.

"… it's because they spray saltwater through the AC vents near the ride, to give people the impression of being at sea. It's a marketing strategy that employs one of our subtler senses, our sense of smell, to drive our preference for the ride. Like how baby stores spray their interiors with Johnson and Johnson baby powder since that is the most recognizable smell of babies, making customers feel comfortable enough to eventually purchase more things at the store."

Raj was always full of these little bits of trivia. After all the fun at Disneyland, Raj's atthe decided to go home a bit early and prepare dinner for everyone, while Raj, his cousins, and Sachin planned to hit an ESPN Zone near Disneyland to watch the Lakers v Rockets NBA Playoffs. ESPN Zone was a sports buff's paradise. There were so many screens featuring so many different games, with scoresheets and stats strewn all around to facilitate betting. Raj and Sachin spent more time checking out the place than catching the game they initially intended to watch. After the game, they headed to Raj's atthe's house, which was more of a mansion in Hollywood Boulevard, to gorge on the delicious food she had prepared. Raj wanted to spend some time talking with his cousins, but everyone was so worn out from the day that they all hit the sack early.

The next day, Gajan drove to Raj's atthe's house early morning to pick up Raj and Sachin for a road trip to Vegas. Gajan told them that the car he would rent was going to be a surprise for them. Raj and Sachin kept guessing what car Gajan would bring for them and settled on the Mustang since it was possibly the best car you could drive into Vegas with. Gajan came in a Camry.

En route to Vegas, Gajan wanted to stop at almost every big diner he came across. Sachin recounted the time in Pune when Gajan would not get off the dinner table till he was completely satiated. He had Dev's grandmom running back and forth from the table to the kitchen to keep the parathas rolling. They figured Vegas would have to wait till Gajan was completely satisfied with all the food he ate.

As the boys journeyed along to Vegas with Gajan's rickety driving, every time they neared a town with lights, Raj would scream, "VEGAS!" And Gajan would say, "NOT VEGAS!" When they did reach Vegas though, there wasn't a doubt in anyone's mind that they had finally reached the right place. The skylight of Luxor, the casinos of New York New York and MGM Grand, Vegas was instantly recognizable from a distance, and Raj was stupefied into silence the one time screaming "VEGAS" would have made sense.

They reached Vegas at around eleven at night and then took an extra half an hour to find a parking spot because Gajan on the wheel and Raj on GPS made a terrible combination. The two of them were screwing around, going in circles, missing turns and doing just about everything wrong. In case they found an empty slot, Gajan would decide it wasn't the right place because it wasn't large enough for him to fit the Camry there, while there were spots smaller than that where bigger American pick-ups were parked.

They stayed in the Luxor hotel itself, which was the first surprise that Raj and Sachin appreciated from Gajan. Gajan and Sachin found the beds too inviting and crashed the moment their bodies hit the mattress. When they woke up the next morning, they found Raj missing.

Sachin assumed Raj must have woken up early once again and stepped out to explore the city just as he had been doing since they landed in the US. At eight, just when Gajan and Sachin were ready to step out, Raj waltzed in. He started abusing them for sleeping through the previous night and was hollering about losing just 200 dollars which for some reason seemed like an achievement, but clearly, Raj hadn't stepped out in the morning. He was out all night, drinking and gambling.

Raj then borrowed Gajan's Oakley shades, muttering something about preparing for a Poker game where he needed to ensure his eyes didn't give him away. After brushing his teeth, he donned the Oakley's, put on his baseball cap, lay down on the bed to read the days Poker agenda, and began to snore.

Gajan and Sachin tried shaking him awake, but all they got were grunts in reply. They decided to step out and explore the city. They walked down the entire strip, from Luxor, which was almost at one end, to Wynn, one of the finest Vegas Casinos, at the other end. They walked in and out of all the big Casinos on the way, checking out malls, shops, the brilliant architecture, the hot waitresses, the slot machines, the cafes, the palpable energy in every street.

By evening, the sleeping giant, Raj, had woken up and decided to meet the two of them at Mandalay Bay, a pub where alcohol bottles were stacked to the roof and the lighting changed colors ever so slowly that you didn't realize it was happening until you suddenly discovered that your red seat was blue sometime back. After getting a few beers, they walked towards MGM Grand to watch a show called Crazy Horse. On the way, they came across a large group of women wearing next to nothing and walking down the strip.

"Women here are like a box of chocolates," Raj said, imitating Forrest Gump.

"You never know which one has nuts," he said, bursting into a laugh.

After watching the Crazy Horse, each of them had a wide smile pasted on their faces that they couldn't seem to get rid of for the rest of the night. Their last stop was Coyote Ugly, which started as a tourist spot following the movie, but the boys stayed on there for long, especially with the final surprise Gajan pulled off. He managed to convince the MC to give them free shots, which he did by announcing, "Oh, we have people all the way from India here."

The next day, they drove to the Grand Canyon, visiting the Hoover Dam and Eagle Point on the way. Gajan kept raving about a skywalk at the Grand Canyon, a structure built jutting out into the crevice of the canyon, made entirely of glass so that you could see the valley below. The real highlight instead was the trek they made to one of the highest points near the Iguana caves, from where they could see the entire canyon below and all around them. They sat there, mesmerized by the breathtaking view, glad they had made this trip to this beautiful country with their closest friends.

They wrapped up the rest of their West Coast trip with a visit to Universal Studios and an evening at Hooters.

The journey back to India was forty-five hours of transiting through airports which was a lot less exciting compared to their onward journey. Towards the end of the flight, Raj and Sachin, sufficiently drunk on the free alcohol and out of movies to watch on the entertainment system, sat down for a serious conversation.

"Do you know that in spite of the violence and disease that wiped out nearly 90% of the Native Americans, there are still over 500 federally recognized tribes in that country?" Raj shared in a contemplative tone some of the trivia that he always had up his sleeve.

"Hmm… but do you realize how important tribes are to every one of us?" Sachin continued, in a similar contemplative tone.

"What do you mean?" enquired Raj.

"I mean, humans are the only animals on the planet that connect socially the way we do. The fact that we can even converse with languages is a consequence of that social behavior. And being such social animals, it's almost mandatory to be a part and fit in within a tribe. You start out with a tribe of just your parents, then friends, teachers, colleagues, all of them get added to it. Eventually, you create a tribe of your own, with someone you want to be with and maybe a family you want to start with them. But all these different circles, be it friends, acquaintances or even your own family, they are all tribes you are a part of, and you need to be a part of it, otherwise you are just lost, there is no feedback loop for you, no one to hold a mirror and correct you if you're going astray. Tribes are essential for our very development, and the lack of it can even be dangerous."

"The alcohol really got to you huh?" smirked Raj.

"I know I've rambled on a bit, but what I was getting to, was that I don't think you understand the importance of being in a tribe. It's almost as if you're scared of being in one, as it may lead you to face the real you. And in spite of all the attitude you throw around, which I think is in fact just a façade for who you really are, deep-down you don't have the courage to face who you really are, and therefore the courage to face anything else in life. Consider learning to drive a car or ride a bike, for instance. It's not about the courage to face oncoming traffic, just the courage to even try something new. The only times you've ever tried driving or riding in the past was when you were drunk and wanted to annoy the people with you. There are other examples, like learning to swim. We had so many opportunities, like the trip to Honnemaradu, and then to Dandeli… none of us knew how to swim back then, but we all tried. Sure, you're lazy, but it goes deeper than that. Like the way you were on that pony in Kashmir. Fear was writ all over your face. I think deep down you're afraid, and then you hide that fear by lashing out at people, being sarcastic or picking fights, just so they don't see through you and notice that fear. And then you use alcohol as an excuse to get away with that toxic behavior. And as we grow older, I think that fear is getting worse.

Nowadays, you seem too scared to even meet new people. You barely attended class over the last two years at b-school. Given how smart and capable you are, you could have made any number of friends and had as many girlfriends as you wished. Yet, the number of friends you made at b-school was infinitely smaller than how many you had at engineering, which itself was so much smaller than your friend circle in school. I started to think you were becoming a sociophobe, spending your time on video games, books, alcohol, things you can do in the comfort of your room, without having to face the fears and challenges that come with every new day. But on this trip, I got to see a different you. I've always been the one to wake up first in the morning amongst our friends, yet you woke up earlier than me on each day of the trip. You went out exploring and did nice things like buy breakfast for us on your way back. US had an incredible effect on you. After a long time, it felt like you belonged to something, to us, to the place, whatever it was, it made you likeable, to yourself even. I just hope it wasn't ephemeral and you don't return to the way you were once we get back to India."

There was so much Raj wanted to say in return, like he would in any other topic of discussion. But this time, he kept quiet. It wasn't so much for what Sachin said, but more out of the overwhelming feeling he had from the trip.

Visiting the US was what he had wanted to do for as long as he could remember. Raj's dad, if he spoke at all, would talk about the life Raj's atthe had in the US and Raj thought he wanted the same. But somehow, after traveling there and doing every touristy thing he possibly could, he was left with a strange feeling of emptiness.

Is this it? Is this all there is to the US?

The plane started to descend over Chennai in the wee hours of a Wednesday morning.

"We're going to continue this conversation on another day," said Raj.

"I know. For now, let's just be glad we had another killer trip."

"Yeah... I guess... We managed to meet a lot of people at least," Raj recounted.

"The only person we missed meeting was Padmini ma'am. She's moved to the US recently too," Sachin replied regretfully.

"Ya right! The last person I would meet there," Raj smirked.

With that, Raj looked out over the Chennai morning sky and began contemplating the start of the new life ahead of him. For the first time, none of his best friends would be a part of the journey that he was about to embark on. He felt an eerie sense of fear and wondered if there was any truth to what Sachin had just said. He pushed the thoughts away for the moment. He needed to see for himself what the big bad corporate world out there was like. Maybe that would have more to offer than what he had expected from the US. And maybe facing it without any of his friends this time would be a true test under fire. For the moment, he looked forward to the fresh start.

The beauty of an overcast morning is all I see,

At least the part that drifts over me,

Fresh beginnings, fresher starts for future smiles,

While I think of brighter stars in bigger skies.

Then there was light.

Screaming over the sound of a hundred jet engines.

A much-admired voodoo doll, pricking me ten pins.

Defiantly keeps bleeding my heart on a reddish carpet.

Gloating about the effortless ease with which it creates,

The intangible mire that sometimes I call my life.

Fury thy be mine during light, all mine?

How do I hate that goddamn fucking light?

Thankfully now it is grey,

Thankfully now I can write.

One day all this will be over.

To die in an endless night,

It will be hard to remember,

The perfect sky I created before there was light…

Second Act.
2020

Reaching out to Padmini ma'am

"Raj is that you?" an old, familiar voice spoke on the phone.

"Yes, ma'am. It's me," Raj replied from the other end of the line.

Raj made the call to his schoolteacher, Padmini ma'am in the US, from his bedroom in his parent's house in Bangalore. There was little else he could do, apart from making phone calls and playing video games. His cirrhosis had become severe. The blood flow through his lungs had slowed down, increasing the pressure in the veins that delivered blood to the liver. This increased pressure in his veins caused edema, fluid accumulation in his legs. He needed crutches to even visit the toilet.

"I heard from some of your other school friends that you have been calling them as well," Padmini ma'am continued.

"Yes, I've got a lot of free time now, so I've been calling a lot of people."

"That's good. You should always keep in touch. I'm surprised at this call though. I've tried to reach you so many times in the past. But ever since you left school, I've not heard a word from you."

"That's true. I'm calling now because I was hoping you would have some answers. You were our class teacher after all. Besides, none of the other people I tried to call picked up, so I figured I'd try your number."

"Then I'm glad it worked out this way. And please, tell me, how can I help you?"

"I was wondering what the point of living is."

"Raj… are you ok? I wasn't prepared for something this ominous."

"I'm serious. I've been thinking a lot about it, and I can't seem to understand the point of life. We are all here by fluke. There is no greater purpose for any of us. None of us get out of this alive. So, what is the point of it all?"

"Look at it this way. Everything that is fun in life, everything that brings you joy, all of it ends when life ends. Might as well make the most of it when you're alive, right?"

"But there isn't anything fun. While I was your student back in school, I dreamt of becoming rich. I thought my life was meant for something great. And I worked hard towards it. I got into one of the best b-schools in India, and received job offers from some of the best places to work. I did it all, and none of them brought me any joy. I switched from one job to another in search of something that truly mattered. But they were all corporate hogwash. Then I started doing something on my own, but that didn't work out either. Nobody supported me. Entrepreneurs come a dime a dozen these days."

"Life is not all about work. The people in your life matter too."

"Every single person I know has deserted me. It's just a matter of time. They either can't deal with me any longer, or they get busy with their own lives. One way or the other, they hurt me."

"Nobody else can hurt you Raj, only you can hurt yourself. It's all up to how we manage things in our heads."

"In whichever case, I haven't met a single person who has mattered to me. It got so bad that at one point I decided to have my own kid. I was truly inspired by the stories Gajan would tell me and figured the only person that ultimately matters is a child you bring up in this world. But then, there's the Indian legislature. They just don't make it easy for a single parent to adopt here. Especially one that doesn't have a stable job and occasionally likes to dabble in a drink or two."

"It's one of those times when I'm glad we have the Indian Judicial System. You first need to sort your own life out before you can be entrusted with another one. I heard what you did with Aishvarya. I meet her often in the US, and the last time we spoke, she told me about the trip she made last year to India to meet you, and you went AWOL."

"That girl was planning to leave everything for me. I haven't managed to hold on to anything in my life. I couldn't risk hurting her if she risked it all for me."

"That's quite selfless… and doesn't sound anything like you. Tell me, what are you hiding?"

"I'm serious. She's always been there for me. Everywhere I went, Mysore, Mumbai, she found a way to be in my life. And now, when she has finally settled down, with a great job and a great husband in a great country… I didn't want her leaving all that for me."

"Listen, Raj, if there is absolutely nothing that gives you joy in life, at least think about the people you bring joy to. So many friends who love you… and your parents, think about them…."

"I do think about them. I'm nothing but a burden to them. I've squandered all my money. Now I'm thirty-seven and still living off my parents in their house. They probably want nothing more than to get rid of me."

"That is not true, and you know it. And yes, you are just thirty-seven. You've got so much of life still to go, to live. You still have plenty of time to figure this out."

"Trust me, ma'am, I've tried. I've spent months trying to figure this out. There is no light at the end of the tunnel. We are inconsequential specks in the universe, simply biding our time on earth. We don't matter to anything or anyone."

"Raj, have you considered therapy? I think you should talk to a professional. They can help."

"What do you think they will do? I've read all of Sigmund Freud. These therapists will simply quote from those books and then just turn my questions back on to me to find answers. I don't need to pay someone to do that."

"I don't know what else to say to you, Raj. Listen, you just take care. It's still daytime for you, but far too late at night for me. I have to get going now."

"Yeah… that's what they all say… but thanks for talking at least for this long. You were anyway the last call I needed to make."

"I'm sure there are others in India who are still in a suitable time zone to talk to you. Please do call them. And we will chat later. Bye now."

Raj put down his phone when the call ended. He glanced at the table next to him. There was a time back when he was in school when it was stacked with Mandrake and Phantom and Archie comic books. Now, it was stacked with medical reports.

The one on top of the stack had just come in. It was his latest blood test report. It stated that he needed to get admitted to the hospital at the earliest. His condition had worsened, and home treatment was no longer a viable option. His parents were downstairs preparing to take him to the hospital the next morning.

Raj looked up at the TV, and then at his collection of video games. He wondered which one to pick next.

Then he looked at his cupboard. A small bottle peeked out from between his clothes. It was a miniature bottle of gin. He recollected picking a bunch of miniatures from a minibar of one of the hotels he had stayed in the US. He had polished off all the others a long time back and left behind only this bottle of gin as he never enjoyed the taste of gin. But it seemed to call out to him now. The only remaining alcohol left in the house. Raj picked his crutches, limped over to his cupboard, and pulled out the bottle.

He smelt it and belched. It wasn't just the smell of gin, but the general smell of alcohol that his body simply couldn't bear any further. He looked around and spotted a half empty can of Red Bull. He poured the gin into it and took a sip.

The Red Bull made the smell and taste tolerable. He glanced around his room again. The room he had grown up in. The safe space he came back to when he couldn't handle the world outside. He had everything he wanted in here. The room grew with him, changing as he did. The Sega video game making way for the PS2. The Windows

95 desktop making way for a MacBook. His comics making way for Russian literature. This room was an extension of him.

He picked up the can to take a second sip, but his arm went numb. He couldn't lift the can. He couldn't even move his arm. As he looked at his fingers wrapped around the can, his face came crashing down on the table, over the stack of medical reports.

Raj went into cardiac arrest.

I'm 12 for a moment,

All the time in the world,

My world is small, my love is new.

I spent that entire moment,

Searching for a way to where you were.

You were my first love,

My first and finest steps into the 'adult' world.

Life was simple, Smiles were automatic.

My life was you. Completely.

I'm 20 for a moment,

Everything feels like change.

You are still right there,

I had to go, had to grow among beer flows and concert glows.

With my friends, my new girl, my blurred memories of beaming smiles.

I saw the world, without comfortable childhood naiveté.

No more sepia tones,

My world has good guitar riffs, harsh neon lights, smoke filled rooms.

Sex, Drugs and Rock and Roll?

(Ehh...some drugs, a lot of Rock and roll, and the occasional 3-month pokie, it's tough to be cool, we are Indian please excuse!)

Youth, so beautifully Brash, Belligerent and Bold.

Maybe it always will be my truest experiment at being alive.

I was constantly busy being me, stopped searching for you,

Finally, you asked, I got scared, Tongue tied, Lied.

Pushed you aside.

Spent another 10 years before I thought of you.

You had gone.

It was (cold? cruel? complete? final?) … fair.

Then,

I'm 33 for a moment.

I'm now a they.

Kid on the way.

It's no longer youth, It's no longer World Vs I.

With a kinder hand I pen my future-proof dream.

Ears used to drumbeats strain to hear faint heartbeats.

Spare a smile for that moment. Spare a smile for my blushing bride.

It is no surprise that I forgot the way which leads to you,

I Forgot you, since I am me no more.

I'm my future kid, my blushing bride, my happy family.

I'm my unthinking smile?

I'm my sense of completeness?

I'm no longer Jack's unsatiated heart!

I'm 45 for a moment.

With a lasting footprint on the sands.

My legacy. My brown eyed boy.

Like proud gods, we celebrate what we have created.

A life. His life. Our life.

We both have aged, aged happily.

All is well on my patch of Earth.

Happiness is a son's curiosity,

Happiness is a loving embrace at days end,

Happiness is a warm suburbia.

I'm my loving wife.

I'm my beautiful son.

I no longer need,

No longer need a way to you.

I'm 58 for a moment.

He has left, Like father before.

To go and grow, impatient for the man he is going to be.

She is my everything now, I'm her everything,

I'm my shielded emotion?

One night as I lay with her, talking about our years together,

Through all that we created, through unshakable bonds,

Through the wall that is a lifetime of love,

I see your face; I see my twelve.

Without preamble, without warning,

My youth is staring into my middle-aged eyes.

Why must it happen now, why must it happen here?

As I lie there in the arms of my wife,

As I Know that I have everything I ever wanted,

A sense of belong, a loving partner, a legacy through my boy,

Why do I still think of you?

Why do I still need a way back to you?

Why now?

I'm 72 for a moment,

She has died. Left me alone, left me broken.

My feeble feet miss her supporting arms.

My feeble mind wishes it remembers everything.

My brown eyed boy is living his life,

Has no time for the old man I have become.

Finally, alone now with my sadness.

The more my body lies, the more my thoughts wander.

They finally settle on you.

I don't know where you are,

Who you are,

Even if you still are.

An old, faded dream of an old man is all that is left.

As the idle Wednesday afternoon breeze blows,

I'm my impending end?

I'm my last mouthful of air?

I'm 99 for a moment,

Still counting the ways to where we were,

I loved my life.

Loved the girl I spent it with.

Loved my son,

Loved it all.

Still, why do I wish I could have found you,

To share these 100 years of mine,

Wish I found you,

Even if that meant missing all of this.

Funny thoughts on the deathbed of a full life.

I'm my unfinished thought?

If I had to choose a time,

12 years old when I walked into school,

12 when I saw you the first time,

A time when I was nervous, but not afraid,

A time when joys were simple and love was pure,

A time when I had all the time to get to know you, be with you,

A time when you had all the time to be with me, save me,

If I had to choose,

12 years, back where it all started,

If I had to choose,

Aishvarya, I wish I had chosen you.

Epilogue

You are usually at the door, opening it for me, or at the end of the stairs, gesturing for me to come up, when your parents opened the door. But this time, you were on the floor. Wrapped in white, from head to toe, with just your face visible.

Your face looked just like the last time I saw it, on Brigade Road in Bangalore, last December. A receding hairline, but everything else still good-looking, like you always were. Even that little beard didn't have a trace of white. So young.

You didn't move an inch, lying there on the floor. I remember you were such a light sleeper. Every time I walked into the hall and found you sleeping on that blue sofa that literally took your shape over the two years at b-school when we stayed together, you always flinched as I moved past. I kept staring at you, waiting for that flinch. But you weren't asleep this time.

Your dad sat next to you, dripping wet as if he had just come out of the shower, and was probably asked to start reciting Shlokas without toweling first. He played the part. Your dad's always been an amazing guy. First, he sat next to you repeating the words the priest said, then he moved over your head and held a straw from your mouth to the sky, continuing the recitation, and finally he walked in a circle around you and poured some water into your mouth.

The rest of the elders followed suit, pouring water in your mouth. Hydrating you after a lifetime of reckless drinking.

I stood next to you the entire time. Looked at your mom during the hydration process and she said kids should not do it. So, I just stared at the others going on about it. Started thinking about the time in Dasarhawaii when you kept pouring me a drink and forcing it down my throat, just as I would throw up with the previous one. It was your turn now to be forced a drink, and I have a room full of people who you don't know doing it for me. Revenge couldn't be sweeter, huh?

An elderly lady came up to pour water. She began to cry. Nobody else did, until then. Not even your parents. I was wondering which bottle you finished when you chatted her up through the night that she's feeling so nostalgic about hydrating you now. Or maybe she just represented all those other people who may have had that night of drinking with you, and left both mesmerized at your wisdom, and sick to their stomach with all the alcohol.

The next ritual was pouring rice into your mouth. You were never into eating much when you drank. And you always found it strange how I would choose to fill that little leftover space in my stomach with food when there was so much more alcohol left to finish. Fitting revenge again. Now it seemed like you were forced to eat as well.

I noticed your atthe at this point. Recognized her face from the time she took us to Disneyland in the US. She was making conversation, and at one point asked how come I didn't know what was going on with you. This was the first time I broke down at your place. It's true. I didn't know. And the thought of not knowing in spite of exchanging messages almost on a weekly basis, a call nearly every month and even a meet for a drink at least every 6 months in the last 25 years of knowing you, not knowing you had cirrhosis just shattered me at that moment. Both your mom and atthe tried to comfort me. I stopped the moment they did that. I wasn't the one who needed comfort. You needed it. Many weeks or months or years before. I'm not going to take that away now. So, I sucked it up and got back to observing the rituals that followed.

Next one was to lift you out from the hall to the verandah outside. The priest asked the men to remove their shirts to do this. Vinay walked in at this time, and we were both about to take our shirts off, when the priest said we need to have our thread on. I told him I don't wear one and Vinay said he forgot his. We were ruled out from lifting you and four elderly uncles came up to the task. They made an honest attempt, but you were always built like a bull. And this time your legs were swollen with edema. The uncles couldn't manage, so I helped them. And from there on, to the ambulance, to the crematorium, to finally the place where you slid in to burn, I lifted you.

A few people came over to see you. Vinay, Aishvarya, Sushmita, Thomas, and some of your neighbors. At most, there were twenty people at your funeral. Probably still a little more than you may have wanted.

My very last moment with you was when the fire lit up around you. I saw your white Nike socks burn. Started to bawl before I could see anything else. The doors shut down as well on cue to not display the disturbing spectacle any further. And that was the end of that.

You would have hated everything about your funeral, dude. You hated Brahminism, you wanted an epitaph, worst of all, you loved yourself too much ("in my head I'm a superstar" is what you always said) to go so soon. But then you left us all. The void that I feel in your absence is unfathomable. And for that, you left this world just as you came into it. For all the things you were when you were alive, you didn't have a choice when you… fuck you, Raj.

- Sachin, January 11, 2020

My Safety Plan

Ways to help myself before and during distress…

Identifying my triggers (thoughts, feelings, comments, situations, discomfort in my body)

____

____

Identifying my warning signs (sleep difficulty or appetite disturbances, unable to look after my body or do daily tasks, substance overuse, self-harm, suicidal thoughts)

____

____

Activities I can do on my own to feel better (Giving myself a complete break, processing my feelings through journalling, relaxation exercises including grounding, deep breathing or guided imagery videos, listening to instrumental music, physical movement, dancing, or a short walk in nature):

____

____

Activities I can do with others to feel better (Eating a meal together, watching sitcom/a light movie, sharing how I feel when I feel okay to, sitting together and doing nothing, playing a game, etc):

____

____

During self harm triggering situations…

Ways I can help myself stay safe: (keep myself away from harmful objects or substances, distraction techniques, post harm care)

____

____

Emergency Contacts: (3-5 people I can reach out to when I am not okay)

____

____

Helpline Numbers:

Vandrevala foundation – 18602662345 OR 18002333330
Available 24/7

iCall 022-25521111 (Mon-Sat 8am-10pm)

nULTA app chat (Mon-Fri 10:30am-5:30pm)

Samaritans - 84229845 28/29/30 (All days 3pm-9pm)

Sampurna 080 25285555 (Mon-Sat 9am-5pm)

Parivarthan 7676602602 (Mon-Fri 10am-10pm)

Women's helpline:

Vanita Sahaya Vani 080 22943068

Sahai Mon-Sat 10am-8pm 080 25497777

Printed in Great Britain
by Amazon

22884050R00199